COZUMEL

Also by the author:

E. HOWARD HUNT
COZUMEL

 STEIN AND DAY / *Publishers* / New York

1096 7559

Mystery

First published in 1985
Copyright © 1985 by E. Howard Hunt
All rights reserved, Stein and Day, Incorporated
Designed by Louis A. Ditizio
Printed in the United States of America
STEIN AND DAY/*Publishers*
Scarborough House
Briarcliff Manor, N.Y. 10510

Library of Congress Cataloging in Publication Data

Hunt, E. Howard (Everette Howard), 1918–
    Cozumel.

    I. Title.
PS3515.U5425C6   1985   813′.54   85-40259
ISBN 0-8128-3040-7

Este librito se dedica a Bill Buckley como recuerdo de nuestra temporada en México.

COZUMEL

I

ONE

I WAS HAVING a few Tecates at the El Portal café and watching the evening tourist crowd along the waterfront. Young people in shorts and T-shirts, some lugging rucksacks or scuba gear, all looking for a cheap place to eat. Travelers from the cruise ship were better dressed and identifiable by painful-looking sunburns.

At the end of the town pier a charter crew was hoisting a sailfish on the weighing scaffold. From where I sat it looked no more than seventy or eighty pounds, and I wondered why they hadn't released it to live and grow. Photographs were taken of the hardy sportsmen posed with heavy rods beside their catch. Snaps would include the scaffold lettering: XXI Torneo de Pez Vela, San Miguel, Cozumel I., Q.R. Mexico. Making it all worthwhile.

I drained the brown bottle and added it to the other empties on the table. An unproductive day in the life of an undercover drug agent, I was thinking, when I saw the blonde come in. Page-boy cut, caramel tan, close-fitting white shorts and a lettered T-shirt covered by fishnet bodice gathered just above her hips with a woven string belt that held a diving knife. Her features were beautiful in an unobtrusive way: snub nose, full lips, and white teeth. Her thighs were perfectly formed, as was what I could see of her calves. They were three-quarters covered by Robin Hood boots of violet suede. An absolutely spectacular young female.

She stood feet apart, hands on hips, and gazed around in an almost challenging way. I wasn't going to challenge her, not with that knife inches from her hand, but then her head stopped moving and her gaze settled on me. Her mouth firmed and she strode toward me, stopping a yard away. "Do you speak English?"

"Daily."

"Is your name Novak? Jack Novak?"

"The same."

She pulled out a chair and folded into it.

"Drink? The margaritas are disappointing and Mexican wine rates about half a star."

She gestured at the empty bottles. "Whatever you're having."

I turned and saw Chela watching. She came over and said, *"Dos cervezas?"*

"Sí. Tecate."

Her dark eyes flashed. *"Cuidado con la rúbia, Juan. No me gusta su estilo."*

"Dos Tecates," I told her. *"Rápido."*

As Chela moved off, the blonde said, "What was all that about?"

"She suggested I be careful."

The bronzed eyebrows lifted. "Why?"

"She doesn't like your style."

"She's rather attractive."

"Half-Mayan," I said, "half-Chilean. Yes, attractive. But so are you."

"Thank you."

Normal male-female tilting, and I wondered where it would lead. Probably no farther than the street. I said, "How come you knew my name?"

"I—we heard it in Mérida . . . at the airport."

"In what connection?"

Chela arrived with dripping bottles and put them down needlessly hard on the table. I said, "A glass for the *señorita.*"

"If you insist."

"I don't really need a glass," she said, "I've drunk from bottles before."

"But not often," I suggested. "You said you heard my name at the airport?"

"Yes—where they service private aircraft. We were asking about planes in Cozumel."

I drew on my bottle. "Lots of private aircraft here. Why me?"

"You have an amphibian."

Chela brought a glass, wiped it on her apron, and set it down near the blonde's bottle. Elaborately I tendered my appreciation.

The blonde said, "What do you do?"

"Watch the Love Boats come and go. Hire out to the wealthy. You?"

12

"I don't mean to be mysterious, so let me introduce myself—Penny Saunders."

"First time in Cozumel?"

Nodding, she filled her glass. I looked over her head at the old sepia photos on the wall: Lindbergh in 1928 at the Cozumel strip, standing beside the *Spirit*; the main drag of San Miguel in 1920; the town Zócalo in '32. Old, old memories. And dreary. "Well, Penny," I said, "you and another party were asking about planes—amphibians."

"Yes. Paul Diehl. He's my lawyer. Actually he's lawyer for the estate— my father's estate."

"And the two of you are looking for an amphibian? Mine's a Seabee built about forty years ago. Republic made them for only a few years, and there aren't any parts. Fortunately, Mexican mechanics are resourceful, they improvise."

"Did you ever hear of my father—Vernon Saunders?"

"Should I?"

"He was well known in Houston."

"I don't know Houston. What line of work?"

"Investment banking." Her back arched and through the wide netting I could read the printing on her shirt: Texas Terrors. The fabric undulated. No bra. I said, "Are you a Texas terror?"

"I was. That's my old high school."

"Cheerleader?"

"How'd you guess?"

"Obvious." I tilted my bottle while she thought it over.

Finally she said, "Is that a compliment?"

"Definitely." The sun was almost gone from the horizon. The evening's violet haze was settling over the Caribbean like a mantle. For a few moments everything was still; no scraping feet or clatter of glasses, no screeching taxis or mariachi music. Our gazes locked, and I knew why she wore lavender boots: the color matched her eyes. She said, "Lived here long?"

"About a year."

"What do you hire?"

"I'm partners with Carlos Paz, who runs a fishing boat."

She half-turned toward the pier.

"We keep it at the yacht basin down the coast road. So you and lawyer Diehl are in Cozumel. What's your interest in me?"

She put down her glass. "I'd rather have Paul give you the details, but we're hoping to find proof of my father's death. I can't inherit until we do."

"He was supposed to have died here?"

"Nearly two years ago. He took off in his plane for Brownsville and never arrived."

"Lot of miles to Brownsville. No trace?"

"Last month Paul came here and asked around. He found a man who remembered a plane coming down offshore."

"The man didn't report it?"

She shrugged. "You know Mexicans—he said he didn't want to get involved."

"That's understandable. Well, I'm sorry about that, Miss Saunders, but we can wrap this up pretty fast. My working papers limit what I can legally do. I can't charter my plane even if I wanted to—the boat is another matter. It's for hire. For fishing or anything else that's legal."

Disappointment turned the corners of her mouth. "Paul might be able to work something out. Would you see us later tonight? We're at the Sol Caribe. Say nine o'clock?"

I would have said no, but for her steady gaze, the depth of those lavender eyes, not to mention the perfection of her form and features. Besides, I hadn't anything scheduled. A stroll around the Zócalo with Chela, ice cream or melon at one of the stands, and early to bed. So I said, "If you'll explain my limitations and Paul still wants to talk, I'll come." I wrote down my phone number. She tucked the paper in a small pocket. "That's fair," she said, "and thank you, Mr. Novak."

"Jack."

She smiled slightly, left the half-filled bottle, and went out. The street light gave her hair a golden aura as she walked to the taxi stand.

I reached for Penny's Tecate before Chela could snatch it away. Brushing against me she said, "I know her kind, she makes trouble. You want to sleep with her, make love?"

"Sure," I said, "but tonight I'm going to see her lawyer. They'll be gone tomorrow."

She snorted. "Maybe she and the *licenciado* sleep together."

"I'll let you know."

"Sinvergüenza!"

I walked through the restaurant and into the back courtyard, where I got into my jeep. From there I drove to the airport and paid the operations guy a thousand peso *mordida* to let me go through flight plans filed the past two years. Then I phoned the Sol Caribe and spoke with one of the reception clerks. Yes, the Diehl and Saunders couple had arrived yesterday afternoon on the hydrofoil from Cancún. They were in separate suites and the clerk didn't know if the *licenciado* and the *señorita* slept together, but in his experience most tourist couples did.

From the airport I drove back through town and pulled in at the yacht basin. Carlos was hosing down the *Corsair*'s superstructure when I arrived. For a Mayan he was tall; muscles rippled under his dark skin, and he gave me a broad smile. "The party caught four sails," he told me. "Biggest sixty kilos. They want to go out tomorrow."

"Take them," I said. "Let's earn it before the season ends."

"I need gas money."

"They didn't pay? Dammit, Carlos—"

"Juan, these *gringos,* they look real honest."

"Then they'll have gas money in the morning. I told you, always have them pay before you come ashore."

"Hey, they'll pay, don't worry."

"I worry," I said, "and if they don't pay it's out of your share, not mine."

"Estamos."

My bungalow was a mile farther along the coast. I'd installed an eight-foot fence on three sides, and before I unlocked the gate I blew a couple of blasts on my supersonic whistle. That told my German attack dogs, César and Sheba, their master was coming in, not some predatory Mexicano. I heard them racing down the wooden pier where my plane was tethered, and before I was out of the jeep they were slavering greetings all over me.

I unlocked the front door, letting them in first as an added precaution, and then I turned on the lights and locked the door. Uninvited visitors were the last thing I wanted in my island refuge, and around Cozumel a lot of strange things went on; smuggling untaxed liquor from cruise ships was the least of them. I fed and watered the dogs and turned them into the yard before I unlocked the radio cabinet and called Brownsville.

After a shower I got into a *guayabera* shirt, ironed and starched by Chela on her day off when she cleaned house and did my laundry. I couldn't have strangers in the place, and the pleasure bond between us had developed into mutual trust. As planned.

I poured a double shot of Añejo over ice and sipped as I listened to the eight o'clock news from Mérida. After that I locked everything up— leaving a few lights on—and drove back to the Sol Caribe. My phone hadn't rung, so I supposed the meeting with lawyer Diehl was still on.

15

Where before I had been mildly interested in Penny Saunders's tale and considered the interview with her lawyer an opportunity to see her again, I was now keenly interested in hearing what he had to say.

No flight plan by any pilot named Saunders had been filed at the Cozumel airport in the past two years, and Brownsville had queried the Houston office about her father.

A Vernon O. Saunders was alive and well and living in the elite River Oaks section of Houston. An agent had made a pretext call to the home and spoken with Vernon, who was irritated at leaving the dinner table where he was entertaining guests.

That being the case, who was the blonde Texas Terror, and what were she and the alleged lawyer really doing in Cozumel?

And what was their interest in me?

It was the sort of strange circumstances I was paid to look into.

TWO

DIEHL HAD ONE of the ninth-floor penthouse suites overlooking the bay. Through the window I could see festive lights festooning a moored cruise ship—the *Song of Norway,* by its size. My host was a lean, sharp-featured man with thinning brown hair. He wore a blue *guayabera* with too much embroidery, so new the store creases were still sharp. In casual attire he looked uncomfortable.

Penny wore a loose white blouse and pleated miniskirt, a black coral necklace and gold wristlet. On her feet, woven leather *huaraches.* Minus the Robin Hood boots, her calves were as great as her thighs. The three of us sipped piña coladas and discussed the island climate, which we agreed was exceptional.

Finally Diehl cleared his throat. "As Penny's told you, Mr. Novak, I represent the Saunders estate. Penny's mother died some years ago—of natural causes—so she's the sole heir. Heiress." He sipped more of the creamy liquid. "Unless I can acquire presumptive proof of her father's death, the estate could be tied up for as long as eight years."

"Was Vernon Saunders a good pilot?"

"He flew for the Navy in Korea and owned various personal aircraft over the years. He passed flight physicals periodically and maintained flying proficiency."

"What plane was he flying when—?"

"A Piper, I believe. Single engine."

"Was he alone at the time?"

He glanced at Penny. "As far as anyone knows."

I said, "In the Caribbean, piracy isn't unknown. Usually it happens to

17

yachts, but planes are hijacked, too. Particularly if there's only a pilot to contend with."

"Good Lord, what kind of people would do that sort of thing?"

"Smugglers, Mr. Diehl. Not Indians bringing in liquor and yard goods, but coke runners. It's a fact of life throughout the Caribbean."

He shook his head and spoke to Penny. "Your father wouldn't have known that."

Without saying anything, she looked away. The loose blouse very subtly showed the fullness of her breasts, and I wondered what she was thinking. I wanted her, but I couldn't let lust interfere with business.

There was a map of the island on the coffee table, and I pointed at it. "Suppose you show me where your informant thought the plane went down."

With his index finger Diehl found a spot off El Mirador on the other side of the island. "About there, as well as I can recall."

"Deep water."

"How deep would you say?"

"Anywhere from twenty to four hundred feet. There's a shelf that drops off abruptly. That's what scuba divers like about Cozumel. Short boat ride and they can go down as deep as they like."

Penny said, "Do you dive?"

"Occasionally. I gather you do, too."

"How did you know?"

"The knife you were wearing."

Diehl allowed himself a brief smile. "Very observant. Now, if you don't mind, we'll get down to business. Penny, would you mind?"

Wordlessly she rose, straightened the skirt pleats, and crossed the room, moving with what seemed unconscious feral grace. She went out, and the door closed. Diehl moved closer. "There are aspects it's just as well Penny doesn't know."

"I thought there might be."

He considered. "What made you think so?"

"You never mentioned approaching the Mexican authorities."

He wet his lips. "I couldn't, Mr. Novak. Unfortunately—as it turned out—Vernon Saunders was a rabid collector of pre-Columbian artifacts. I'm sure you're aware their export is strictly controlled, but his enthusiasm and means were such that he let nothing stand in his way. He had come here on a collecting trip. By flying alone he was able to land where he chose and bring his trophies into the U.S. without declaring them. Customs, of course, would have confiscated them on the spot, returned them to Mexico, and prosecuted my late client."

"Saunders could have done well here. There're at least fifteen Mayan ruins and a *cenote*—holy well—identified and under protection of the Archeological Commission. There could be any number that haven't been found. And very little work's been done—officially—on the known ruins."

His fingers tented.

"But with Saunders dead he can't be prosecuted, even if his plane was filled with jars and relics. What's the big deal? Why not tell Penny the truth?"

"I decided not to inform her of her father's proclivities . . . not wanting to tarnish his memory."

"She's of age," I said. "How old—twenty-four, five? Surely she could forgive her father his hobby. Even if it means he was a thief."

The idea seemed to shock him. "She's been raised in a rather cloistered atmosphere, understand, and I prefer she not be disillusioned. Following her mother's death she and her father became very close—inseparable, you might say. Vernon had the means to shelter her from anything unpleasant."

I grunted. "The Texas Terror? With that bod she'd have had ample opportunity to grow up fast."

"That's an unpleasant thing to say, Mr. Novak," he said in tones of reproof.

"I'm not a very pleasant fellow. What's your proposition?"

He straightened. "I have to find that plane, *must* find it if probate's not to drag on for years."

"That's very considerate—and ethical. Most lawyers would love to drag it on, collecting fees indefinitely. You still haven't told me just what you want from me."

"Putting it simply, I want to hire you to fly and search for the plane."

"What you're asking is illegal—as I told Penny. How much did you have in mind by way of hire?"

"Five hundred dollars a day. There's a limit to the funds at my disposal."

"That's unfortunate," I said. "In so delicate a matter I'd need double that to ease my conscience, and compensate for the considerable risk."

"Seven-fifty, then."

"Eight and I pay the gas."

"Very well." The smile he gave me was the kind an iguana would smile if it could. We shook hands, and his palm was as moist as it was soft. I said, "Got a card?"

"Card?"

"The kind lawyers are always shoving at you. I like to know who I'm dealing with."

"Unfortunately I didn't bring any. It didn't occur to me I might need one."

I could have asked for his Texas Bar credential, but I'd pushed him far enough. "I'll take half now, half in the morning."

He swallowed. "Personal check?"

"I've a supply from last year. Shuck out."

Reluctantly he got out a sheaf of traveler's checks and began signing. I said, "I'll have the plane off the beach at nine o'clock. Tell the taxi driver to take you fourteen kilometers from town—that's about ten kilometers from here." I made a pencil mark on the shoreline. "Coming alone?"

"I'd prefer to, but Penny's determined to take part in the search."

"Commendable. When you reach the beach get one of the boats to bring you out. Too rocky to risk the plane's hull. I can fly about three hours before refueling. You can lunch while I'm taking care of that."

Handing me four checks, he said, "What are the chances of finding the plane?"

"Poor. If it hasn't been seen by now it's probably sunk beyond visibility. How was it painted?"

He stroked his chin, finally saying, "White body with, I think, blue stripes."

"Too bad. The blue will blend with the water, but if it's in visible range the white should show up." I tucked away the checks. "Anything else I should know?"

"I ask you to be discreet."

"If I'm not it's my ass. And if we find the plane, what then?"

"Someone will have to go down and examine the wreckage."

"After two years in the water there's not going to be much resembling a human being. Maybe a jawbone."

"That would be useful for dental identification."

"And the artifacts—if any?"

"I . . . I hadn't thought about them." He looked up at me. "What would you recommend?"

"After you've got what you want, I can let the authorities know—anonymously. Then we'll both feel better about Mr. Saunders's hobby."

He sighed, wiped a bead of perspiration from his nose.

"Nine o'clock," I told him. "If you leave here at eight-thirty you'll be there in plenty of time, so try to be prompt. If I have to fight the current to keep from drifting, people are likely to wonder."

I went out and closed the door. From the balcony I gazed at the lighted cruise ship and felt the night's warm humidity surround me like steam. Penny's suite was a few yards distant, so I walked to the door and listened for her telephone to ring. After a while I knocked.

In a few moments I heard her voice from the other side of the door. "Paul?"

"Sorry," I said, "it's Novak."

The door opened enough to show her face. "What do you want?"

"Couple of things. First, had it been up to me, you could have stayed while the lawyer and I made arrangements."

"Then you'll do it?"

I nodded. "Second, you owe me a drink."

She hesitated, but the door swung inward. She was wearing a frilly white peignoir, knee-length and translucent. She looked as cool and fresh as though she'd just stepped out of the shower. I let her close the door as I walked to the Servi-Bar and opened it. "What's your pleasure?"

"I'd love a piña colada, but I suspect it's fattening."

"I don't think that's a problem you'll ever have."

"So I'll—oh, what would you suggest?"

"Añejo on the rocks." I got out the little bottles, four glasses and ice, and poured dark rum.

Our glasses touched. Her eyes were darker in the dimness of the room. Like a chameleon, she seemed to take on the coloration of her background. *"Saludos,"* I said, "and you say, *'y tiempo.'"*

"Y tiempo." We drank.

She said, "I don't like being excluded from things that concern me."

"Me either. We were talking money, bargaining, Paul and I."

"Paul told you I'm going?"

"He insisted."

Penny smiled, lowered herself onto the sofa. Her suite was smaller than Diehl's, sitting room and adjoining bedroom. The bed covers looked rumpled. We drank and looked at each other until I said, "There's a pretty good disco in town, the Scaramouche—it's opening about now."

"Thanks, but I'm comfortable here, and tomorrow will probably be a long day."

The telephone rang.

Before she could lift the receiver I said, "Tell him you're tired, got a headache."

She frowned. "I don't know why I—"

"Do it," I snapped, and she picked up the phone. For a few moments she listened, said, "I'm really too tired tonight, Paul ... Very well, breakfast at

21

seven-thirty." She replaced the receiver, and I drained my glass.

"What makes you think you can give me orders?" she said sharply.

"Just testing," I told her. "If you were sure of yourself you'd have told me to go to hell, kicked me out, and let Paul come over. But you haven't figured out how much I know or how I fit in." I opened another miniature and drained Añejo over my remaining ice while she watched silently. I sat on the sofa beside her. "Giving you the benefit of the doubt, I'd say you don't know the full extent of the scam."

"Scam?"

"Penny—whatever your name is—I think you're in a dangerous spot."

She laughed thickly. "You drink too much."

"But not tonight." I sipped the chill rum and smacked my lips. "I know a great deal more than you have any reason to imagine. Paul—if that's his name—thinks I gobbled it all up like the big booby bird, and we'll keep it that way. This talk of missing men and great fortunes, a waterlogged corpse in a sunken plane—heavy stuff. I can guess why you're along, and you can tell me if you want. Point is, things are likely to get very dicey—once we've found the plane."

"Then you believe there *is* a plane—at least you believe that."

"Oh, I believe ardently. But your father won't be in it."

Her eyebrows drew together. "Why not?"

"You really want me to tell you?"

Her face turned away. Tightly she said. "I guess not."

I drew the robe from her foot and examined it. She resisted until I said, "Don't make me hurt you," and found what I was looking for on the inside flesh of her big toe. I touched the old track marks, and her muscles went limp. "Smack," I said. "Still hooked?"

"Not for a year," she said tremulously. "What made you . . . ?"

"Your arms are clean. You on anything?"

She shook her head, and I saw tears welling in her eyes.

I found her purse and shook it out on the coffee table. A small prescription bottle rolled out. Mexican Quaaludes. I put the plastic bottle in my pocket and checked the medicine cabinet. Empty. I dumped her suitcase on the bed and went through the pocket liners. Another Lude bottle. I now had her drug supply.

She watched listlessly as I went back to the sofa. "Diehl is an elastic executor," I remarked and studied the bottle labels. Cancún pharmacy, Cancún doc, probably from the hotel where they'd stayed. I opened one bottle, took out four tabs, and placed them on the table. "That'll get you through tomorrow."

"What about the others?" she said pleadingly.

I went to the toilet, dumped the rest of the Ludes into flushing water.

"You must be a narc bastard," she sneered.

"You make it sound like a disease. But Diehl's your candyman, he supplies your drugs to keep you in line. Get your head together—where the hell are your values?"

"Washed away in the sewer." She began sobbing silently, chest heaving.

I sat down and took her hand. "You don't want to be part of Diehl's action," I told her. "It can only be big trouble for you."

"What . . . should I do?"

"Don't let him think I know more than I'm supposed to. Do that and I'll get you out of this mess."

She swallowed, dabbed at her eyes. "How?"

"A flight ticket anyplace you want to go—and cash for resettlement."

She sat up. "Who *are* you?"

"San Nicolás. Santy Claus. That's all you need to know."

She shivered, drew her arms tightly around her breasts. "I'm scared," she whispered.

"You don't need to be, not any more. But cross me and you'll be in more trouble than you could imagine." I sipped from the glass and set it down. "I want a straight answer, and if you lie I can easily find out. Is Diehl his name?"

She nodded. "Paul Diehl. And he's a lawyer."

"Houston?"

"Miami."

I stared at her. I hadn't expected that. Miami added a new dimension. For a while I stared at my glass, the melting ice. Then I said, "Who picked Vernon Saunders?"

"I did."

"Why you?"

"Because I know Houston . . . and Vernon."

"Well?"

"He . . . kept me. Two years."

"Bad choice," I told her. "If a man's supposed to be dead, make sure he is."

"Paul didn't think anyone would check."

"And . . . ?"

"Vernon was the only man I knew wealthy enough to have the kind of money Paul wove into his story."

"Where are you from?"

"Galveston," she said and her mouth twisted. "My name is Astrid Nordstrom. I used to be a dancer. That's how Vernon met me. I did everything I could to get out of the stick shanty where I lived."

"But you're educated."

"High school—and you'll never know how hard it was to try to study, car hop for decent clothing. Ma was a drunk—still is, if she's alive." Her lips trembled. "I shouldn't say that—she did what she could for me."

"Father alive?"

"Who knows? He was a sailor, knocked up my mother and sailed away." Her voice was bitter. "All I got from him was my name." She laughed mirthlessly. "Now you know the kind of trash I am. Still want to help?"

"A deal's a deal, and you're not trash—far from it."

"I'll live with you if you want."

"Thanks—I take it as a compliment. But I have to live alone."

"That waitress . . . what about her?"

"Chela cleans my place, takes care of it. If we go to bed occasionally it's an investment in loyalty."

The lavender eyes regarded me. "Strange way of putting it—but you're a strange man. Are you . . . were you married?"

"Once."

The telephone rang. I said, "You know what to tell him."

Lifting the receiver she said angrily, "*No*, Paul, I'm too damn tired. Don't wake me again." And slammed it down. Turning to me, she said, "I'll have another drink."

I made two more. The Añejo supply was diminishing, but an assortment of bottles remained. And plenty of ice. I wondered where the night was leading.

She said, "Paul told me he's a big defense lawyer—narcotics. It's made him wealthy."

"He could have fooled me. That kind of work takes guts."

"Look under my pillow."

I went to the bedroom and lifted the pillow. Under it lay a Colt .380 automatic. I replaced the pillow and went back to her. "You take it through Customs for him."

She nodded, sipped her drink, and raised her arms to stretch. The robe opened, revealing the smooth swelling of her breasts. She said, "Too late for the disco?"

"Another time," I said. "Diehl's nervous about you. If he bed-checks, you should be here."

Either the liquor or my assurances had restored her confidence. She was the same cool goddess who'd come to my table a few hours ago. The difference was I'd made her my confederate. Brownsville would be glad to know about Diehl, and the Miami office. This was growing like fungus in a hothouse.

She said, "I was to persuade you to cooperate with us."

I twirled ice with one finger. "Diehl got my name in Mérida?"

"They said you had the only amphibian plane."

I nodded. "Are you a certified diver?"

"Absolutely. Vernon had me take the course. We used to dive from his yacht . . . the Bahamas, Grand Cayman. Once we flew to Bonaire for a week." She sighed. "Before his wife found out."

"Sounds good while it lasted."

"Very good. It was a way of life I'd never known—then it ended with a crash. I went back to dancing in a topless bar—twelve-hour nights." She looked away. "Another girl turned me on to horse, without it I couldn't have endured the life. It was degrading."

"You don't have to talk about it."

She shrugged. "How many girls like me have you known?"

"Druggies? Too many. But never one like you." I felt awkward. Now was the time to leave. I started to get up but she said, "You don't have to go."

I wet dry lips.

She said, "If I'm alone I might start feeling sorry for myself and pop all four tabs. That would upset Paul. And I wouldn't be able to dive."

"True."

"Shouldn't you confirm my loyalty?"

"There's that," I agreed, and against all office regs I leaned over and kissed her lips. They were sweet and cool, and when they parted, her tongue was smooth as velvet.

In the dark bedroom we shed our clothing, and as we got into bed she pulled out the Colt and set it on the night table. "Just because Paul looks like a nerd, don't think he won't try to kill you. He's boasted he's killed three men."

"I'll try not to be the fourth." We lay side by side in the dark, cool room. In the silence I could hear her soft breathing. My hand stroked the smooth outlines of her body, caressed her full breasts. We kissed, and passion overwhelmed me. Her thighs parted and we were one.

25

THREE

BEFORE DAWN I was driving back to base. I could have used more sleep, but I had too much to do. Coffee and a cold shower brought me back to reality. I carried air tanks and backpacks, masks, fins, and BCs down the pier and loaded them into the Seabee's baggage compartment. Even with three of us plus the heavy gear we were still under the thousand-pound limit. I topped the tank from my drum of hundred-octane avgas, dipsticked the oil reservoir, and checked the alternator connections. In the cockpit I started the 260HP Lycoming engine, heard it purr smoothly, and shut it down. From under the seat I took my Astra .44 magnum, opened the cylinder, and checked the six soft-nose bullets. No corrosion. I replaced them and twirled the cylinder before reinserting the revolver in its hiding place.

I hoped I wouldn't have to use it.

I didn't like shysters who fattened off drug defendants, got them freed on technicalities or by bribing jurors; but that wasn't sufficient reason to waste this particular lawyer. Even if he was part of something very big in South Florida.

I had a pretty good idea what Diehl wanted to recover from the ocean bottom, and it wasn't Mayan artifacts.

Dawn was beginning to change the ocean's gray into dark lavender, deeper in hue than Astrid's eyes. I went back to the house, fed César and Sheba, and made contact with Brownsville, reporting the situation and what I'd learned. They told me to stand by for response in a quarter of an hour, so I shut down the transmitter and made breakfast, eating eggs and bacon on the patio as morning light turned the ocean green and blue. Except for evening, it was my favorite time of day.

I got into shorts and old *huaraches,* a salt-faded T-shirt. I didn't know how competent a diver Astrid was, so if she got into trouble down below, I wanted to be ready to help.

As I finished my coffee I realized I was no longer uncertain about finding the plane. Diehl wouldn't have mounted so complicated a mission if he wasn't confident of results. After that, of course, he'd have to protect himself. By silencing me. Forever.

After fourteen minutes I turned on the set and heard Brownsville come in. The office said Diehl was Luis Parra's principal lawyer, Parra being the big Colombian dealer with ten murders to his personal credit. So they wanted Diehl sufficiently alive to cooperate with the South Florida Task Force that had been trying to locate Parra for a year since his escape. Two federal marshals had been slaughtered in that episode, and Parra had vanished. He could be back in Columbia, Miami, or even Mexico. Anywhere. Making Diehl precious property. I was to bring him in without reference to the Mexicans. If they got him, Diehl could stall extradition for years.

Or take a bullet in the brain from one of Parra's hitmen.

Astrid, they said, was an essential witness: not only to Diehl's plot, but to whatever came up from the plane. Once in Brownsville she'd get protective custody under the federal witness program; name change, steady pay. Not a bad deal for her, I reflected after I'd shut down the set. A second chance at a life she'd been excluded from first time around.

Interesting that Luis Parra should drift onto my scope again. Two years ago he'd been on DEA's most-wanted list, when I picked up his trail in New Orleans through Superdome box tickets he'd bought from a scalper. After the Saints game, Parra flew to Freeport, B.I., where I located him in the Casbah Casino blowing a big wad of dough at the tables.

I bribed two Bahamian cops to distract his bodyguards while I dragged Parra out of a bed he was sharing with two broads. He was so drunk I had to pull on his pants, and that was all he wore during the night crossing to U.S. waters.

Figuring his boys would be waiting for Parra in Miami, I landed at Ft. Lauderdale and kept him tied in the gear locker until agents from the Miami office arrived and took him away.

After that his lawyers got busy, charging kidnapping, physical abuse, violation of Parra's first-through-Twentieth-Amendment rights, and they'd probably have gotten him out of the Federal Correctional Facility, charges dismissed, or at least on bail. But being a typical wise guy Parra couldn't wait while the judge thought things over, and went the escape route.

Which made my own shortcutting moot, though the U.S. attorney and the Strike Force chief chewed me out and had me transferred u/c to Cozumel where, they said, I'd have fewer opportunities to exercise initiative.

But Diehl looked like a live lead to Parra, and I was ready to follow wherever it took me.

Eight-thirty. Diehl and Astrid should be leaving the hotel. I secured the base and walked down the pier, both dogs frolicking around me, licking my hands, nipping my calves. I climbed into the cockpit, cast off the snub line, and closed the door. Light breeze turned the nose seaward, and I started the engine, waggled the rudder, and lowered flaps for takeoff.

Mixture rich, taxiing into the wind, I shoved the throttle forward, and after a few bounces the Seabee rose on its hull step and the wing floats lifted free of the sea. I drew back the control column and watched the surface receding below. The flight was so short I didn't raise flaps; I climbed a few hundred feet and headed for the rendezvous beach.

I was picking a landing spot when I saw the two of them coming down the sand to where small fishing and snorkeling boats were beached. I dipped my wing, turned seaward, and eased the throttle. Heading into the wind, I set a long flat glide to touchdown and taxied back toward the beach. By then a small outboard launch was heading out. I kept the prop turning enough to hold against wind and current, caught a bow line from Diehl, and snubbed it as they climbed into the rear of the small cabin. "Buckle up," I said and tossed the line back to the boatman.

"Right on time," Diehl observed. "I like that."

"I like it myself," I said, half-business but in keeping with the semi-holiday spirit that invests strangers going where they've never been before. "Sleep well?"

"Marvelously," Astrid said, and Diehl nodded. "Me, too."

I gave them binoculars, and Diehl handed me his map. Pretending to study it, I said, "We'll cross the island's southern end, cruise at two thousand feet, and if you spot something, we'll drop down for a look. I brought diving gear."

"Good idea," Diehl said. "You're thorough."

"I'll take that balance now." I reached back and felt crisp traveler's checks against my palm. "I'll give you a receipt when we're ashore."

"Whenever."

I folded the checks into my wallet and ruddered into the wind. "Miss Saunders," I said, "do you find this exciting?"

"Very. It's such a funny-looking little plane."

"Like the Model A it's reliable. Are you frightened?"

"A little."

"Cheap thrills, eh?"

Diehl scowled. "What's your range?"

"Four-fifty miles without headwinds, cruising at one-twenty. In practical terms I could make Veracruz or Guatemala City—but I've never tried."

"But not the States?"

"I could fly about two-thirds of the way, paddle the rest. Did Mr. Saunders's plane have auxiliary tanks?"

"I assume so," Diehl said. "Can we get started?"

I shoved the throttle forward, bounced on a small wave to lift onto the step, and then we were hit by cascading spray until I pulled back on the stick. I climbed in wide spirals that took us across the ceiba jungle below —just as the pilot of the lost plane had two years ago. I showed them El Mirador beach, the departure point, slowed to a hundred knots, and began circling.

Holding the column between my knees, I glanced back and saw them looking down through binoculars at the smooth surface of the Caribbean. Astrid was wearing what she had at the café—except for the high-fashion boots. What I could see of her T-shirt read *error,* and I found myself wondering if it was an omen. She turned slightly and I saw the initial T. It made me feel better until I remembered Diehl would have the Colt where he could get it out fast. But until we located something he'd keep it out of sight. So in a way I could time things. And thanks to Astrid I knew about his pistol.

But did *he* know I knew? Had Astrid told him? Did all three of us share his secrets? The thought troubled me, but I told myself I was in my elements—air and sea—and he wasn't. Diehl's turf was the courtroom— lousy bastard. I looked down at the mottled sea. The dark areas were reefs, kelp, or deep crevices in the ocean floor. Most of the sport diving was at Palancar, off the southeast bend of the island, and even for an experienced diver the reef was awesome in size, depth, and variety of marine life. Coral heads ten feet across.

To the north, half a dozen charter fishermen were trolling for sail, outriggers splayed widely. I could see baits skipping over the water, chalking the flat green sea. *Corsair* was one of them, and Carlos had better collect for two days' hire. I could have reminded him by radio, but there was no need to let Diehl know our communications link.

I extended my turn another half-mile seaward and heard Diehl shout, *"There! Down there!"* Pointing excitedly, he handed me the binoculars. I banked left and, fitting the lenses to my eyes, looked down.

FOUR

I SAW IT, too. A whitish sliver far below that could be a wing or the fuselage panel. Whatever it was lay on a shelf less than a hundred feet deep. Keeping it in view, I spiraled down and dropped a marker above it. The smoke showed wind direction as I came in, and we touched down only yards away. I cut back the engine, idling just enough to keep the pusher prop turning, opened the door, and tossed out the sea anchor to retard drift. On the deck behind their seats was a styrofoam float with a center section of plexiglass.

"Miss Saunders," I said, "perhaps you'd like to take a look."

She nodded, but Diehl said, "You're familiar with aircraft. You go."

I grimaced. "All right, but don't let the line get away from you—and haul me back when I signal." I shoved the float through the door and gave Diehl the nylon tether cord. I pulled off shorts and sandals and went over the side.

The water below was cool and refreshing. I surfaced and pulled myself onto the float, shouted at Diehl to pay out line, and began drifting from the plane. Then I gazed down.

Below, it seemed the surface of another planet, where everything moved in slow motion: kelp and purple sea fans waved ponderously in the current, grouper and parrotfish orbited their nests under coral heads, the mottled brown body of a large Moray slithered into a rocky crevice. I sculled over a massive coral outcrop and saw what we'd spotted from the air.

It lay on its side, lapstrakes white and barely stained by algae. Before plunging to rest on the sea floor, it had been a two-masted yawl, about forty feet long. Its red-lead keel slanted out like a broad scimitar, and I could see the broken masts, the silt-dulled sails. The rudder was gone, there was a jagged tear amidships as though a torpedo had gone through, but my guess was reef puncture. I wondered if men had died, but all that was history and irrelevant.

Looking up I waved at Diehl and sculled toward the plane. While he secured the float, I clung to the wing strut and worked my way back into the cabin. "Well?" Diehl demanded. "What is it?"

"A boat." I began hauling in the drogue, squeezed water from its bucket and passed it back to Astrid to stow. After a shot of rum, I got on my shorts and sandals and closed the cabin door. "We'll keep looking."

I TOOK THE plane to three thousand feet and another half-mile beyond the island. While they scanned the sea, I began trying to figure out why a pilot wanting to fly west by northwest toward Texas would have gone down southeast of the island. That course would have taken him near the western tip of Cuba—hardly safe airspace—en route the Florida Keys. Another explanation was that the pilot had filed a false plan and flown another heading.

Or his compass failed.

Astrid tapped my shoulder. "Sharks down there."

I scanned the school through her binoculars. "Dolphin," I told her.

"How can you tell?"

"Sharks' tails are vertical—dolphin have horizontal tails, flat."

"Hell with the fish," Diehl snapped. "You sure we're looking where I told you?"

"If you can do better, take the wheel." I lifted my hands and looked around. His face was frozen. "Jesus—no, for God's sake, Novak, keep steering!"

I put a hand on the column. "Maybe your info was bad. The Indian could have seen a falling star."

"No, I'm sure it was Saunders's plane. I questioned him closely."

Astrid said, "Maybe we're too high."

"Possibly," I said, "so we'll try from five hundred."

Down we went, scouring the smooth surface, back and forth, out and around without seeing more than a couple of obvious wrecks. Finally I said, "To anyone watching us this is getting a little obvious. Let's knock off for lunch while I refuel."

"Fine with me," Astrid said. "Paul, maybe you could talk with that man again."

"God knows where *he's* gone," Diehl said irritably, "I had a hell of a time finding him before."

"Maybe I could help—my Spanish is pretty good."

"Never mind, I can get a translator from the hotel."

"Interpreter," I corrected. "Break for lunch?"

"Yeah."

I flew back along the coast, touching down near the beach off Chancanab. The bottom was smooth, so I eased into shallows and let them out in less than a foot of water. Diehl peered at the big, open-sided thatched huts shaped like kilns. "What the hell are they?"

"*Palapas.* You can buy food and drink but avoid the water." I looked at my watch. "Back in an hour."

They waded ashore and up the sand. The wind turned me seaward, and I took off again. This time I landed at the airport and had a light lunch while they gassed and serviced the plane. I considered calling Brownsville but had nothing to add to what the office already knew.

Where the hell was the sunken plane?

An army captain named Jaramillo came over and, uninvited, sat down. He was an airport hanger-on and a lover of freebies. I ordered him a Carta Blanca and he pushed back his cap and opened his collar before tilting the bottle to his thick lips. He clasped it in a pudgy hand, fingers like thick cigars. When the bottle was half-drained he set it down. "All morning you fly off the south end."

"You're well informed."

He pulled a toothpick from the table jar and began working on his stained teeth. "What interests you there?"

"Spotting sail for Carlos."

"Find any?"

"A few, but far out. The party won't care—they'll settle for shark and barracuda."

He shrugged. "Good money, eh?"

"Occasionally."

"Maybe I'll buy a boat like yours."

"Too many boats already," I said, "not enough gamefish."

"That's a nice *casita* you've got. Why don't you ever invite me there?"

"I haven't gotten around to having guests."

"I know some girls—we could have a fine party on the beach."

"Not a bad idea. Bring a whore for yourself. Your wife will do for me."

While he was working on the inner meaning, I paid the check and got up. "Have a splendid afternoon," I told him and went back to my plane.

As I checked tire inflation I wondered if I'd ever get to be alone with Astrid. Already I was losing hope of finding the downed plane.

THEY WERE WAITING at water's edge when I taxied close to the sand. Diehl's skin had a slight burn from eating in the sun, but Astrid looked fresh and vital as though the sun pumped vitamins into her body. Breeze feathered her lovely hair, and as she climbed in, her thigh brushed my arm. I wouldn't mind flying forever with her, I reflected, but Diehl was excess to my needs. Still, he was what interested the office.

During the morning I'd noticed his professional patina peeling away; as anxiety grew through the hours of searching, he'd become curt and nervous. The sea-change made it easier to visualize him as a shyster who did Parra's slimy work.

I glanced around to check seatbelts and noticed Astrid's eyes; there was a vacant glitter and I realized she'd popped another pill. I shifted the rudder to catch the breeze, the outgoing tide took us into deeper water, and in less than a minute we were airborne.

Back over the search grounds, I cruised at five hundred until Diehl grabbed my arm. "Down there, Novak!"

I banked around and flew back at fifty feet, looked down, and shook my head. "Sand," I said. "A patch between two ridges."

He swore.

"We've got a better chance now the sun angle's changed," I told him, "if the plane's shadowed by a ridge."

I climbed to a thousand feet and began spiraling outward. El Mirador was still my reference point, but from the ground those beaches looked pretty much the same. Diehl could have mistaken one for another.

On the other hand, if the plane had exploded in the air, its debris wouldn't be recognizable on the bottom. Not after two years.

If that was the interval.

Drug pilots collected for the loads they carried, so most of them strained their planes' limits with deadly results. The depths off Colombia's Santa Marta peninsula were an aircraft junkyard.

Gradually I turned north and began scanning beyond an adjacent beach. Offshore, a mile or so away, a boat was fighting a sailfish. It lifted from the water in bursts of foam, tail skittering across the sea. Not my boat, unfortunately, for it looked like a trophy-size fish.

Dark clouds were gathering on the horizon; a summer storm was moving in. I gestured, and Diehl growled, "So what?"

"So we can't fly much longer."

He swore again. Astrid's face was impassive. I wondered if she was immune to his coarseness or zonked on pills.

I turned on the radio and listened to the weather report. Barometer falling, front ten miles distant and moving toward Cozumel. Unwelcome news. I said, "We'll try another few minutes, then secure."

"So you can milk another eight hundred tomorrow?" he sneered.

Astrid said, "Paul!" but I snapped, "If you don't like it get another pilot."

While we snarled at each other I'd let the plane ease northward, and when I next glanced down I saw a light angular shape at the edge of a dark irregular area. Taking Astrid's binoculars, I banked for a better view. Something definitely there. Prow of a smashed boat? I had a feeling it wasn't.

I banked to the right so Diehl could see and began spiraling down. The clouds looked ominous, and I wondered if there was time to use the float and get airborne before the storm hit. In a front like that, there could be winds strong enough to tear the Seabee apart.

I dropped a smoke marker and went down, full flaps, onto the sea. Taxiing back, I said, "Penny? Want to splash around?"

"Love to."

Diehl snapped, "Like hell you will," so I shoved out drogue and float and jumped in.

Advance winds were whipping up the sea. I stroked with the current and began looking down through the plexiglass.

It was there, all right, about eighty feet below, a white geometrical shape not found in nature. Nearby there seemed to be a bulky mass, shrouded by kelp, that could be broken fuselage. I drifted further and saw a wing trailing edge-up like the blade of a knife.

No wonder it hadn't been spotted before. Of course, I wasn't sure this was the object of Diehl's search, couldn't be until someone went down and checked the numbers. I looked up and felt wind tugging at my wet hair. I waved at Diehl, and he began hauling in.

Back in my seat I said, "It's a plane."

"God damn!" Diehl shouted exultantly and grabbed Astrid around her shoulders.

"It's broken up, and I can't see the registry numbers because of the way it lies."

Astrid said, "How far down?"

"Less than a hundred feet. On a shelf edge with deep water beyond. How deep have you been?"

"Hundred-twenty, but not for long."

We were about three hundred yards offshore. A heavy stand of gray rock jutted onto the beach: the landmark.

Diehl pounded the back of my seat. "Maybe you can dive after the storm."

"The bottom will be stirred up. We'll try tomorrow. Seatbelts." I hit the throttle and took off toward the storm, banked around, and fled from it toward the shelter of a lagoon off the coastal highway not far from their hotel. Waves bounced us around, and I saw Diehl's sunburned face pale at the cheekbones. Poor sailor?

As rain spattered the fuselage, Astrid pushed the tail around and waved goodbye. Diehl was sitting on the beach, knees apart, head down. I knew the posture and smiled as I took off again. I flew to the airport, cranked down the wheels, and landed, taxiing to a tiedown area to wait out the storm. I was barely inside when rain struck like bullets.

ASTRID SAID, "I was beginning to think we'd never find it."

We were sitting poolside at the hotel, drinking mango daiquiris and gazing at each other across a decorative table. The storm had passed, and now in early evening the sky was clear, only the hint of onshore breeze. Her eyes were normal again, their lavender so rich and deep that my breath caught. "Too bad about Paul," I said and twirled my glass.

"Not the bourbon, bad water in the ice cubes." She smiled. "I thought I'd never get him to the elevator. It wasn't . . . very pleasant."

"He'll survive."

"So the doctor said." She sipped from her glass. "I love the way you fly that plane. Where did you learn?"

"Navy." The subject was one I wanted to avoid so I said, "What's the plan tomorrow?"

"While we were lunching, Paul said he wanted me to dive with you when we found the plane. And I'd feel safer if we're together. You're supposed to search the pilot for ID and stay out of the cargo compartment. That's my job."

"He told you what to look for?"

"Aluminum suitcases—that's how he described them."

"Remember, that's supposed to be your father down there, so be appropriately sorrowful and horrified. Any remains won't be pretty to look at."

The *Sunward* was backing away from the pier. Festal music drifted over the water. The sounds clashed with my thoughts of death. "We'll be conspicuous out there. I'm surprised Paul didn't want a night dive."

"I'd be terrified to go down in the dark."

"With lights?"

"Even with lights." She was wearing a coarsely knit cotton top with a fashionably drooping neckline. "Ever make it underwater?"

"In a pool, but it's an overrated amusement."

She laughed. "Okay, we'll stick to business down there. But all the time I was sitting in the plane I wanted to put my arms around you, kiss the back of your neck, nibble your ear."

"I hoped you would." I took her hand and pressed it. "How does he plan to get the stuff off Cozumel?"

"He might hire a longer-range plane, but he hasn't said. Remember, I'm part window-dressing, part diver. I don't know much else."

"If things should turn nasty, stay out of it, understand?"

Carlos appeared at the table, stared at Astrid open-mouthed, and recovered himself enough to exclaim, *"Que garota!"*

"Um?"

"He says you're attractive."

"Thank him for me."

"Pendejo," I said pleasantly, "stop staring at her and state your business." This in Spanish. *Pendejo* is *not* a nice word.

"What tits," he observed, also in Spanish. "You're lucky, partner."

"We're not going to stay partners long if you keep that up. Carlos, *Señorita* Saunders. Penny, this fishing bum is Carlos Paz, and he has a truly foul mouth."

"I'm sure I've heard it all. You can't imagine the joints I worked in."

Carlos said, "We boarded three sails, Juan. Kept two for weighing."

"And the money?"

He flashed a thick roll of pesos. "I know who to trust."

"You were lucky." A thought came to me and I turned to Astrid who was watching bathers sitting around the water-bar. "We'll take my boat tomorrow and have the comforts of home."

"That *would* be better—if Paul goes along with it." She glanced at Carlos. "I don't think he'll want your friend."

I shrugged. "Tell him I might get suspicious if he excludes the captain."

She nodded slowly. "I'll explain it's easier and safer to dive from a boat than from your little plane."

To Carlos I said, "We've got a charter tomorrow."

"Ya sé."

"No, a new one—us, plus a *gringo* upstairs with *turista.*"

He frowned. "I gave my word, Juan."

"Give the charter to Casimiro or Rolando. This is private."

He shrugged in his expressive Mexican way. "What time?"

"We need to be off El Mirador by eleven."

"Leave at half-past eight."

To Astrid I said, "Eight-thirty at the yacht basin. I'll have tanks, buoy, a raft, and diving gear. Some lights."

"Sounds good."

I said to Carlos, "We'll be doing some diving. Bring food and beer and water. We won't need the rods. I'll be at the boat by eight."

"Okay. What's the sick *gringo* like?"

"You won't like him," I said. "Just run the boat and don't worry about him. Anyway, he's a *licenciado* and not built for rough stuff."

"I've known some tough *licenciados.*" He used the word *duros.*

"Not this one."

He shrugged again. "I'll see Casimiro." Bowing to Astrid, he went away.

"So," she said, "it's arranged?"

"As far as I'm concerned."

"And when the cases are on board you arrest Paul?"

I tried to keep it light. "I can't arrest anyone. I can't even write traffic tickets."

"Well, you're involved with the government—in some way."

"I cooperate from time to time—when I see things I don't like. Since we know the dead pilot isn't Vernon Saunders, who might he be?"

"Paul didn't say. Someone he hired, I guess."

I finished my drink. "Ever occur to you I'm planning to rip off Diehl?"

"I thought of it."

"Would you care?"

"Not if I weren't hurt."

"That's sensible. Keep your eyes and ears open tomorrow, and we'll get out of this with what we want." I looked up at the top floor balcony, and there was Diehl in a bathrobe, looking down at us. I waved casually and gave him thumbs-up as if wishing him well. Abruptly he bent over as though in spasm and disappeared from view. Nosy son of a bitch, wondering if I planned to screw his girl. His ex-girl.

"How many Ludes left?"

"One—for tonight."

"You don't need that shit."

"I'm accustomed to it."

"Get unaccustomed," I told her. "We'll be down too deep too long for kidding around. Diving on a high is like jumping from a plane without a chute."

"God, you're straight," she said with the first anger she'd shown me.

"Like a lance," I told her, "and all the way."

She swallowed. "I'm sorry—it's just that you can make me feel so . . . uncomfortable." She glanced up at Diehl's balcony before reaching for my hand. "Your place or mine?"

"Yours. Then dinner in town—maybe hit the disco."

"Swinger, huh?"

"Sometimes."

So we went to her room, closed the curtains, and made love, expending all the accumulated passion of the day; falling asleep then and waking after dark. Except for bikini patches her body was evenly tanned, her pubis a shade darker than her sunbleached hair.

In some ways she reminded me of my former wife; beautifully formed body but lacking a few degrees of what I used to think of as character. Irresolute; a drifter, accepting the easy way.

But I didn't want to think about Pamela—not then, preferably never. But in the quiet of my bungalow at night when I couldn't get to sleep Pam came back to me, and I thought of her beauty and her wasted life. Together we'd been two sides of a coin that turned false, counterfeit. Who to blame? Her genes? Mine? So different, so unlike . . .

Lips moving over my throat. For an instant I thought it was Pamela, but the hair was too golden, too silken. I closed my eyes and kissed her hairline. Remembering . . .

WE ENTERED MORGAN'S courtyard, an atrium of tropical plants and flowers, sheltered tables around the sides. Pleasant to see the handsomely varnished wood, so reminiscent of old New England, and pass time over a beer with the breeze coming gently through. The adjacent restaurant was air-conditioned, with deep carpeting and white linen napery. We could have been in a good restaurant in Mexico City or New York. Coming in from the old cobbled streets of San Miguel, we entered another world, one few Migueleños got to see. Or could afford.

Afterward, we drove down the coast to the Kayab ruins and walked along the trail until we could see the ancient castle's dark gray outline against the lighter sky. It stood on a high promontory, waves breaking on the rocky fall below, water phosphorescent where it caught the moonlight.

She gripped my hand. "It's magic," she breathed, "fantastic."

"They were builders," I said, "and mathematicians. This *castillo* was standing when Moses wandered the desert."

"It's just incredible," she murmured, caught up in a rapture of her own. "What happened to the Mayans?"

"They created something—and were enslaved by it."

"What?"

"A calendar. They lived by and for it. It was their narcotic."

I saw her face turn downward. She moved away, but I plucked a red flower from a nearby bush and threaded it into her hair. For a fractional second I remembered doing the same for Pam—on our honeymoon.

Astrid linked her hand around my neck. "That was nice. It's been . . . oh, so long since anyone did that." She kissed my cheek. "John, Juan, Jack Novak, you're a very nice man."

"Diehl doesn't think so."

"Why did you have to spoil the moment?" she said tightly. "You're always thinking of him. I'm just a way to get at him."

"You were his way of getting at me."

Her fingers touched the flower petals and she looked away. "Are you going to kill him?"

"Would you care?"

"Not especially." She took my hands, nails digging into my palms. "Why?"

"Because he plans to kill me."

FIVE

AN UNDERCOVER MAN lives a lie. He lives it even when he sleeps, if he's going to survive. Some live their role so well and so long it consumes them, and they forget which side they're on. I was fully conscious of the dividing line that separated me from traffickers and hit men, but I harbored a disposition to waste Diehl.

Erase him from Astrid's life.

I sniffed morning breeze and decided to shelve that kind of thinking. I had a job to do, and so far I'd done it well. Carlos came up from the cabin, saying, "Everything stowed—water, beer, food. Shells in the shotgun."

Four air tanks in gunwale racks. Masks and regulators, weight belts, fins, and buoyancy compensators. Orange buoy for the wreck. Leg knives, rubber boat, drum of nylon line. And my Astra in the map drawer forward of the wheel. "Gas?"

"Filled tanks last night. Fifty pounds of ice in the chest." He looked landward down the pier. "They're late."

"Yeah. I'd rather he purge himself ashore than here."

Carlos grinned. "You make love to the *rúbia*, eh?"

I'd left her bed at five-thirty, but I said, "She's the *licenciado*'s woman."

"Maybe—but yesterday when I was with the two of you—*hombre*, it was like a whorehouse. I could smell the lust."

My throat was dry, but I made myself swallow. "*Indio*, you've got imagination. You should be a writer."

"What would I write about, fish?"

"A *gringo* did—and got the Nobel Prize."

I saw them leave the taxi and walk toward us, Astrid in the lead, Diehl trailing behind. He looked older and thinner than yesterday, and he walked carefully over the planking. I knew where my gun was; I wondered about his.

Diehl sort of grunted at me when I told him my captain's name. Diehl licked his lips. "I didn't want this setup. That man reliable?"

"He's an *hombre de confianza,* as we say—and very proud. Watch your mouth around him."

Diehl peered out at the ocean. I said, "Anyway, what's so secret about diving on a sunken plane? You want the stiff's name, not the loot. Right?"

"Is there a berth below? I think I'll lie down."

"Help yourself—but I'll take the day's pay now."

He might have been sick but not too weak to argue. So I said, "You've hired an expensive boat, master and captain, diving gear, and the services of a qualified diver. Eight hundred's cheap for that—lunch included."

Sitting down, he endorsed traveler's checks, and I noticed a bulge under his shirt—too irregular for fat and about the size of a Colt .380.

Astrid said, "I think I'll stay up here." She was wearing designer sunglasses and a cute little visored cap; otherwise she was ready to strap on a tank and dive. As I gazed at her, I wondered what we'd find below.

I cast off the lines, and Carlos started the engines, and we swung out and away from the pier. Three well-fed pelicans watched from guano-streaked pilings.

Above, a Mexicana 727 was coming in for an airport landing. One of the cruise ships was leaving port. In Cozumel another day was taking shape and form.

Once outside shoal water I took the wheel, and Carlos opened bottles of chilled Garci-Crespo water and passed them around. Astrid took one, but after going down into the cabin Carlos came back with the bottle. "The *licenciado* says he's not feeling good."

"Well," I said, "maybe sea air will help." Astrid smiled, stretched her long legs on the transom where the sun could reach them. I got out a backpack and fitted it around her body, adjusting the straps to her waist and shoulders—and managing to brush her breasts. "Don't do that," she whispered.

"That's bad?"

She wiggled inside the harness. "Feels good. But I know what would feel better."

We smiled at each other—knowingly, like school kids in love.

Carlos turned on the sonar ranger, and I watched a developing profile of the bottom. Astrid said, "I'd better see if Paul needs anything." She undid the harness and went down to the cabin. I fitted her harness over the nearest tank and locked the stainless steel loop. I added regulators, checked pressure at three thousand psi, and added a drop of detergent to each facemask, smearing it around to prevent condensation. Behind me Astrid said, "He seems to be sleeping. Poor man, the bug took a big, big bite."

"It'll do that," I agreed, "so he ought to keep up his strength. Maybe a thick slab of fried pork liver with onion gravy and chilis for brunch. Stiffen his spine."

She doubled over laughing. "Or destroy it."

Carlos grinned, too, getting the general idea.

After that we calmed down and watched the sea and shore. Soon we passed Chancanab, where Diehl had consumed the impure ice cubes. The kiln-shaped *palapas* were distinctive landmarks for boats. Already some were gathering over Palancar Reef a mile ahead, and I found myself wishing I were taking her there instead of to the deeper wreckage of a contraband plane.

From her belt she removed the diving knife and strapped it around her right calf. Today's T-shirt was high-visibility orange; no Texas Terror legend across her breasts. I said, "How long since you've been down?"

"Four months."

"In case you've forgotten, bottom time at ninety feet is only thirty minutes. Don't ascend faster than your smallest bubbles. We'll need a reasonable rest before a second dive to bleed off nitrogen." I looked at her. "*If* there's a second dive."

She nodded thoughtfully. Pointing shoreward I said, "There's Kayab."

"I'll remember it—always."

I went down to check on Diehl. He was asleep, body moving with the easy roll of the boat. I should sleep that well, I thought. Well, they say murderers sleep best of all. I went past him and began to unfold the bundled rubber boat, remembering my pre-dawn contact with Brownsville. Some office asshole was practically airborne wanting to come down and lend me a hand wrapping up Diehl, and I'd said for God's sake if I couldn't handle him alone, they ought to fire me. They didn't want to risk a flap in the middle of an op, so they agreed on hands off. But they'd send an unmarked Lear, on signal, to pick up my client and fly him to Miami. With suitable escorts.

But would it be so easy? Chance had landed Diehl in my lap, and he had no idea how welcome he was. I'd taken his girl, and now I was going after his money and his freedom. It seemed like a lot, but he was an unwholesome presence in the world of drugs. His kind corrupted courts, the system of justice itself. He deserved no mercy; didn't deserve to live.

43

Diehl moaned, sat up quickly and grabbed his belly, lurched off the bunk and into the head. I closed the door on a volley of unattractive sounds. Poisoning him hadn't entered my mind; nature and *E. coli* had taken charge.

Topside I filled my lungs with fresh air. "It's unsanitary below," I told Astrid, "better stay here."

She glanced around. "Is there a spot where I can get a—let's say— complete tan?"

"Up forward. I'll rig a screen and tell Carlos not to peek."

So we worked it out, and she lay back on a pad, naked to sun and sky. I applied tanning oil to her front and nearly blew my mind. Then I went over the chart with Carlos, showing him the outcrop landmark. He drank a beer and chomped an onion sandwich while I steered around Punta Sur and took a bearing on the lighthouse at the island's southern tip. The sonar chart showed more than twenty fathoms below. A hundred feet off the starboard bow a gray dorsal sliced the water, and I estimated the shark's length at nine feet. I had a bang stick aboard and decided we might as well take it down. In shark waters I liked better odds than a single knife. The bang stick's 12-gauge magnum shell was instant death to anything smaller than a killer whale.

Turning the wheel over to Carlos, I went forward and stared at that gorgeous body. Shading her eyes Astrid said, "Will you do my back?"

"I'll do you standing on your head."

"Not here you won't." She tapped the oil bottle and turned over. Great buns—I'd admired them before and longer. Kneeling, I oiled my hands, started at the base of her neck and worked down, massaging her spine, flattening the little lumbar dimples, kneading the streamlined handholds, and delicately working the base of her spine. "Uh-uh," she murmured, "that's enough."

I'd forgotten Diehl, the basket case, until a shadow warned me, and I looked up to see him lurching toward us. In one hand was a gun and it pointed at me. "What the hell you think you're doing?" he snarled. "I oughta shoot you now!"

SIX

THERE ARE TIMES for fast physical response, others for non-
chalance. I figured Diehl's illness had diminished his common
sense, and jealousy had taken charge. So I shrugged. "Penny's
idea."

She sat up, hands covering her breasts. "Oh, Paul, don't be so emotional.
If I need protecting I'll let you know."

"Yeah," I said. "Just because she's sunning without a nappy's no reason
to think I'm preparing to rape her."

He glanced at her, then back to me, and I knew he was feeling foolish
and out of line. He stood uncertainly, swaying with the roll. Rising, I said,
"You finish the job, pal—I've got things to do," and walked past him,
ignoring the gun.

In the wheelhouse, Carlos lowered the hand that had been gripping the
overhead shotgun. "Gracias," I said, "but I don't want any gunplay." I
went below and dragged the rubber boat topside, inflating it with the
compressed-air bottle. From a corner of my eye I saw Diehl make his way
unsteadily to the cabin. If he draws on me again, I thought, I'll shove it
down his throat.

We rounded the island and headed toward where we'd found the plane
the day before. Diehl hadn't come off well in our faceoff, so he was likely to
try to improve on it when we got down to basics. Letting me know he
packed iron hadn't been prudent, and he was probably regretting it in the
comfort of his bunk. Trouble was, while I was busy with the sunken plane
he'd be able to arrange things topside to his advantage. He was smart—
had to be—and any effective defense lawyer can improvise on the spot. Of

45

course, he'd have Carlos to contend with, but I had confidence in my captain.

Another half-hour and I signaled Carlos to throttle back. Then I woke Astrid and told her to get ready. Brushing hair from her face she whispered, "God, that was close! Suppose we'd been making it?"

"We wouldn't be talking now." I kissed her lips, she said, "That's nice," and I took the wheel from Carlos, maneuvering the boat until it was where I wanted it. The depth ranger showed sixteen fathoms when Carlos began to pay out the anchor, and I saw Astrid getting into her diving gear. Carlos lowered the stern dive platform as Diehl emerged from the cabin. I got out of my shorts and into trunks and T-shirt, and lugged air tanks aft to the transom.

Diehl said, "If the pilot's body is down there, bring up anything that might establish identity."

"Hell, I'll hand you the whole corpse."

"That won't be necessary," he said tautly. "Just follow instructions, Novak. You don't seem to realize how important this is."

To whom? I thought, but said, "Okay, if there's a body there not Saunders's—what then?"

"I try to think positively, suppose you do the same."

"Yassuh." I strapped on my tank, helped Astrid over the transom onto the platform, and looped nylon line around my upper arm. I slipped into the BC, pulled on fins, and rinsed my mask. To Astrid I said, "Ready, partner?"

Nodding, she fitting the regulator mouthpiece inside her lips and pressed the purge valve. Carlos handed me the bang stick. I looped its lanyard over my left wrist, bit down on the rubber mouthpiece, and eased off the platform.

Coolly refreshing water enveloped me as I dropped downward in a mass of bubbles. As they cleared I glanced up and saw Astrid's fins above.

The underwater world is silent, the only sound the bubbling of your breath, and once your consciousness excludes it, the silence becomes overwhelming. In every dive I feel like an intruder in another level of existence; motion slows, and as you descend, colors gradually fade until at ten fathoms there's only black and white and gray.

When Astrid reached me I looked around and spotted the plane farther away than I'd expected. I pointed, she gave me thumbs-up, and together we slanted down. From now until we surfaced, communication was through the hand signals divers use.

Below us, a patch of lime-white sand surrounded by tall fronds. There were coral and flint-dark volcanic rock, sea fans and brown beds of kelp.

We glided across a ridge, and I saw that the far-side wing was missing—probably fallen into the deep canyon beyond.

The plane lay on its side, wing twisted down over the cockpit door. It was a Piper all right, painted white and striped in a color that could have been blue. I glanced at my depth gauge: ten fathoms, and farther to go.

A silvery yard-long barracuda flashed past, and I felt Astrid grip my arm. His turf, not mine, so I slowed descent until he was vanishing in the deep beyond.

The plane didn't seem to have been two years on the bottom. Very little silt dulled the horizontal surfaces, and no algae to speak of. We reached sand bottom near the tip of the wing, and I tied nylon line to the strut, yanking it a few times to let Carlos know we'd bottomed. He'd attach a marker buoy and let it drift. In an emergency he could follow it down to where we were, but I didn't expect any problems. Not until we reached the boat again.

Astrid swam over to the cargo hatch, and I realized I was going to have trouble with the cockpit door. The wing lay partly across it. I tried shoving the wing aside, but the bent metal didn't budge.

I'd used a lot of air in the effort and rested to slow my breathing. Then I drifted onto the nose, noticed the bent prop—it had been turning on impact—and looked in through the windshield.

Ahead of me a swarm of tiny fish—purple wrasses—moved among black strands that looked like fine ocean grass. My shadow frightened them and they darted away, following the alpha fish. Now I could see what they'd been feeding on. Dark hair moved in the slow current, but it was all that was still attached to the skull—except for sunglasses whose metal frames glinted dully. Behind the opaque lenses, empty holes where little damselfish darted and played.

Nose, ears, and facial flesh were missing, devoured by crabs, eels, and other scavengers. Above the collar of the leather flying jacket thrust a column of bone. The chest seemed strangely flat, and what I could see of the trousers billowed emptily. Of the corpse only the bony structure remained.

The arms hung down, finger bones still intact.

It was a gruesome scene, one I'd never seen before and hoped never to see again.

I checked my wrist chronometer; nearly fifteen minutes had passed, half our bottom time. Looking along the fuselage, I saw Astrid had opened the cargo panel and was tugging something out. The shape glinted brightly. Well, that was her job.

Mine was to get at the corpse and locate ID. I used my knife to pierce the plexiglass windshield until I'd made a puncture big enough to saw with the serrated edge. It was slow work, but I managed to cut and pry a hole big enough to get one arm through. I unsnapped pocket buttons and pulled out a leather billfold. A driver's license was sealed in plastic. With difficulty I read the name, Fernando Guzmán, and a street address in Port Arthur, Texas. There was a wad of greenbacks and nothing else. I decided I didn't want to bring up the identifying license and dropped it back into the plane. I tucked the billfold in my trunks and swam over to Astrid. She was half into the hatch, and on the bottom rested a metal suitcase. As I watched, her body moved backward until I could see that she was pulling out a second case. She let it drop to the bottom and glanced at me. I showed her my chronometer and checked her air pressure: 1800 psi remaining. My gauge showed under 1500.

Through faceplates we gazed at each other, and I knew we were both thinking the same thing: what to do with the loot?

I swam over and peered down into the cargo hatch. There was a jumble of spare clothing: raincoat, rubber sandals, an umbrella, a bundle of tie-down cords; but no more containers. Astrid had brought out what Paul Diehl wanted.

I picked up one of the cases, walked it over to where I'd tied the nylon buoy-line, and returned with the other. Then I unknotted the line from the strut and ran it through the case handles, knotting it securely. They could be hauled to the surface when the time was right. I gave her the "let's go up" signal, and we pushed off the bottom. But instead of heading for the stern platform, I slanted toward the anchor cable, and we went up slowly, hand over hand, surfacing below the bow. I pulled out my regulator and looked around. About a mile off the island stood a good-sized yacht. Aft of amidships a small chopper rested on a pad. It was the kind of floating palace Greek shipping tycoons customarily command, and I wondered why it was cruising the Caribbean. Astrid noticed it, too, but said nothing. In a low voice I said, "When we get aboard, go forward and keep busy with your gear. I'll handle Diehl."

"Please be careful." She touched my arm.

"If he gets the drop on me, my revolver's in the map drawer by the wheel."

She nodded, let go the cable, and submerged. I waited a few moments and followed her under the boat.

I saw her climb onto the platform and pull off her fins. She kicked her feet a few times, and I took it as a sign everything was cool.

I lifted onto the platform and pulled down my mask. Carlos was helping her shed the heavy backpack, and Diehl was watching us from the transom. "Well," he snapped, "what's down there?"

"Gimme a break." I unsnapped the backpack, Carlos lowered it into the boat, and I pried off my fins. When I was in the boat, I pulled out the water-soaked billfold and tossed it at Diehl. He went through it eagerly, dropping the wad of bills on the deck in his haste. "That's *all?*"

"That's from the pilot's jacket. I had a hell of a time getting through the windshield."

He swallowed. "Could . . . was there any way to tell who . . . ?"

"The teeth are in good condition." I grabbed a towel and dried off. "The ID on the wing is Charlie Bravo four-one-five Nan."

He seemed to be thinking. Finally he said, "That's Vernon's plane."

"I could photograph the wreck—if that would help."

"Circumstantially it could." He turned toward Astrid, who was drying knife and mask.

I said, "Penny found two metal cases in the cargo compartment."

"Oh, that's great! Why didn't you bring them up?"

"If they hold contraband artifacts we don't want to be caught with them aboard. Besides, a sand shark took a sudden interest in us, and Penny thought we ought to get out."

He had a problem now, and he thought it over. Finally he said, "There might be clothing with a tailor's label—something to identify the pilot. Anyway, I'll take a look at the cases. You'll have to go down for them."

"Later."

"Now."

"Listen, my man, I've been doing hard labor ninety feet down. That means nitrogen in my blood, and it takes time to work out. I'll dive when it's safe, not before." Some color seemed to have returned to his face. I said, "How's your health?"

"Better."

"Sometimes it leaves as quick as it comes. You look dehydrated, so I'd recommend bottled water. Or beer if you feel up to it."

Carlos brought me a flask of Añejo and Diehl a bottle of Tehuacán. After a sip I said, "I've been wondering why a high-priced corporation lawyer like you packs a gun. Scared of Indians?"

He shrugged. "One never knows."

"That's an old Fats Waller line. In case you don't understand the law of the sea, the captain's in charge here. He and I are responsible for your

49

well-being. If pirates attack, we'll repel. Besides, I don't know how good a marksman you are, and Stella Novak's son isn't about to get knocked off by a stray bullet." I thrust out my hand. "Give."

He seemed frozen.

"Sometimes a man doesn't see where his best interests lie—until he's made a mistake. Now, either you hand over your piece like a gentleman, or Carlos and I'll take it off your body."

The Indio had come up behind him and was standing so close their shadows merged on the deck. Diehl blurted, "You have no right to do this," but he brought the pistol from his pocket. Carlos reached around for it, tossed it to me.

I withdrew the magazine and gave the pistol back to Diehl. "Let's have lunch."

Carlos broiled steaks in the galley and served them with salad and cold drinks. Astrid ate with Diehl while I went forward with Carlos, who said in Spanish, "The *licenciado* lacks balls."

"Making him dangerous." I gave him the pistol magazine. "Don't fool with the marker buoy until I tell you. I've got something on the line. It's what the *licenciado* wants—what this whole trip is about."

"Sounds interesting."

"It is. The girl knows."

"*Coño, chico,* why not get rid of the *licenciado?*" I told him part of what I was planning to do; there'd been no reason to until we'd found the right plane—and cargo.

"Okay, Juan, be careful." He licked steak grease from his thick fingers, and I finished my water. Beer is no good when you're diving because it bubbles in your belly.

Carlos gestured at the yacht. It seemed nearer than when I'd first noticed it, and crewmen around the helicopter seemed to be putting on floats. Maybe someone was going to drop in on us, offer to buy a big juicy grouper so the chef could turn out a major *pièce de résistance* for a finicky Greek.

Astrid walked forward and knelt beside us. "Are you going down again?"

"After lunch settles I'll photograph the plane—and cargo. Did he ask about it?"

She nodded. "Plenty mad we didn't bring it up."

"What did you say?"

"Didn't want you to suspect anything."

"What's his mood?"

"Eager. My God, is he eager! And pissed off that you took his gun."

"Well," I said, "he won't need it. You can go down with me if you want."

"If you don't need me to hold lights or anything, I'd just as soon get a little more sun." She gazed at me. "Who knows when I'll get another chance?"

"Yeah." In Miami they'd want her isolated for a while. Under methodical interrogation she might reveal things she didn't realize she knew.

Carlos took our plates and went off to the galley. Astrid touched my lips with her fingers. "After . . . this is over with, you won't leave me, will you? I don't want to have to deal with things alone."

"Never fear when Novak's near."

"Don't joke."

I held her hand. "Nothing to worry about. Trust me."

"I do—I've been trusting you almost since we met. I . . . I don't want things not to work out. The thought frightens me."

"I wish we could make love—now."

"So do I."

Diehl bellowed, "How much rest do you need, Novak?"

"Less than most," I called, touched her face, and walked aft.

I got out my underwater camera and strobe rig. To check them I posed Astrid by the gunwale and photographed her several times against the skyline. Flash and shutter were synchronous, so far as I could tell. Diehl came over and Astrid moved away. I said, "I'll photograph the plane so the numbers show, and try to get a shot inside the cockpit."

"Of the pilot."

"What's left of Vernon Saunders." I glanced around. "Daughter's bearing up remarkably well, don't you think? Of course I didn't let her see the remains. You'll need specialized equipment to get them out, by the way—one of the commercial dive shops can do the job. Then you'll need an official or two on hand to take charge of the remains for shipment home."

"I suppose so," he said thoughtfully, "but one thing at a time. Take the photos and bring up the cases."

I rigged a line to the lights and camera and lowered them over the side. Diehl had asked for photos as part of his charade; my office wanted them as evidence.

I fitted a fresh tank into my backpack, donned weight belt, BC, fins, mask, and knife. When I was sitting on the platform, Carlos handed me the long tubular bang stick. Diehl was watching intently. Astrid peered down over his shoulder. Silently she blew a kiss, and I nodded, bit down on the mouthpiece, and slid off. Now that things were at the final stage I didn't

51

want to waste time. I photographed the plane, the pilot, and the two bright cases on the sea floor beside the plane.

I took a final look around, saw a moray slither into the open cargo hatch, and was glad I wasn't there. I hated the vicious creatures, but this would be my last dive for a while, and I had other creatures to worry about.

I blew enough air into the BC to drift slowly upward, keeping just below the bubble rise, slanting my ascent toward the dive platform.

Carlos helped me out, and when I was standing on the deck Diehl said, "Well, where the hell are they?"

"Relax, man." I pointed at the marker buoy. "Haul them up—I've done my work for the day."

Astrid was sitting in the steerman's chair, long legs outstretched. Carlos winched up the anchor, and she left the chair so he could bring the boat alongside the buoy.

This was the critical moment. Diehl hauled in the line, grunting and straining. I pulled shorts over my wet trunks and fitted my tank into the rack. Astrid had gone down to the cabin.

I'd been watching Diehl and doing other things, so I hadn't realized the yacht's helicopter was airborne. I heard the loud flutter of the blades and sensed it was somewhere in the direction of the sun. I remember thinking they'd picked a hell of a time to pay a social visit, just as the metal cases surfaced. Diehl yelled excitedly, and Carlos went over to help lift them aboard.

Both men were crouched beside the gunwale when the chopper opened fire. Rotor noise covered the popping explosions, but I saw the deck splintering, and when I glanced up I saw a man firing down with an automatic rifle. Wedged in the doorway, he was aiming at Carlos and Diehl. Carlos yelled and fell back; Diehl screamed and raised his arms as though to ward off the bullets, then was slammed violently against the gunwale. I scrambled for the map drawer, grabbed the Astra, and was spinning around to return fire when something struck the back of my head.

I dropped into bottomless depths. As I submerged in blackness I knew I lacked a tank. I gazed blindly, looking for Astrid.

Where was my beautiful blonde buddy? What had happened to her?

II

SEVEN

"J ESUS, NOVAK," THE inspector sneered, "that Mexico livin'
musta beat your brains into guacamole."

His name was Phil Corliss, and we'd worked together out of
Norfolk. We hadn't liked each other then, and there'd been no improve-
ment since. He was what guys in the business referred to as an empty suit. I
said, "What makes you say an odd thing like that, Phil?"

"Because of how you handled—excuse *me* if I say screwed-up—the
Diehl case."

He was sitting at the head of a conference table; toadies and factotums
ranged between us. The tape recorder was on, and the office legal counsel
was sitting in. Bored, but present. Corliss's idea of an administrative
hearing.

I'd been over it all before, superficially with the Mexicans and in detail
with the shooflies sent down to bring me back. I was getting very tired of it
all, and my skull still ached.

"So what's the theory?" I asked. "That I killed Diehl and my buddy,
Carlos, stashed the loot, and whacked myself on the head? So I could drift
around the Caribbean until someone got curious enough to board the
Corsair?"

"What about the girl—this Astrid Nordstrom? Where's she at?"

"If I knew, I'd be with her—in the unlikely event she's alive."

"You didn't see what happened to her?"

"After Diehl began hauling up the cases, I didn't see her again. She went
into the cabin."

"Sounds like she knew what was comin'," he said nastily.

"Or took a full bladder to the head rather than squat on deck with three guys watching."

One of the anonymous toadies snickered. Corliss eyed him irritably. "Not a laughing matter, Petoski."

The legal counsel yawned. "Let's get back on track, men. I've got a meeting in chambers in about ten minutes." He stared out of the window at the high-rise Miami skyline. Probably wishing he were with an affluent old-line firm on Brickell Avenue, defending drug clients for megabucks. Like the late Paul Diehl.

Corliss stared at him for a moment, then turned his gaze on me. "You didn't have all that tough a job in Cozumel, Jack—coast-watching, sniffing leads—"

"—that developed the Amsterdam case, the Malta distribution net."

He shrugged. In his book, that was a lot of yesterdays ago. "Okay, you brought in a few things. But you got this basic problem, Jack, you showboat, screw the organization."

"I don't think the record bears you out, Phil. Anyway, to continue—everything was on track until the chopper showed up and started blasting away."

"You're the only one who saw a chopper."

"The only one alive."

"And the phantom yacht—what about that?"

"I've described it before. Sorry I didn't think to check flag, name, and registry. I had no reason to."

"But you wish you had."

I shrugged, stifled a yawn.

Legal counsel said, "That would certainly help your case, Novak."

"I'm a case? What case? You guys tootin' white evidence? Crawl down to reality. Why should I lie? More importantly, why shouldn't you believe me?"

Corliss said, "Okay, okay. How long between the time you passed out and rescue?"

"Roughly six hours. They boarded after dark, found me, and took me ashore. I was in the clinic until next day when Burrows barged in."

Corliss said, "For your information, we checked on Astrid Nordstrom in Galveston, Houston, Bay Town, and Texas City."

"And?"

"Nothing."

"I'm not shattered by that, Phil. As she told it, she had a rather colorful

56

background, including topless dancing in dives around Galveston Bay. Of course, she could have been lying."

"Prolly," Petoski remarked. "Don't exactly sound like no Girl Scout."

"Girl Scouts seldom get close enough to drug action to make good informants."

"You call her an *informant,* for Christ's sake?" Corliss demanded.

"By any standard. You would too—if she'd lived."

"So she's dead, is she?"

My throat tightened. I'd been able to suppress shock and sorrow, but these guys were rubbing me raw. "The chopper gunman shot Diehl and Carlos Paz—funny, the name means Peace—landed on floats, came aboard, and removed the cases. After killing Penny—Astrid, I mean."

"Or she helped them take the cases and flew back to the mysterious yacht."

"No way—chopper wasn't big enough. It held pilot and gunman."

"So you believe she was killed, too? Where's her body?"

I looked away. I didn't want to think where it might be, how the scavengers were working on it. Tears blurred my vision.

"Well?"

I took a deep breath. "This is pointless—unless I'm charged with something." I glanced at the legal counsel, whose eyes carefully avoided mine. "In which case I get myself a lawyer, and we lay everything out in the open."

"Now, now, Mr. Novak," the office lawyer said soothingly, "no need for hostility. You've got a good record with us, and you had an outstanding record as a Navy Seal. Understand, there's a difference between bringing charges against you and subjecting you to official criticism for—"

"—mishandling a case?" I shook my head. "I don't accept that. If anything, you guys screwed up. No one warned me about the yacht and its chopper. Someone should have known about it, known it was there and why. You couldn't expect me to have that kind of information."

Legal counsel said, "Things would be greatly altered if, say, there were some evidence of the yacht's proximity. Even its existence."

I remembered something, but the hell with surfacing it. Instead I said, "It doesn't take forensic genius to determine the bullets in the deck were fired from above, port side. I remember holes in the cabin roof, too."

Corliss shoved a stack of photographs along the table. I'd seen them before. They showed two bodies sprawled on the well deck, bullet holes in the planking and overhead, my diving gear . . . I pushed the stack aside.

"Bottom line," Corliss said. "Where're the coke cases?"

"By now," I said, "I imagine the contents have been cut and distributed all over the southwest."

"But you don't know."

I looked around the table. "What you seem to ignore is that I managed to breach the periphery of a major narcotics organization. One that disposes of a multi-million-dollar yacht and some well-trained killers. Who heads it—Luis Parra? I think Diehl was killed because he'd been trying to screw his own organization. Carlos and Penny—Astrid—were killed because they were there."

"And *you,* Jack?"

"Left for dead." I spread my hands. "What else?"

Petoski said, "Could be your payoff for helping out."

I shook my head. "Considering the source, I'll let that pass. None of you were there, I was. So unless you intend to fire me, I'll get on back to Cozumel, pick up the pieces, and continue the investigation."

Corliss said, "Whatever we decide, you won't be going back to Cozumel, Jack."

"No?"

"I think we can agree you should be suspended for the time being—while an independent inquiry is made."

My hands opened and closed. Clammy. My face was damp and cold. "After which?"

"A less challenging assignment—say, Albuquerque. Making friends among the *cucarachas.*" To Hispanics it was an offensive word. "Of course, if you brought in the Top Taco legally, without all the inadmissable strong-arm stuff you used before, you'd get the Medal of Freedom."

I drew back my chair. "Tell you what, fellows—if that happens, tell the President to keep the Medal and grant me letters of marque and reprisal."

The office lawyer yelped, "Privateering? You can't be serious."

"Try me. And in the meantime, to uncomplicate matters, I'm resigning."

The lawyer said, "Now don't act in haste."

"Why not? You have."

"Sit down, Novak!" Corliss exploded.

I shot him a bird and walked out. In the reception room I scribbled a resignation and left it with the girl. Legal counsel stepped into the elevator with me and got off at the *Judges Chambers* floor—without saying a word.

I got out at street level and walked through the lobby to a taxi stand. The driver took me back to my motel near Miami airport, and when I was in my room I swallowed two prescription painkillers—remembering Astrid's pills—and lay on the bed in my darkened room.

Silence, unbroken but for the whisper of air from the a/c vents. I was glad to be free of them, I told myself, and, yes, I *was* going back to Cozumel and they couldn't stop me.

How long had we been together—three days? Four? Astrid haunted my thoughts. I wanted to remember her alive, vibrant, warmly passionate— but macabre visions interposed. Was she—like the pilot—a ravaged corpse, eye sockets refuge for tiny fish?

Yes, I'd go back to Cozumel, start looking for her killers.

But first I had a call to pay.

As a widower I knew how it felt to lose a loved one.

How much did the widow Diehl miss Paul?

THE DIEHL HOUSE on Bay Harbor Island was set well back behind high grillwork fencing. Biscayne Bay lapped at the rear of the estate, and a thirty-foot competition speedboat snuggled up to a private pier. I drove through the untended gate and parked my rental behind a steel-gray Corvette near the entrance. To the left of the house a wide garage sheltered three late-model Mercedes: white, beige, and brown. I rang the doorbell.

Chimes echoed through the recesses of the house, and presently the door opened. A uniformed houseman said, "Yes?"

"Mrs. Diehl, please. She's expecting me."

"You're Mr. Novak?"

I nodded, and he stepped aside. "Follow me, sir."

The Japanese sand garden was ringed by Italian tile that glinted in the afternoon sun. Toward the Bay was a screened tennis court and a large free form pool with a three-meter board. I paused to watch a bikinied girl climb the diving tower, bounce once, and snap into a reverse three-and-a-half somersault that astonished me. "Is that Miss Diehl?"

"No, sir. Mrs. Diehl's daughter by a prior marriage—Miss Melody West."

"She must practice a lot."

"Diving?"

"Let's not restrict it to that."

"Miss Melody is a precocious and talented young person." He led me around the austere arrangement of rocks and bright sand to an imposing, mission-style door. I wondered if the inhabitants were as eclectic as the décor.

The houseman rapped on the carved panel, waited a moment, and opened it. "Mr. Novak, Madam."

The long room was carpeted in beige. Chairs of polished teak and fawn leather. There was a long sofa near one of the tall windows, and a shiny Coromandel cellarette.

The woman reclining on the sofa had dark hair, a full bosom, and expensive legs. The man lounging against the cellarette, drink in hand, had wave-styled hair of a hue so light as to resemble platinum. The effect was gorgeous. He wore what goes for business attire in Florida: pastel turtleneck, collarless ice cream jacket, and matching slacks that showed his crotch to advantage.

"So good of you to come, Mr. Novak. I'm Delores Diehl, and this is my husband's—my late husband's—associate, Larry Parmenter."

His long thin nose seemed adapted for scenting money. He sniffed, "Drink?"

"Anything cool, thanks."

Mrs. Diehl indicated a spot on the cushioned sofa and beckoned me over. She looked in her early forties. Her hairdo and makeup would have been exotic in Middle America but routine in Miami. Behind me Parmenter said, "Juice and vodka suit?"

"Admirably."

Mrs. Diehl said, "So you were the last to see Paul?"

"Not entirely." I took a frosted glass from a well-manicured hand and sipped.

"But I thought—"

"I don't know if he was dead when I went down. After that someone came aboard—probably the men in the chopper." I drank again. Liquid papaya was not my idea of juice, but it was well-diluted with vodka.

Parmenter said, "How do you know someone came on board?"

"Because a number of things were missing."

Mrs. Diehl's eyes caressed me.

"A couple of cases from the downed plane. Paul—Mr. Diehl, that is—said they contained artifacts." I looked up at Parmenter's bland face. "Illegal artifacts. Contraband."

He shrugged. I said, "In what sense were you an associate of Paul Diehl?"

"Member of his law firm. Senior member, that is."

Delores Diehl said, "Larry, why don't you mix me something agreeable? It's so distressing to think of Paul dying so brutally—and here's the man who saw it all happen."

60

"Just like a story, isn't it?" he said and went back to the cellarette. Ice clinked on crystal; something burbled when poured. "Any chance you could identify the killers?"

I shook my head and looked at Mrs. Diehl's attractive face. "They came in from the sun—closest I saw the rifleman was about fifty feet. Never saw the pilot at all."

"Shocking." Mrs. Diehl touched my thigh. "But I'm glad you survived."

"Me, too." My gaze followed her fingers as they toyed with her neckline, lowering it as if by chance. Nature had been bountiful indeed.

"Unfortunately, though, Miss Saunders was also a victim."

"So I understand." Parmenter came around to hand our hostess her drink. "And that's a point needing some clarification."

"Because her body wasn't found?"

He gave me a tolerant let's-be-realistic glance. "Because her presence was—shall we say—unanticipated."

"She was his client."

Delores Diehl said, "Paul told you that?"

"And she confirmed it." Through thermal windows I saw her daughter come out of the pool, towel hip-length hair, and stroll toward one of the poolside cabanas. For a kid she was extremely well developed—and coordinated. I wondered how she was taking it all.

Parmenter said, "That raises a series of problems, Mr. Novak. You see, she wasn't an office client."

"You've checked?"

"Of course."

I drank from my glass. "And the Saunders estate?"

"I . . . I'm afraid I don't know what you mean."

Delores Diehl sighed and put down her glass. "Some cock-and-bull story to explain why he was traveling with a woman." Her eyes regarded me. "Don't be shocked, Mr. Novak—"

"Jack, please."

"—Jack. But my husband, my *late* husband, was human—like all of us, you understand."

"Only too well. Nevertheless, the lady existed. They booked separate suites, so I don't think you should draw any negative inferences."

"My, my," she murmured, "the very picture of propriety."

I let it pass.

She said, "Forgive me, but this hasn't been the best of times for me."

"I quite understand." I looked at Parmenter. "One thing—not very important—confuses me."

61

"Oh?" Nostrils flared like a rabbit's.

"Why would Mr. Diehl tell me he was from Houston?"

They exchanged glances. Parmenter looked down at his drink, and I noticed that his lashes were long and silky. He was going to provide a lot of emotional support to the widow—I could foresee that. After a few moments he said, "I could speculate that our firm does business in Houston from time to time, but the truth is, I don't know why Paul would have said such a thing. Perhaps he was embarrassed about being with the girl—as well as the nature of his business on Cozumel."

"I won't press that one," I told him and finished my drink. "Know anyone with a helicopter-carrying yacht who had a grudge against him?"

"Goodness, no," Delores said in tones of distress, and Parmenter shook his head.

"I'm naturally interested in those things, because the work I did for the late Paul Diehl—and its outcome—has left me in rather an uncomfortable position."

"Uncomfortable?" Parmenter inquired. "How so?"

"Certain authorities theorize—ridiculous as it seems—that Paul was dealing in narcotics."

"Typical of federal snoopers," Parmenter remarked. "Exactly who was entertaining such slanderous thoughts?"

"Afraid I'm not at liberty to say."

They didn't like it. Delores said, "It's only fair to let you know that I'm going to sue."

"Who?"

"You, for beginners," Parmenter said. "Negligence in operating your boat, bringing it into harm's way. And perhaps contributory to Paul's death."

"I appreciate the warning, and in return I'll suggest you sue someone able to pay."

Parmenter's eyes glittered. "It could get fairly nasty."

"I can well imagine. Especially when attorneys start looking into Paul's reasons for being on Cozumel, his books, and clients. All aired for the record . . ." I put down the glass and stood up. "Thanks for the refreshment. I—"

"Just a minute," Parmenter said, "you're leaving it at that?"

"What choice do I have?"

He licked his lips. "If Delores—Mrs. Diehl—changes her mind, where can we contact you?"

"You can't," I told him. "I came on a courtesy call. Suddenly I'm facing adversary proceedings. You can't reasonably expect me to cooperate." I turned to the widow. "I'm sorry about your husband's death. I didn't know him long, but I don't think he deserved to die as he did. Or Penny Saunders." I took a deep breath. "*Or* my captain. And I don't think we can overlook Diehl's culpability. He was in peril before he ever reached Cozumel. Despite that, he went ahead and exposed the rest of us to lethal violence."

Parmenter sneered, "How do we know *you* didn't kill them all?"

I didn't want to disfigure him, so I slapped his cheek just hard enough to sting. He reeled back, covering his left cheek, and I said, "I've heard that before—and I don't want to hear it again from you."

"You attacked me!" he screeched.

"Sue me," I told him and walked the length of the room and out of the door. I let myself out without the houseman's help and found the girl sitting on the lawn, looking at my unimpressive car. She was wearing designer shorts and a salmon-colored blouse with a floppy bowtie. Some circles would have thought she needed a bra, but I didn't mind. Her face was oval and thoughtful, deep-set dark eyes, and black hair drawn back from her smooth forehead with what looked like a jade barette. She watched me approach, and when I stopped to open the car door she said, "I'm Melody West—not Diehl, West. Who are you?"

"My name is Legion. No, that was yesterday. Today I'm John Novak."

"Could you give me a ride?"

"You don't know where I'm heading."

"Maybe I don't care."

I pointed at the garage. "The place is bulging with Bavarian iron, Melody—run through your gas allowance?"

"I have my *own* credit cards. But my license was suspended for thirty days." Her expression was petulant.

"Speeding, no doubt."

"Well it wasn't overtime parking. Anyway, I need to talk with you."

I opened the door. "About what?"

"Mother said you were with Paul when he died. I want you to tell me about it. The truth."

"Get in."

EIGHT

"**W**HERE DO YOU want to go, Melody?"

"Someplace cool where we can talk. I've had enough sun today."

"I saw you diving. You're very good."

"I won the Southeastern Women's Three-Meter last month."

"Thinking of the Olympics?"

"If I survive the Nationals. But I don't know how long I could take all the discipline and training."

Conversation lapsed, and she sat quietly beside me as I drove over the Causeway, parking behind a quasi-club called The Players. As we walked to the door I looked her over. "One thing—are you old enough to drink?"

"Don't I look it?"

"Um, but do me a favor—if the waiter wants ID don't make a scene."

"He won't—I've been here with Larry."

"Why, the bounder," I said as I opened the door for her. "Corrupting a juvenile. And him an officer of the court."

"Don't say that—not that he wouldn't like to." She tossed her head. "Anyway, Larry's a space case. Totally."

"Of course there's Mother," I said. "And Mother's come into a lot of money. Makes a difference."

"She always marries—well."

"Some women have a knack for it." We found a small banquette in the nearly empty lounge. I asked for Añejo on the rocks, and Melody said she'd take the same. The waiter was poised to question her but decided against it. I said, "What grade are you in?"

"You ask a lot of questions, Mr. Legion."

"Novak," I corrected. "You're a senior?"

"Was. Are you married?"

"No."

"You don't have the married look."

"That's a compliment?"

She began fooling with a coral bracelet I hadn't noticed. "Have you got herpes or anything?"

"Would I admit it?"

"A decent man would. Unless he's gay."

"A decent man wouldn't be talking dirty with a kid."

"Sex isn't dirty—it's therapeutic. Or didn't you know?"

"I know a lot of things, but we're here to reprise Paul's final moments. You liked him—or you didn't?"

She shrugged. "He was okay, I guess. Sort of a wimp, but he never tried fooling around with me. And he *was* good to my mother."

"Well, that's nice to hear. She and Larry were sort of putting him down—that surprise you?"

"Not really."

The waiter delivered our drinks, and I paid him. It was that kind of place, cash on the line. She touched her glass to mine. "Chin-chin."

"Salud."

We drank. She said, "You speak Spanish, don't you? I mean, living in Cozumel you'd have to."

"Living in Miami you almost have to."

"I get along in Portuguese."

"How's that?"

"I was born in São Paulo. My real father owned some mines."

"Nice work," I remarked. "By the way, that rum is high-test, so take it easy."

"Don't worry, I don't get drunk and sloppy. I've got too much respect for my bod."

"That's the sort of thing I like to hear from the younger generation. Anyway, here's what happened to Paul Diehl." I related a bland version, and she listened without changing expression. Her glass was empty before mine, and as I signaled a refill I said, "The blonde who called herself Penny Saunders—ever hear of her? See her?"

"Not that name or description. But I suppose Paul could have any woman he wanted. He had an awful lot of money." She looked away. "I sure don't want Larry Parmenter to get it."

"Let's hope Mom retains a good attorney to handle probate." I twirled my empty glass. "Funny . . . Diehl told me he was settling another man's estate, now his is up for grabs." The waiter came over and removed our glasses. After he went away I said, "Paul was known as a top-flight drug lawyer. Ever meet any of his clients?"

"No."

"Ever hear of Luis Parra?"

She shook her head. "Who's he?"

"Very big in Colombia, Miami, and around the Caribbean. He could afford a yacht like the one with the attack chopper."

"Should I ask my mother?"

"No, in fact, I don't think you ought to say anything about our tête-à-tête."

She laughed scornfully. "Think I want her to ground me?"

After I paid for our drinks Melody said, "I like this," as she tongued the chill rum.

"Seductive," I agreed and felt her hand on my thigh. "Hey, I'm the one supposed to do that. Trying to diminish my machismo?"

"Just being honest about the way I feel. You're very attractive."

"And you're jail bait. Haven't you got a regular boyfriend or anything?"

"You mean, do I ball the Ransom-Everglades backfield? No. But if it salves your conscience, I'm not a virgin." She looked at my wristwatch. "I don't need to be home until eight. Let's go somewhere and get acquainted."

I'd had enough unsettling frustrations and drinks that it sounded like a swell idea. "If you mean what I think you mean my toes are curling. Ah . . . where would you like to go?"

"One of those places with waterbeds and adult movies." Her hands had gotten busier. To keep her from unzipping me I said, "Okay—but let's wait till we get there."

"You won't be sorry." She opened her mouth on mine, her tongue thrust and curled. Her breath was sweet and hot. My head began to pound. Perhaps a cool shower . . .

The Morningstar Motel was just off Collins Avenue. I took the key from the room clerk and walked behind Melody to our second-floor room.

Turning on the air conditioner, I said, "Here's some quarters for the movies."

"Hell with them." I heard the rustle of dropped clothing and turned to stare.

Without shoes she stood about five-four, a compact Godiva in long hair; absolutely ravishing in her tanned nakedness. Voluptuous hips and thighs, firm breasts with pointed pink nipples, and a black, well-trimmed delta.

She pressed into me, and within seconds I was as horny as a stallion. Her fingers did spidery things with my sensitive flesh, and if she'd been a nun I couldn't have stopped.

Presently I lay back and stared at the ceiling. "Damn you," I said tightly. "You lied to me."

"So what's a lie? I couldn't be a virgin forever."

"Why choose me?"

For a while she was silent. Then she said, "My mood, lover. And you attracted me. I said to myself 'Why not?'" Her lips brushed the side of my face. "You're a lovely lover."

"I shouldn't be your lover, Melody."

"So I'm precocious. Be cool, don't fight fate." She rose on her knees and made an adjustment. Then she leaned toward me and gripped my shoulders. Her hair fell forward, brushing my chest and face as she moved sinuously and sensually, taking possession, dominating our lovemaking. After a while I drew down her face, and we joined in a long, deep kiss. First time out, and this kid was something to fantasize about.

Finally she rolled aside, breasts heaving. Trying to control her voice she murmured, "Can . . . we . . . meet . . . tomorrow?"

"I won't be here."

"Cozumel?"

I nodded.

"Can't you postpone awhile? Even a few days, Jack?"

"Have to go."

One hand trailed the contours of my face, fingers resting on my lips. "Take me with you." She kissed the lobe of my ear, began to nibble with her small white teeth. I said, "We've done basic exploratory work, Melody, but we can't have everything at once. A year or so from now—*Ouch.* That hurt!" Her teeth lacerated my ear lobe.

"Don't treat me like an infant!"

"Have I?"

"You meant we should wait until I grow up."

"Seems sensible."

She made the waterbed undulate. "Taking me to this slimy whorehouse, making me watch dirty movies, raping me. Now you want me older. You *are* a bastard." But she was still smiling.

"Some ways you're older than I am."

"Please don't tell me you're old enough to be my father."

"Probably am."

"An hour ago age didn't matter."

"That was . . . before."

"I want to go with you."

"Not this time."

"Then make love to me. Do it. *Now.*"

SHE WAS SOBER and *triste* when I left her at the gate with a vague promise of staying in touch. My lips were puffed and almost raw; she'd used the drive back to excite us both, and when I saw her walk up the drive I was sorry we couldn't meet tomorrow.

As I turned back toward the airport, I remembered that after plebe year at the Academy I was let in on a secret by some upperclassmen who disdained the celibacy rule. Around Annapolis there were a lot of retired CPOs, and some had young daughters. And Navy widows rented rooms on quaint side streets. Saturday afternoons midshipmen and nubile kids would rendezvous in a mating frenzy that made the rest of the week's servitude easier to sustain. So in my teens I got accustomed to San Quentin Quail—as underage girls were called—and in responding to Melody, I had few scruples to overcome. Besides, she said she was seventeen, which was what she looked, and not only was that old enough for a girl to make up her own mind, but it kept that old statutory rape shiver from cruising up and down my spine.

Melody was a passionate young female, and I'd remember her a long time. But if I ever returned to Miami I felt sure she'd be gone. Her mother's household wasn't one she'd want to stay in longer than necessary.

In my room there was a phone message: *Call Delores.*

Why? I wondered. For what? Coy fencing? Or an open proposition like her daughter's? The hell with Mom; I wanted to leave with the good memories I had.

Of Melody.

So I collected clothing, packed my bag, and drove back to the rental office. Two hours later I was on a Mexicana flight to Cozumel.

I had to try to put things together, make sense of the murders, and where it happened was the place to begin.

But from now on I was working on my own.

NINE

MY HOUSE WAS empty, but I was glad to find the dogs fed and watered, bed made, and food and beer in the refrigerator. Two crisply starched *guayaberas* hung in my closet. Chela had kept house, assuming I'd eventually return.

I strolled out on the pier, looked at the Seabee moving with the changing tide, and remembered Astrid flying with me. So much I hadn't learned about her, so much to remember.

I sipped beer and watched the moonpath on the calm water, thinking that from the office point of view I'd probably screwed up. Diehl had been my target, and I hadn't delivered. They had a point, but they hadn't been here. Even federal marshals occasionally lost a witness to hit men; the office should have understood. Someone other than Phil Corliss might have, but that was the luck of the draw, and no sense looking back.

My head was beginning to throb again, and I'd had a long and unexpectedly active day. The more rest I got, the better tomorrow would go. I finished my beer and turned in.

I'D KNOWN THAT seeing Carlos's widow wouldn't be easy, and it wasn't. Carmelita sobbed when she saw me and began beating her bosom while the two little children ran around in a frenzy of confusion.

But after she calmed down I told her I was going to get *Corsair* fixed up, and when I left Cozumel it would be hers. That made her feel a lot better, and she gave me a wet kiss and a big hug. In Miami I'd cashed Diehl's traveler's checks, and I gave her the whole eight hundred as a kind of death benefit, telling her it was Carlos's share for his last days of work. The money improved her spirits even more, and I left with her blessings and an implied offer to warm my bed should I ever desire companionship.

Next the El Portal café. Chela spotted me when I came in and she burst into tears—I was having that effect on females this morning. She grabbed me and covered my face with kisses as patrons watched in astonishment. Then I took a corner table, and let her bring me eggs, ham and fried bread, coffee, and piña juice.

She sat across from me, clasping my free hand. I thanked her for taking care of my bungalow, and she brushed tears from her cheek. "What else would I do, *padrón*? It was my responsibility." She'd never addressed me so respectfully before. Was it because I was back from the dead, or just back? But she couldn't resist adding, "I warned you about the *rúbia,* eh? And see what happened."

"You warned me, and that's all I want to hear about it. Where's the boat?"

"At the marina."

"Anything happen I should know about?"

"The police asked questions about you—so did Jaramillo."

"They hurt you?"

She shrugged. "The Captain—Jaramillo—called me your whore. Said you ran drugs. Called you *contrabandista.*"

"Coming from him, that's the laugh of the year."

"*Sí.* He has eyes for me."

"He's got eyes for anything in skirts."

"He's a pig. If he touches me I cut off his *cojones.*"

"Right."

"Shall I come out tonight? Cook a good dinner?"

"Fine idea." She pecked my cheek and went off to wait on a customer. I drove out to the yacht basin and found *Corsair* settled on the shallow bottom, deck awash. I opened hatches, put on my mask, and went down to check damage. Some of the bullets had penetrated the hull. I forced hemp plugs into the punctures I could find, borrowed a bilge pump, and soon *Corsair* was afloat and tugging at the line. I got a tow to the boatyard where it was hauled out on the marine railway. The mechanic said he wanted the engines drained and dry before he disassembled them, and that would take a day or so. I pointed out hull damage to the shipwright and asked him to repair deck holes as well. Seawater had cleansed the blood I remembered on the deck, and if I could keep my eyes away from the bullet holes, it would be all right.

I drove to San Miguel's police station.

The *comandante* was surprised to see me and unsure how to react. I said, "You've been asking questions about me, Elpidio."

"A few necessary ones, *Señor* Juan."

"Anything you want to put to me?"

He stroked his Zapata mustache. "I can't think of anything. What are you going to do now?"

"What I did before." He offered me a bottle of José Cuervo, and I filled my mouth with tequila, swilling it around to freshen teeth and gums. A guaranteed microbe killer. "*Gracias.* Has anyone been able to identify the big yacht from which the helicopter flew?"

"Lamentably, not yet."

"But it was seen."

"*Sí.* But not its flag or name."

"A yacht that size . . ." I spread my hands Mexican-style.

"I understand. Strange, is it not? I thought so myself."

"And the Coast Guard?"

"Busy chasing *contrabandistas.*"

I grunted. "Like Jaramillo, eh?"

"The *Capitán* has his own thing going."

"I'm going to tell him to stay away from mine."

He said nothing, stroking both sides of his mustache.

"I don't want trouble with him," I said, "and he's a fool if he brings it."

"Assuredly."

"Well, I wanted you to know." I stood up. "Thanks for the drink."

"*Su servidor.*" We shook hands and I went out.

As I got into the jeep I thought it just as well the boat wasn't ready. I needed to get to the wrecked plane again, but today would have been too soon. I needed time for memories to recede. Elpidio hadn't mentioned the plane, so perhaps it was still undisturbed. Along with the camera I'd left on the bottom.

I drove back to the bungalow and tuned in some smuggler frequencies, drinking Añejo and listening to boats and mother ships talking with each other. There was a lot of drug business going on in the Caribbean, most of it conducted with impunity. Well, that wasn't my problem any longer, and the lease on the bungalow had months to run. The office might repossess the radio, but they wouldn't try to oust me. Corliss didn't have the balls for that.

So here I was with a boat and a plane and a good woman to keep house. Most men would have settled for that, but I couldn't. Forget Diehl— Carlos and Astrid were dead, and I wanted their killers.

73

All I had to start with was a camera.

After siesta, I freshened up, shaved, and played with the dogs as I strolled down the pier. Sheba looked as though she might just possibly be pregnant. Well, it would be nice to have a litter of little wrigglers around the house. César could do double guard until they weaned.

I pulled the plane's bow to the pier, stepped on the nose, and looked inside. Everything watertight. I opened the engine hatch and checked the oil; down about a pint. I was closing the hatch cover when I remembered something. So I opened it all the way and peered in.

It was reasonably well concealed, but I'd glimpsed it anyway: the olive-drab end of a plastic block. Sure enough, detonator embedded, wires leading to the coil. One touch on the ignition button and the Seabee would vanish in a ball of flame. Me with it.

Someone, somewhere didn't like me. They'd failed on the boat, and this was a catch-up try. Logically it should have succeeded. Despite the sun's warmth I shivered and began very carefully to disconnect the wires. Demolitions had been a big part of my Seal training, the sort of technique you never forget.

I wondered how they'd gotten past the dogs?

Easy—come by sea, letting the dogs yelp from the pier; do the dirty job and shove off.

Who?

I separated the detonator from the C-4 block and tossed both into deep water where they'd disintegrate.

In the house I took a Vera Cruz panatela from the humidor and lighted it, wondering how much Larry Parmenter knew about his late partner's affairs. He hadn't revealed much at the Diehl house, but both of us knew we were adversaries. Maybe he thought I had designs on the widow Diehl and her fortune. Well, he could rest easy on that, but my dislike was instinctive.

Parmenter was one of the drug mouthpieces who took fees in cash, dope, cars, real estate, or any combination. They knew how to get a client's bond reduced from ten million to one, and have a secretary rush a Bogotá ticket to the courthouse before the judge changed his mind. The client was on the next plane, the shyster had his loot, and the government had no defendant. The scenario was one Luis Parra could have followed, but for his lack of patience. And if by some incredible miscalculation he'd actually gone on trial, Parmenter's kind of lawyer knew the many ways to intimidate jurors, bribe judges and witnesses, and get charges dismissed. I'd seen the script played out too often to have any respect for that slimy side of the legal trade.

But sometimes a drug lawyer would promise what he couldn't deliver and later be found dead in his office, or the Lincoln Continental would blow up in a parking lot. Or a "random" burglary would leave the shyster dead, his wife or girlfriend bloodied beside him.

But while it lasted, life was incredibly lush and rewarding for the fast-trackers, and Larry Parmenter's career had barely begun. He'd take over Diehl's clients now, pocket those huge fees from Parra and other cocaine cowboys, and transfer them abroad by courier. Because of treaties, Suisse was no longer chic, *hèlas,* but there was no shortage of depositories around the world, many conveniently in the Bahamas, Caymans, and Netherlands Antilles. From there the profits could be funneled back into Miami condos, restaurants, resorts, and porno movies.

Everything seemed to be on their side. Who was going to stop them?

I heard tires skidding on gravel, a horn honked. Clamping down on my cigar, I went outside and saw dust settling around an old Army jeep. Captain Jaramillo at the wheel.

He was all smiles when he saw me, jumped down, and rattled the gate. "Heard you were back," he called. "Let's have a drink."

I went up to him and we faced each other through the galvanized fencing. "Maybe tomorrow," I said, "in town. I'm tired and I've got things to do."

His fat face showed an exaggerated expression of sorrow. "You don't invite me in, *amigo*?"

"No, *Capitán,* I don't invite you in. I'm sure you'll forgive me. Don't move." I went back into the house, got a Tecate from the refrigerator, and brought it out, twisting off the cap. "So you shouldn't leave thirsty." I passed it through the fence. He took the bottle stared at it, then at me.

Slowly he lifted it and drank, wiped his thick lips. "I need to ask you some questions."

"About what?"

"The killings—your boat."

"There's nothing left to say. Besides, airport security is your business, not piracy."

"As you know, I have interests in many places."

I yawned.

"We should have a friendly talk," he persisted.

"Maybe another time." The dogs had trailed out after me and taken guard position beside my legs. Jaramillo stared at them, wet his lips. "You don't want to make enemies here in Cozumel."

"I don't want to make enemies anywhere. So what are we talking about?" I smiled. *"Hasta luego, Capitán. Tengo mucho que hacer."* Turning, I went back into the house. The dogs stayed, watching him carefully. Jaramillo drained the bottle, flipped it over the fence, and drove away, raising another cloud of dust.

What the hell was all that about? He was sniffing around for something. Had he expected to find the Seabee destroyed, me with it? As an Army officer he probably had access to explosives, but so did a lot of Migueleños and off-islanders. Besides, what did he stand to gain?

He neither frightened me nor did I really consider him an enemy. He envied the *gringo,* and perhaps that was the dimension of the problem.

Around the cottage I had weapons cached. A sawed-off 12, an M-16 assault rifle, a boot knife, and a Navy-issue .45 pistol. When I inspected my boat I hadn't found my .44 Astra, so it must have been taken when the chopper crew came aboard to kill Astrid and grab the metal cases.

I checked the weapons and replaced them; not even Chela knew where they were. Not knowing, she couldn't be forced to tell.

I carried a beer out on the seaside patio and relighted my cigar. Diehl had set me up—or tried to—but before that he himself had been fingered for death. He hadn't been the only one aware of the Piper's cargo, and the others played him like a puppet on a string—until he recovered it from the plane. Then they moved in. Had it been theirs all along, or was the attack only what it appeared—an act of piracy?

Astrid knew more about Diehl than she'd told me—and Delores must have known where Paul was going. I was willing to bet my final paycheck that Parmenter knew considerably more. What I'd seen of the widow didn't suggest she had the cunning to conspire against her husband, but I'd been wrong about women before. Delores was drawn to luxury the way iron filings flow to a magnet, and Diehl had shared an ample lifestyle with her. Of course, it was possible domestic trouble was brewing, and he'd planned to cut his losses. To her that would have been the equivalent of a death threat, one she might have moved to forestall. Probably his insurance policies were double indemnity—and he'd certainly died a violent and unnatural death. So she stood to collect a great deal from that alone, aside from his real estate, investments, and bank account. Did she own the law firm now, or was Parmenter the beneficiary?

I thought about these and other matters until sunset, when the town jitney dropped Chela at the gate, string shopping bag bulging with fruit, vegetables, and fresh-killed meat.

We swam off the pier and started making love in the shower. She cooked a fine Yucatecan dinner of pork and plantains; we drank some rum and went to bed early.

Things were almost as they were before Astrid found me in the harbor café.

Almost.

TEN

IN THE MORNING, after driving Chela back to town, I stopped at the boatyard to check *Corsair*. Engine parts were sunning on a long worktable, and the shipwright was drilling out bullet holes and patching with teak dowels.

The mechanic told me the gas tank hadn't been punctured, so unless there was afternoon rain, he thought he could have the engines running by nightfall. Until the boat was operational I was stalled, so I bought fresh chemicals for my makeshift darkroom and took them back to the house.

Parked at the gate was a white Beetle with a rental tag, someone behind the wheel. I got out of the jeep, and a man opened the VW door. "Hold it," I called, "let's see your hands."

Two empty hands appeared. "Okay," I said, "out slow and easy."

He was about my size, with reddish hair, wearing a white mesh shirt and a two-piece tropical suit. "Mr. Novak? I'm from the Embassy." He flashed a Treasury credential in the name of Joseph Milton.

WE DRANK TECATES on the patio while he told me he'd been seconded to the South Florida Strike Force and traveled between Mexico City and Miami. "I'm out of it now," I said.

"The word got around, and that's why I'm here. Some of us knew Phil Corliss and don't think much of his judgment. We thought DEA's loss might be our gain."

"What way?"

"Well, your cover hasn't been blown—you could stay operational. I'm authorized to offer you a pay jump and the usual perks. For working basically on the same matters."

I wiped foam from my upper lip. "Interesting idea—you go by Joe, do you?"

"Right."

"I appreciate the offer. Right now, though, I'm not prepared to work for anyone but myself."

"May I ask why?"

"This last fracas personalized things."

"You mean . . . the girl."

"And Carlos, my captain. Those killers opened up like it was Tet all over again—we never had a chance. When I say I was unbelievably lucky to survive I'm not kidding."

"So you want revenge."

"That's the bottom line. I doubt it's compatible with Strike Force goals." I looked out at the horizon—a thin line of green met the pastel blue of the sky. "The trouble with law enforcement is the law. It tends to bind both arms behind my back, while the bad guys are free to do any damn thing they want. How many repeat arrests are made—only to have the trafficker jump bond and disappear? A year later he's caught again, and the same thing occurs." I shook my head. "Sometimes I think judges, even prosecutors, are in a giant conspiracy to aid and abet traffickers, insure no harm befalls them. But when something happens to a guy like me, the office turns against him. Suddenly I'm an outcast."

"You don't need to be." He sat forward. "If you didn't know, Treasury eased careless Corliss into DEA to get rid of him—he'd been a substandard agent too long. Naturally he resents a self-starter like you, who produces without complaining all the time. Nobody in the Strike Force holds you responsible for Diehl's death or the disappearance of whatever was in those cases. But Corliss saw a chance to eliminate competition. Will you think over my proposition?"

"Sure—but until I've made progress against those killers, I wouldn't be much good to you. And I could be a source of embarrassment if I screwed up."

He leaned back. "You're not taking on just one or two men, you know, it's a whole organization."

Nodding, I told him about the booby-trapped engine while he squinted at the Seabee.

"Any ideas who might have done it?"

"Someone working for the people on that yacht. They see me as a threat—because they don't know how much I learned from Astrid or Diehl. And they realize I know the Piper crashed during a drug run."

"You say 'they.' Who do you think's behind it?"

"Luis Parra for one—Diehl was his principal lawyer."

Milton nodded. "Diehl's backup was his partner, Larry Parmenter, who has a continuing interest in what's disclosed."

I told him about meeting Larry with Delores—leaving out Melody West. That was entirely private and very personal.

He stretched long legs and loosened his tie. "So where do you take it now?"

"I need to identify the yacht—and the girl Diehl was traveling with."

"Yes—Ingrid, no, Astrid Nordstrom." He frowned. "Computer turned up nothing on her. I don't suppose you have a photo?"

"I was coming to that." I told him about my pre-dive camera check and my intention of recovering the film. "With luck the yacht'll be on it, too."

"We can help there. Can't be too many that big, cruising the Caribbean. I'll pass prints to the Naval attaché and the Coast Guard. How soon can you have them?"

"The boat might be seaworthy tomorrow."

He drained his beer. "I'd offer to go with you, but I'm a lousy sailor, get seasick in a rowboat."

I exchanged our empty bottles for cold ones from the refrigerator. Handing Milton one I said, "Perhaps we could just cooperate for the time being—share knowledge. Nothing formal."

"I'd go along for sure. An informant's entitled to reciprocity."

I settled back in my chair. "There're so many inconsistencies and loose ends involving Diehl's arrival and death, that I haven't been able to make sense of it. He knew the plane was where we found it and was mighty eager to get the cargo. But a high-priced lawyer seldom gets that close to drug action."

"Unless it was a private venture."

"He had plenty of money."

"But a man can always use more. His travel's been checked, and for the past couple of years Paul Diehl was damn near everywhere—Madrid, London, Houston, Amsterdam, Zürich, Panama, Curaçao, Grand Cayman, and of course, Miami. His travel involved setting up dummy firms, making foreign investments and money transfers, also dealing in diamonds. . . By one estimate, he moved close to two hundred million dollars."

"Everything offshore."

"Yeah, couldn't touch him. We kept waiting for a false move so we could collar him and offer him a deal."

"Parra."

Milton nodded.

"There's the dead pilot," I said, "Fernando Guzmán, late of Port Arthur."

"He was just that—a pilot who flew loads in from time to time, mostly pot, nothing major."

"Vernon Saunders keeps coming to mind."

"Clean—as far as anyone knows. Owns a private banking house, makes a lot of money for clients—and himself. Backed a football franchise when the new league was getting started. I don't think Diehl would have used his name if Saunders were really involved."

"The girl explained that . . . sort of."

"In retrospect, how do you see her?"

"I don't think I can be objective, Joe. She was extraordinarily beautiful and probably too intelligent to have led the kind of life she described."

"As a go-go dancer around Galveston Bay. I read all that."

"I'd like to know if Saunders really kept her. It would go to her credibility. And his."

"Sure, but I doubt the Houston office is going to want to ask him straight out. Or Mrs. Saunders, for that matter. If Astrid—let's call her—were alive and headed for the witness stand, it would be important to know. But that's not the case."

I thought of the cool lavender eyes, the ultra-casual boots, the T-shirt and its bravado legend. I missed her terribly; would mourn her a long, long time.

Gently he said, "She had quite an impact on you."

I swallowed. "I wasn't ready to lose her. But that's my luck with women I care for."

"There's that Big Appointment Book in the sky. My name's in it, so's yours."

"Can't accept fatalism. My wife's death . . ." I didn't go on.

"Sorry. Where were we?"

"Vernon Saunders." I lighted another cigar, and smoke hovered between us. "My hunch is he's linked to Diehl."

Milton had taken out a pad, and now he made a note. "We'll have a look at his tax returns—maybe he's been paying fees to Diehl's law firm."

"You might scan Parmenter's, too."

He looked up and shaded his eyes. "The girl ever hint what the cases contained?"

"No."

"What did you think?"

"Coke, horse, gum opium—high-value, low-volume narcotics."

"Gems?"

"Never considered it—until you mentioned Amsterdam." I shrugged. "I was looking forward to seeing the contents, believe me."

The sun was high above us, the sea a glitter of silver slashed with green. "If you're not too particular we'll have what passes for lunch."

"I'd appreciate it—that was a non-meal flight." He got up and stretched. "Radio working? I've got some frequencies for you in case you want to reach the Embassy office."

I fixed a salad and grilled beefsteaks. With fresh hard rolls and icy beer it was a good impromptu spread.

Milton said, "If it turns out you can't dive tomorrow, I'll fly back to the capital. Meanwhile, can you put me up overnight?"

"Easiest thing in the world." I showed him the spare room and encouraged him to take a siesta. He accepted gratefully, pulled off shoes and coat, and lay down. He was close to sleep before I left the room. A nice young man, I thought, and probably too decent for the corrupt underworld we worked in.

TOWARD FIVE O'CLOCK I returned to the boatyard and found *Corsair* in the water, engines burbling nicely. The mechanic was making final adjustments, and while he completed them I inventoried my diving gear. All there. The killers hadn't bothered it. Three partially filled tanks and a full one—more than enough for tomorrow's dive.

I let Milton buy dinner for me at Pepe's on the waterfront. He said it was expense account so I ordered *langosta* risotto and a bottle of Riscal *blanco*. Usually I took visitors to Morgan's, but I wasn't ready to return there—not while Astrid's memory still enshrouded me.

Afterward I escorted my new ally on a walking tour of souvenir shops to settle dinner, then drove back to the bungalow.

Milton took a shower and turned in, and as was my custom, I sipped Añejo on the patio while darkness cloaked the sea. I hadn't wanted to brood about Astrid, and so I welcomed a vision of Melody that penetrated my mind. I saw her on the diving tower, gazing moodily at my car, sitting beside me in the cocktail lounge—and the smooth perfection of her young body next to mine. I wanted to see her again—if only for therapeutic sex. Her phrase, not mine. But would I?

Tomorrow I'd dive down to the sunken plane. Alone in the gray depths, what would I find?

ELEVEN

W E SLEPT LATE. Over breakfast I told Joe Milton I'd develop the camera film—assuming it was there—and make prints he could take back to the Embassy. He said, "I feel I should go out with you if only for moral support, but the sea and me we don't agree."

"That's okay. You look a little pale from office work, so grab some sun while I'm gone. We're about the same size and there's extra trunks. Take a pad down on the pier and relax."

"Good idea."

"The dogs won't bother you. If anyone comes by they'll insure privacy."

"But you're not expecting callers."

"None."

AT THE BOATYARD I topped off the gas tank before heading down the coast. Clear day, hardly a ripple on the water. Because of new gaskets, I held the engine at 2,200 rpm for an indicated speed of twelve knots. No hurry.

I tied the wheel, went to the stern transom, and opened a bottle of cold water. It seemed strange to be back on *Corsair*. Almost as though I were reliving those murderous events. Diehl and Carlos had been over there by the gunwale when the chopper came blasting down from the sun. Astrid . . . *Jesus*—she'd been below.

If only she'd stayed there, I thought, but the shooting must have brought her up. So they killed her, too, thinking I was already dead. The blood was gone from the decking, but ghosts seemed likely to remain.

The wreck was farther out than I remembered. I'd planned to use the rubber boat but found it bullet-punctured, no repair kit handy. That left me without the help it could have provided in an emergency, and I found myself wishing Joe Milton had come along to watch the store. I wasn't expecting trouble below, but if it cropped up I'd have to handle it as best I could—alone.

Corsair was anchored by the bow. While it swung into the current I got ready to dive. In addition to normal gear, I took a hacksaw and bolt cutter in a mesh bag, then I looped the bang stick around my left wrist, and dropped off the platform.

Bubbles obliterated vision, but I was descending while they headed for the surface, so in a few moments I could look around.

I was dropping toward the plane's white stabilizer, and too close to the abyss, so I slanted toward the plane's nose and glimpsed the camera rig where I'd left it more than a week ago. A barracuda, glinting like stainless steel, came over and examined me from a yard away, turned abruptly, and vanished into the cobalt deep. Probably the same fellow that frightened Astrid. The wreck was his hunting zone.

My fins touched bottom. I went over to the photo rig and picked it up. Everything seemed intact. I prayed the film was undamaged. The camera's plexi-housing was guaranteed for double the depth, but if water had seeped in, what was I going to do—sue the maker?

With the bolt cutter I snipped metal from wing surfaces so I could get at the bent longerons that jammed the cabin door.

The hacksaw bit cleanly through the twisted metal tubes until finally I was able to shove the wing aside. Only a strut attached it to the fuselage.

The effort used a lot of air, nearly half a tank. For a while I rested, normalized my breathing, and checked my chronometer; about ten minutes' bottom time remained. More than that and I'd have to ascend by stages, gripping the anchor line.

A face mask restricts peripheral vision, so I didn't see the shark heading from the right. I glimpsed the white underbelly, the open, teeth-lined jaws, and backed against the plane just in time. His moving tail belted me as he swerved past, leaving pain in my ribs. The fuselage protected me from rear attack, but he had a full half-circle to play with.

This time he rocketed in from the left. I bounced the bolt cutter on his nose and he veered away. But the rough shagreen hide scraped flesh from my thigh like coarse sandpaper. I didn't want him bleeding, but in sparing him I was bleeding myself. Red tendrils curled outward from my thigh.

So it was Mr. Bang Stick or nothing, and seconds were passing fast. As soon as other predators scented my blood they'd join in, and the shark stick held only one shell.

I saw him off in the distance, twenty or thirty feet away, a gray shark, three meters long. His walnut-size brain seemed to be thinking things over. When he decided, he'd attack with jet speed. I readied the stick with two hands. Waited.

Levered by his powerful tail, the shark lunged straight at me, jaws spread so wide I could barely see his eyes.

I'd hoped for a head shot, but the angle was wrong. So at the last second I ducked and shoved the bang stick hard against the roof of his mouth. The explosion hurt my ears, and the turning body crushed me against the plane before it sank slowly to the ocean floor. The closing jaws had crushed my metal weapon like a hairpin; the body writhed and flopped, whipping up clouds of sand. I decided to move before everything was obliterated.

Opening the cabin door, I searched until I found Fernando Guzmán's driver's license, dropped it in my bully bag, and exited the plane. From somewhere a big moray appeared to watch the gray shark's agonies, and other fish were gathering. Sharks don't travel alone, so I could expect more trouble if I waited. Blood seeped from my abraded thigh.

I grabbed the camera rig, blew air into the BC, and headed for the surface. All the way I kept looking down, knife in hand in case I had to fight again for my life.

Finally I broke surface forty or fifty feet from the dive platform. The current was against me, but I never stroked harder or faster in my life. I didn't have a lot of strength left, so after setting the camera on the platform, I slid out of the backpack and hung the heavy tank there by its straps. Then crawled out.

For a while I sat there, eyes closed, breathing deeply until I felt I could get over the stern.

When I opened my eyes there was a launch off the port quarter. Two men in it, one casually pointing a rifle at me.

TWELVE

"**H**OLA, SEÑOR. TODO va bien?"
I waved weakly. "*Sí*—everything's fine."
I thought the gun might lower, but it didn't. And the launch kept coming. I got the camera rig over the stern and climbed to the deck.

The man with the old Mendoza rifle was smiling toothily. "We want to come aboard, see your fine boat."

I made a casual welcoming gesture. Hell, they were going to come anyway. I dropped my weight belt, pulled off the BC, and walked into the wheelhouse.

"Help with the line," the other man called. He had a revolver and a patch over one eye. A *tuerto.*

"Tie it yourself." I pointed at my raw thigh. "I have to bandage this. Shark," I explained and opened the map drawer as though looking for my first-aid kit. The Astra wasn't there, of course, but my boat wasn't entirely defenseless.

Both men wore the straw hats and loose white cotton garb of fishermen, machetes thrust down through waist sashes. The rifle was explainable—for sharks—but there was no touching of the forelock, no respectful *"padrón."* They were *contrabandistas* trying their hand at piracy. I was today's target of opportunity.

The rifleman was clambering over the stern transom where I reached up as though still searching for the kit. My hands closed around the 12-gauge scattergun I hoped he hadn't seen. *El Tuerto* left the wheel, revolver in hand, and started to board.

Snatching the Remington from its clamps, I dropped flat and fired a burst over their heads. Thinking it would frighten them off.

89

Maybe dive fatigue slowed my reactions, but I wasn't doing what I should have done. The nearest *bandido* fired from hip level, and a white-hot needle stung my left shoulder. He was aiming for a better shot, and his partner was pointing the revolver at me when I blew them both away.

The magnum loads slammed them back against the gunwales, and I had a flash replay of Carlos and Diehl dying. I squeezed my eyes shut, opened them to present reality and, still holding the shotgun, moved aft. I toed the rifle from curling fingers, saw life ebbing from dulling eyes. From the hole in his chest, the pellets had shattered his heart.

The one-eyed *pirata* lay in a pool of blood, his face red jelly. I kicked his revolver aside and knelt to press his heart. It would never throb again.

Standing up, I looked around. The horizon was clear of boats, the sound of firing couldn't have carried ashore. No one visible on the distant beach.

I took a long pull of Añejo and studied the old, scarred launch bobbing astern. Several woven baskets lay on its duckboards. Dry goods, liquor probably; I didn't care about the load.

And I didn't want to try to explain a second deadly encounter to the San Miguel police. The truth would strain even the *comandante*'s credulity.

Warm liquid on my left hand. Blood.

It trickled down my arm from the shoulder wound. Gently I felt for the bullet, but it had passed on, leaving a clean groove through the flesh covering my bursa. I took another pull from the bottle and got the first-aid kit from the port bulkhead.

I used a gauze compress on my shoulder, taping it tightly down; Milton could improve on my field expedient after I got home.

I shook antibacterial powder on my thigh. What the shark's slimy hide forced into my flesh threatened infection far more than the bullet graze. Putting away the kit, I turned my attention to the bodies.

I considered weighting and dropping them to the bottom, but that would link them to the plane, possibly to me. If I dumped them over the side, current would carry them ashore before nightfall.

So I dragged each corpse over the stern and into the launch. Next, their weapons. I wrestled the rifleman aft and put his arms through the wheel spokes, leaving the other *chingado* on the planking beside his cargo. I covered his faceless head with a straw sombrero. Number Four pellets had provided additional ventilation to the already loose weave. I tied the other hat on the wheelman's head. The eyes were flat and dull, staring sightlessly ahead. That wouldn't be noticed from a distance, though the big red hole through his chest might attract attention. The sooner we parted, the better.

The launch engine was in neutral. A clutch engaged it, and the propeller began to turn. I unfastened their bow line and coiled it near the prow, holding to *Corsair* with one hand. Slowly I walked the launch forward until it was pointing at the open sea, then climbed onto my foredeck. The launch putt-putted along, distance increasing. A gull dropped down for a look at the motionless men, squawked, and gained altitude. For a while I watched the launch moving off toward Cuba, satisfied it would keep going until fuel gave out.

Then I started *Corsair*'s engines and hosed pirate blood from the planking. Sun and salt would bleach the shadows that remained.

By now adrenalin was leaving my bloodstream. I felt pain in my ribcage, thigh, and shoulder. I picked up the BC to stow it and saw that the protective nylon envelope had been torn by the shark's body. My back ached from being slammed against the sunken plane.

I had another long pull of rum and winched up the anchor. Then I unscrewed the camera housing from the light bracket, wrapped it in a towel, and tucked it in the empty ice chest away from sunlight.

I replaced the spent shells in the Remington and clamped it to the overhead, glad I'd never have to visit the crash site again.

The launch was half a mile away when I turned *Corsair* around and headed home.

I DROWSED A good part of the return trip; the combination of fatigue and alcohol dulled my senses. I didn't want to reach the yacht basin bandaged as I was, so I cruised beyond it, turning in when I could see the Seabee and my pier.

I honked the boat horn to bring Joe Milton to the pier. The sound fetched both dogs, but not my new friend and collaborator. Well, maybe he was still on siesta.

But as I neared, I could see him in my borrowed trunks, lying on the sun pad toward the end of the pier. I honked again, but somehow sensed he wouldn't respond.

It was an eerie feeling as I guided the boat alongside, almost knowing what I'd find.

His flesh was burned deep red from hours of sun, but Joe would never feel discomfort or pain. Never again.

Above his right temple, partly hidden by breeze-blown hair, was a pencil-sized puncture. The left side of his head had exploded across the planking in a welter of gray brains and crusted blood.

My stomach shrank and I retched, vomited again and again, until even the bitter bile was gone.

THIRTEEN

W EAK AND SICK, I lost patience with the Embassy radioman who finally answered my call. "Identify yourself," he kept repeating, "or get off this frequency."

"You idiot!" I yelled into the mike, "I'm at Cozumel, and I want Joe's supervisor."

"Joe? Joe who?"

"Joe-who-wrote-*Paradise Lost.* Get him."

A man identifying himself as a supervisor came on the air, "Listen, good buddy, this is no CB frequency, so get off. It's reserved for official traffic."

"This *is* official."

"Let Joe do his own talking."

"I can't. I mean *he* can't."

Awareness gradually dawned. After a while the voice rasped, "Fatal?"

"How do you want to handle things?"

"I . . . we'll call you back."

I kept the receiver on while I wandered through the house. Jesus Christ! I kept repeating like a worn record. *Christ Almighty!*

They took long enough replying for me to make black coffee and get into dry clothes. My bandages couldn't be seen, but the pain remained, and very bad. Finally I heard the speaker say, "Diver?" so I went back to the radio. "Diver here."

"You have the frequency list?"

"Yes."

"We'll go third from the bottom. Now."

I dialed the new frequency. "As we were saying, it's a retrieval problem."

"Can't get a plane there before dark."

"Poor idea. After that massacre ten days ago, I have to stay clean."

"What's the alternative?"

"Hate to do it, but Joe can't feel anything now. So after dark I'll take him out to sea."

Long pause. "Will he be found?"

"I know the currents."

"That's satisfactory, what's your personal situation?"

"Not secure. When I got back there was a pound of C-Four hugging my engine. Joe was wearing my trunks today, sunning while I was off on a dive. They shot him, thinking it was me."

Another pause. "Sounds as if you're under siege. Maybe you ought to vacate a while."

"I'm giving it thought." I remembered the camera still on the boat and told him what the film might contain.

"Want someone to come for pickup?"

"Don't risk another man. Give me a mail drop."

For that we switched to another frequency, and when I'd written it down he said, "Could you call back later? I'd like to make sure the job's complete—and you're okay."

"Around eleven," I told him, "possibly later," and turned off the radio. Just sitting there had stiffened my back and chest muscles. I'd vomited all the rum I'd drunk and needed a painkiller.

Alcohol thawed my stomach. I fed the whining dogs and looked out to sea.

The killer or killers wouldn't be around now. Through telescopic sights they'd seen the body jump when the bullet struck, and gone off satisfied with a clean kill. Wouldn't try again until someone realized they'd wasted the wrong man.

His body still lay out where he died. Because someone might have been watching, I hadn't covered it. Now there was no reason to.

Less than an hour to nightfall.

I put Joe's shoes and clothing—everything but his wallet—in a bag and weighted it. Depending on what scavengers did to Milton's blown-apart head, a determination of violent death might or might not be made. I decided to take him out about a quarter of a mile, up-current from San Francisco beach. There were always bathers there, and his body would soon be found.

It was like *The Man Who Never Was,* I mused. And this too was war, though civilians didn't like to think of it that way. Poor Joe Milton, poor bastard. A sensitive stomach killed him—and spared me.

How long?

I got out my issue .45 and a shoulder holster with two spare magazines. If I'd been showing iron earlier, the pirates wouldn't have tried boarding. I put on the harness and felt better.

I'd lost energy and blood during the afternoon. I needed food but didn't think I could keep it down; not yet. So I chewed a mango and sipped orange juice with two ounces of dark rum. Then I walked out to the road and peered around. No cars, no bearded hitchhikers with *schlepsacks.* Just the uneven dirt surface, the wall of ceiba trees beyond. The dogs sniffed around, pointing their long sensitive noses into the wind, scented no aliens, and returned with me to the house.

By now the sun was below the horizon. Afterglow lingered, and there was no hurry for the funeral. I considered caching the camera in the house, but for all I knew it could be torched before I got back. So the camera and I would go together, return together. Or not at all.

I lighted another Vera Cruz panatela, but after a few puffs tossed it away; the taste was like stable-scrapings, though not the tobacco's fault. My whole system was reacting to the vomiting.

Along with the clothing bag, I carried a flashlight down the pier to where Joe Milton lay.

In darkness and death the undamaged portion of his face looked incredibly young. Tears welled in my eyes, rage tightened my belly. It would only get worse if I stood doing nothing, so I grasped his outstretched hands and dragged the body onto my boat.

Onshore breeze cooled perspiration from my face as I headed *Corsair* to sea. Joe's body lay on transom cushions like a statue. Automatically I started to switch on running lights, decided against visibility. I dumped the clothing bag offshore in four hundred feet of water as I turned for the unloading point.

Awkward with pain, but gently as I could, I lowered Joe's body over the side. Current took it quickly away. Moonlight glinted in his dead eyes, and I grimaced before shoving the throttles hard. I didn't ever want to meet his widow and tell her what I'd done.

I ran the boat back as fast as I could and tied at the pier across from the Seabee. Camera in hand, holster strap unbuttoned, I walked into the house and found the dogs curled up, asleep.

In the darkroom, I removed the film cassette and found no water contamination, so I mixed chemicals and began developing the strip. When it was fixed and dry I held it up to the light. Of 36 frames I'd exposed seven. I ran the negative through the viewer to check images and found what I hoped would be there: Astrid—the yacht silhouetted distantly behind her. My heart skipped. My golden girl. And wished it had been color film.

Other frames showed the wrecked Piper and its two cargo cases, the aluminum brightly reflecting the photoflash.

I printed two enlargements of each negative and left them on the dryer while I raised the Embassy radio operator.

"This is the Diver," I told him. "The message is—Done."

"Anything else?"

"Signing off." I locked the cabinet and went back to the darkroom. The prints were dry. I separated them into two piles, and fitted one set into an envelope, addressing it according to what I'd copied down. I wound up the negative, put it into an airtight film container, and dropped it down a hollow poster of my old brass bed. If anyone came they'd have to wake me to get it.

I pulled down the sheet and was unbuckling my holster when I heard the dogs setting up a clamor at the front gate, where an engine was idling. When I floodlit the yard I saw a taxi and someone getting out. The driver handed down a bag, and I wondered who the hell it could be.

I turned off the floods and left the house, pistol ready. By then the taxi had driven off, and someone was standing just beyond the jumping, baying dogs.

I whistled them down from the fence, squinted through darkness, and made out a petite female form.

"All that rumpus—is *this* how you welcome visitors?"

I felt as if the great gray shark had slammed me a second time. *"Dear God!"* I blurted. "Sweet child, you couldn't *possibly* have come at a worse damn time."

III

FOURTEEN

I CARRIED MELODY'S bag into the house and bolted the door. The dogs trotted over to their *serape* and sat down. Looking around she said, "What is this, a fortress?"

"Close to it." Resignedly I sat on a chair arm.

She came to me, kissed my cheek, and shook out her hair. There was something about the gesture suggesting permanent residence. "How inconvenient am I? Have you got a woman here? I don't do threesies."

"I haven't asked you," I replied, "and my girlfriend isn't around."

"Then why are you so uneasy?"

"You."

She shrugged. "You *said* we'd stay in touch, *told* me you wanted to see me again."

"Well, that's true. But I—"

"Later. Honey, I could really use a drink. Some of that rum you like. With or without ice." She plunked herself down on the sofa and stretched sculptured legs. "What have you been up to, lover?"

"Up to?" I felt a wild urge to shake her. "Let's take today—I killed two men and buried one I didn't."

She sniffed. "Been smoking—or in shock? I think you need help. Please, darling, I'm thirsty."

I limped off to liquor stowage and built us a pair of strong drinks. A lot of rum and a little ice. God, but she looked beautiful: white teeth, fantastic smile. Our glasses touched. "Chin-chin."

"Salud." She drank deeply and shook herself. "I don't know how you can drink this stuff all day long."

"It's the tropics. Abstainers aren't comfortable here."

99

"Then I'd better get accustomed." She drank until I put a restraining hand on her arm. That made her smile. "You *do* care for me."

"Madly."

"You haven't asked why I'm here."

"You'll tell me when you want to." I drank again. "Had dinner?"

"Just that little cold plate they hand you on the plane. But I'm not hungry." She sat forward. "I'm not going to be a burden, so tell the Mex her services aren't required. I can cook and wash *and* clean house."

"Now how the hell would fortune's darling learn such menial stuff?"

"From servants, sweet. *They* raised me in Brazil, not my biological parents." She twirled her glass making the ice chips tinkle. "Satisfied?"

"What can I say? I didn't hear a choice."

"But you're not kicking me out." She smiled provocatively, "Why don't you come over here and relax?"

"Well . . . I will."

"Please—remove the artillery. I don't want it gouging my tender young flesh."

I'd forgotten the harness, so I slid out of it, wincing with pain as it came off the wounded shoulder. I sank down beside her, wondering if all this was real.

"You poor man," she said solicitously—and stroked my thigh.

I yelped and shoved her hand away. Gritting my teeth I said, "I've got physical problems," unbuttoned my shirt, and let her ease it off my body. She stared at the blood-crusted bandage but said nothing. I let her undo my belt and stood so she could slide down my pants. When she saw the thigh bandage she paled. "My God, did the dogs attack you?"

"Shark."

I thought she was going to faint, so I sat down to steady her. Her eyes opened, she drained her glass and blinked. "I *hate* sharks—did you kill it?"

"I did."

"All alone?"

"Solo."

With that, she pressed my hands between hers. "I *knew* you were right for me. But, oh boy, how *completely* right you are. It's fate, lover, absolutely nothing less."

"Look, Melody, we have a very short history."

"But a long and fascinating future—believe me. Now, where do you stash the booze?"

I gestured, she dropped her sandals and padded away with our glasses.

In a few moments she came back and sat on the floor like a yogi. Looking up at me, she said, "Tell me about yourself."

"Maybe tomorrow."

She tilted her glass and sipped. Her smile was sly. "I'm so glad I'm here. Have you realized you love me?"

"I've only seen you once in my life."

"Is this a numbers game? Listen to me—I could tell . . . the way we made love."

I shook my head. "That was therapeutic—remember? Besides, you were a beginner."

"Well, it may have started therapeutically, but it sure turned out differently."

I forced my gaze from her dark eyes, that beautiful, memorable face. Jesus, and only a kid. "What are you doing here?"

"Here—this house? Or Cozumel in general?"

I made a face. "You know what I mean."

She sighed. "To put it briefly, things got intolerable at home. After you left things got very stale. Also, Mom's supposed to be in mourning—like Electra—so she hasn't been going out to the spots she used to frequent." Her nose wrinkled. "Frequent—I like that. Well . . . the upshot is because she can't be seen in public with Larry, he spends his time *chez nous.*" She drank again. "I know what goes on—I'm not a child—"

"You're not?"

"—but people could at least be discreet, right? I mean, you took me to that sordid motel so we would be off the street."

"What's the point, Melody?"

"It happened last night. As usual, Larry had dinner with us, and I went up to my room to watch TV and think about you, but the damn tube stopped working so I came downstairs to watch the set in the library and heard them talking." She paused. "Your name was mentioned."

"I trust nothing malign was said."

"Oh, they don't know we made love—if *that's* what worries you."

"Last thing in the world to worry me."

"Anyway," she went on, "they were discussing who you really were—if you worked for anyone."

"Like who?"

"Whom. The government. It made you sound very mysterious." She kissed the lobe of my ear, and I felt her tongue begin to move inside. "That tickles," I said, "so tell your tale and we'll get to the other."

She smiled, gratified. "So I watched my program, and on the way out I saw them."

"You mean . . . ?"

"Like two chipmunks. That bastard Larry was on the sofa with Mom, humping her."

"I see. Well, that's what grownups do sometimes."

Her lips trembled. "But she was *letting* him, Jack. I mean, Mom had her legs around his *hips* and was moaning—the way I sometimes do. And he's such a complete *shit.*"

"Probably a lot of bedrooms in that house," I remarked. "Bad form making it downstairs. So what did you do?"

"Couldn't help it—started yelling at him to stop balling my mother."

"Did he?"

"You just *bet* he did. And when he was pulling up his pants I ran upstairs and locked myself in."

I drank more of the delicious rum. "Usually a girl-child runs away when a male drops his pants."

"Oh, you're impossible," she snorted, "and me at an impressionable age."

"Think of the trauma, the possible effect on your future relationship with males." I shook my head. "So, what then?"

"I packed a bag, got my credit cards, and sneaked out before dawn. I checked into the Pavillon and considered what to do."

"And it boiled down to Cozumel?"

"Mostly. But I'm supposed to compete in the Nationals at Stanford, and this is partly on the way."

Putting my right arm around her shoulders, I kissed her lips. "I'm glad you came."

"And I can stay?"

"Until the Nationals—whenever they are."

She kissed the tip of my nose. "What's the age of consent in Mexico?"

"Never asked."

"I don't want to put you in danger."

"Danger?" My laugh was hollow. "In days ahead I'll tell you about danger, little one."

"Brazil is very strict," she confided. "If a man takes an underage girl's virginity it's practically a death offense."

"Lot of that go on?"

A fey smile touched her features. "Know how they avoid it?"

"I can guess."

She leaned over, cupped her hands, and whispered.

"Listen, Melody, why is it every time we get together we talk obscene things?"

"What other chance do I have? Besides, I like to, and it turns me on."

"Oh."

"Do you want me?"

"You know I do, battered as I am."

"I'll be careful. I really will. Where's our shower?"

"Second door on the left."

We disengaged, she picked up her bag and trotted off. I saw the light go on, and in a few moments heard the shower.

Not wanting to wet my wounds, I gave myself a sitz bath in the guest room tub and went into my bedroom. The light was out and Melody was under the sheet. Awkwardly I leaned over to kiss her. Our lips met, the sheet moved down and bared her breasts. They were cool and damp, her body lightly perfumed.

"Cat out, precious?" I asked.

"Yes, pet."

"Lights off, darling?"

"Yes, dear. And there's a note for the milkman."

"Table set for breakfast, honey?"

"First thing in the morning, doll. How do you like your eggs scrambled?"

"Dry, baby. Phone off the hook?"

"We'll never hear a thing, love. Now leave everything to me. Lie back and relax."

"What about you?"

"I can take care of myself." She slid down, her body arched, and her hair fanned over my groin. There was a large lump in my throat. Impure emotion.

As she worked her wiles I closed my eyes and thought that it had never been so good. Not even with Penny. Not ever in my life before.

FIFTEEN

I'D GONE OVER the Seabee very carefully before we took off, checking nooks and crannies where explosives might be hidden, inspecting control cables for hacksaw marks, and giving the plane a thorough shakedown. I'd made Melody wait down the pier just in case I tripped a tiny bomb. She wore an immodest bikini, Carrera sunglasses, and a hint of Shalimar. I climbed out on the pier and gestured her to me. A pleasure to watch her walk!

She said, "I've never seen a plane gone over in such preflight detail. Do you go through that every time you fly?"

"Only recently. I'm going to taxi around and go up for a test hop before taking you. So be patient, okay?"

"Anything you say, love."

I did as described, the plane didn't blow up or fall apart, so I nosed it against the pier and helped her in beside me. I pointed at the seat belt and shoulder straps. "Ever fly?"

"Ever fly *in* a plane—or fly a plane?"

"Can you handle an aircraft?"

"Sure. My father showed me when I was ten. He had planes and a private strip at the mines. Will you let me fly this little old thing?"

"Love me, love my plane. Now follow what I do. Remember when doing a water takeoff, keep wheels up."

"Elementary."

"Switch, ignition, flaps, throttle, mix . . ." I pointed them out, told her about running on the hull step before lifting off.

"What's the takeoff run?"

"Very short—you'll feel it when it's right and ready."

"I'm ready now." Her hand trailed over my groin.

"Ready to join the mile-high club?"

"Heard about it for years—let's." She undid her halter, wiggled out of the bottom, and for the first time in my life I was in a plane with a naked girl. I ran up mercury and headed into the wind.

First I flew over the center of the island, pointing out ruins visible through the undergrowth. Then I followed the coastline until I could see San Francisco Beach. A crowd was gathered near the waterline, and I felt sure Joe Milton had come ashore. I must have been staring because Melody said, "We're losing altitude. Let's get to six thousand, okay?" Watching the altimeter, she drew back the yoke.

Presently she got into my lap and did everything necessary for qualification. Then she got into her seat, leaned sideways, and kissed me. "Letcher."

"Nympho."

We both laughed. I said, "That was fun—all of it. Pay attention as we land."

"Sí senhor."

I pushed the column forward and spiraled slowly down until we crossed over my pier. I turned back into the wind and dropped gently to the surface. Melody watched everything I did, and I felt that if need arose she could fly the Seabee.

On the pier again, I led her over to *Corsair* and told her we'd take it to where I'd left my car. "Can you handle a boat as big as this?"

"Did you see the Saber behind Paul's house? He gave it to me. Five times the horses in this tug."

So I got off at the boatyard and drove my jeep back to the house. She brought *Corsair* in competently, with just a tad oversteering, but no damage to hull or pier. This was an all-around girl, the kind of companion I'd never had—though Astrid might have been.

I let Melody make lunch, and then I drove into San Miguel to show her its few sights: bars, restaurants, the town pier where fishing and dive boats docked. "Not much to see," I remarked.

"Well, it's compact."

We strolled into the El Portal, took a table, and Chela sauntered over, wiping her hands on her apron. *"Para servirle,"* she said in a edged voice.

"Chela Lopez, Melody West." They nodded at each other. I said, "Chela, she's my late wife's younger sister, here to spend a short vacation. Right, Melody?"

My housemate nodded, and Chela stared at us in obvious disbelief. Melody said, "Tell her I'll take care of things from now on."

I swallowed. "Melody's learning how to cook and keep house, so . . . I'd like you to come back after she's gone."

"Perhaps. You want something, Juan? Passion fruit for the *niña*?"

"Ah . . . well, I guess we'll just go along." I swallowed. "Wanted you two to know each other."

"*Cuidado,* Juan," was her parting shot. "I warned you about the other one." She looked at the ceiling. "Some men, they never learn."

Melody murmured, "I got most of that, and I think we've worn out our welcome." I followed her to the street. It was one of those difficult situations most men handle ineptly, including myself.

Back at the house I let Melody change my bandages before I went into the darkroom. So many things had happened since her arrival that I'd postponed sending off the photos. I'd planned to include Joe Milton's wallet, but decided to keep it for possible use, especially his Treasury ID. I brought out the envelope and showed my set of prints to Melody.

She glanced at those of the sunken plane without much interest, but when she came to Astrid she paused. "She was traveling with Paul?"

"Called herself Penny Saunders—later said her name was Astrid Nordstrom. I asked about her—remember?"

"Her face *is* familiar—I think somewhere I've seen her. She's striking-looking."

"She was," I agreed. "Try to remember where you saw her."

"I have an excellent memory—now I'm sure I've seen her."

"Paul's office?"

"No, it was . . . I've got it. Larry drove her to the house once, and while he was talking with Paul she walked around back and watched me diving."

"No introductions?"

"I was practicing for the Regionals, and concentration was the thing. When Larry came out she went back to his car."

"The silver-gray Corvette."

She nodded. "I assumed she was one of Larry's fancy broads."

"Maybe she was." I pointed out the yacht in the photo background. "See the chopper? That's what did us in." I explained about the film and how I'd had to recover it. Melody said, "So what are you going to do?"

I tapped the envelope. "Hope the yacht can be identified."

"Think there's a chance?"

"Should be."

Her finger outlined my ear. "Isn't it siesta time?"

"It is."

"I'll have to adjust to tropic routine. I'd ask you to scrub my back, but not while you're bandaged." She frowned. "That shoulder wound doesn't look like a shark bite."

"Bullet."

"Really?"

"Told you I'd killed two men—that's why."

She touched the bandage tenderly, "I thought you were just . . . exaggerating. Will you be in trouble?"

"Not from that."

"Unzip me, please." She turned, and I opened the back of her blouse. She shrugged it off, baring her torso. I kissed the back of her neck, and she said, "I've been thinking about what Larry and Mother said. *Do* you work for the government?"

"No."

"If you do, I'd never tell."

"I was in the Navy."

"But you got out."

"It involved my wife's death."

"I won't pry—but there's so much about you I want to know." Rising, she pressed my head between her breasts. I felt her body quiver as she whispered, "God, I want you."

Under the ceiling fan, on the coverless bed we made love and slept through the afternoon. I woke and left Melody asleep, wrote her a note, and took the envelope of photos to the San Miguel post office. It was near the police station, and as I walked back to the jeep the *comandante* came out and beckoned to me. "The body of one of your countrymen was found on a beach this morning."

I said nothing.

"He rented a car at the airport two days ago."

"Well," I said, "I'm not missing anyone."

"I thought he might be a friend."

"You haven't mentioned his name."

"Milton. Joseph Milton. The name under which he rented the car."

"Maybe he was from one of the cruise ships."

"No, he flew in from Mexico City. The Embassy has been informed."

"You're a good officer, Elpidio."

"*Gracias.* I like you, Juan. I don't want you in any trouble. You have a visitor, a young one."

"My late wife's sister. *Mi cuñada.*"

"Enjoy her company."

We shook hands, and I drove back to the house. Melody was drying her hair on the patio, dogs curled about her feet. A tranquil scene, I reflected, one that let me feel comfortable and secure. She blew a kiss, and with the towel, twisted her hair into a toque. "Did you bring supplies?"

"We'll dine at the Sol Caribe."

"Sounds enticing. But you don't have to spend money on me."

"While you're here I want to display you."

She smiled. "My first public date with a grownup male." Her eyes appraised me. *"What a male!"*

We had evening drinks on the patio, and when the sky was deep purple I drove her down the highway to the hotel. Our meal was well served. I chose a bottle of good Chilean Riesling and noticed admiring glances directed at Melody; envious ones at me.

Later in bed I kissed her forehead and she snuggled close.

I hadn't been so contented since Astrid's death. But from experience, I felt it couldn't last.

When Melody's breathing became soft and rhythmic, I left quietly and went outside with the dogs. The half-moon illuminated the grounds, glinted from the Seabee's windows. I remembered cutting into the sunken Piper while Astrid brought out its clandestine cargo.

I wondered if the pilot's widow knew who'd hired him for his final flight. Someone should inquire.

SIXTEEN

MELODY AND I could have been mistaken for honeymooners. We drove around the island, had beach picnics, visited some of the accessible ruins, took out the boat for nude swimming, and flew over to Cancún for a day. The return trip was her check flight, and after minor help on takeoff she had the controls all the way.

One afternoon I raised Mexico City and learned my envelope had been received, contents appreciated. There was more, the supervisor said. "We got a make on that yacht. It was built for the late Shah in Holland, outfitted in Barcelona and the UK. In Alexandria it was sold to a Lebanese banker, resold to a Greek shipping magnate who got into debt. At auction it was bought by a Netherlands Antilles corporation located in Curaçao. It flies a flag of convenience, Nigerian registry—currently named *Solimar.*"

"So the owners aren't identified."

"The only name on its papers is the Dutch lawyer who processed the deal."

"Familiar pattern."

"Also, we've sent copies of the girl's photo to various agencies, but I don't think they'll be productive. Not unless she had a criminal record."

"She might have been booked for nude dancing, but that's only a guess. Incidentally, a few weeks ago she was seen in Miami with Diehl's partner, Larry Parmenter."

"Well, she was part of Diehl's scam, wasn't she? Oh, the *Solimar* fueled at Progreso about a week ago, then disappeared. Nobody went ashore."

I could have flown there in an hour—if I'd known.

The speaker crackled: "For the record, did you accept Joe's proposal?"

"I like things the way they are. No offense."

"None taken. Stay in touch."

"Likewise." I switched off the set.

Melody came in from feeding the dogs, and I put my arms around her. "If I haven't said so before, I'm glad you're here."

She kissed the point of my chin. "That's because you love me." Her smile was elfin. "You're not up to more complications in your life—I understand that—but I tell you now our future's together."

"Must be a comfort to have foresight. Mine's limited to an hour ahead—if that."

"You know I'm gifted, precocious, too. So you can bet money on my prediction." She touched my cheek tenderly. "Does the idea distress you?"

"You're weird," I told her. "At your age shouldn't you find the whole idea of an enduring relationship—marriage, in short—overwhelming, gross, or both?"

"I'm not my age."

"Of course you are."

"Qualitatively speaking—surely you can understand that? Good grief."

I sighed. "It's a fantastic idea—only, how to get through the next few years? You in college—me ekeing out a living with my boat . . . doesn't sound terribly stable."

"I'll bet Chela never attended college—why should I?"

"So I won't have to apologize for my life partner, if that's what you intend to be. With your athletic skill, you could probably get a full scholarship."

"I've been offered one—U of Miami. But I don't want academic achievements—I want you."

"That's because you haven't met many fellows past the acne and bubble gum stage. Give yourself options—you're gorgeous, talented, and very bright. Hell, you might want to go into law or medicine. You don't know, because you've never been exposed to academic disciplines."

"Why are you so obstinate?"

"I care for you. Life isn't a big bon-voyage basket of tasty fruit, Melody. Some things we get, others elude us. I started out to make admiral and dropped out. So I'm trying to explain to you, be content when something good comes along, and don't complain when it doesn't repeat every day."

Her lips formed a straight line. "Meaning what?"

"Meaning we should make the most of your vacation. Let the future do what it will."

"I love living with you—I've never known anything close to it, so I don't want it to end. Without you I'd be . . . incomplete." She pressed close against me. "Are you afraid of a commitment because of . . . your wife?"

"She has nothing to do with now."

"I think you should tell me."

I'd been dreading the question, knowing eventually it would come. Now was as good a time as any to answer. I poured myself a drink, carried it back to where she sat.

"I was just out of flight training when I met Pam at a Philadelphia dance. She'd gone to a fashionable Maryland school and was a model hoping for cover assignments. My carrier was on the East Coast and I could usually get to New York for the weekend. In six months we married with the understanding she couldn't be a Navy wife, following me around from port to port."

"Quite a concession."

I sipped more of my drink. "Her career began to take off. A classmate told me my carrier was headed for the Indian Ocean for a long tour, so I volunteered for the Seals. Training kept me in the Virgin Islands for a while, but I managed to visit New York even from there. Pam was on a near starvation diet, compensating for that and long working hours with cocaine. I begged her to knock it off, and she promised she would. Then my Seal team was sent to 'Nam for the last months of the war, and when I got back she was on horse—heroin—and badly addicted, looked like a skeleton. She'd sold everything we owned to pay for her habit. I had a nasty brawl with her pusher, and it ended up with her screaming at me to get out." I finished my drink. "A month later she OD'd, and I left the Navy, figuring it had cost me my wife. I was wrong, but I had to lay the blame someplace. DEA took me in and let me do what I wanted—fight the narcotics traffic."

"I'm sorry," she said softly. "And you ended up here. Are you still . . . ?"

"They trashed me for losing Diehl. I told them to shove it."

"I . . . needed to know. Forgive me."

"Bringing us to unfinished business. I have to go away for a while, Melody, and I can't leave you here."

"The dogs would protect me."

"Not from bullets."

"But I'm not—"

"They'd assume you know everything I do. When do the Nationals begin? When are you due at Stanford?"

"Three days—but I've decided not to compete."

"I want you to."
"Who'll take care of the dogs, the house?"
"Chela."
"She has a forgiving nature?"
"We'll see."

I GAVE MELODY half a day's scuba instruction before letting her dive Palancar reef with me. Her confidence and water skills fitted naturally into the sport, and the following day we dived the Santa Rosa. That's where the offshore reef sheers away into a thousand feet of water, and I wouldn't have dived it with someone I didn't trust. But now and then when I'd glance at her moving body, I'd remember Astrid, and how we'd gone down to the sunken plane. The memory didn't do me any good, and I realized how Melody's arrival had postponed all I'd resolved to do.

We parted at the airport, and I took a later flight to Houston wondering if we'd ever meet again. During the flight across the Gulf I tried to push Melody into the recesses of my mind so I could plan what I was going to do. Finding the pilot's widow came first.

SEVENTEEN

THE GUZMÁN HOUSE was single-story concrete block on a small plot of land featuring a bumper crop of weeds. Most of the old houses in the subdivision had a sagging roof or porch, or the foundation was giving out. One of those thirty-house postwar developments whose builder cashed in fast and left town before complaints came in.

Some of the backyards had pens for chickens, and I saw rabbit hutches as I drove down the potholed street looking for the number. Last night I'd rented a compact at the airport and checked into a cheap hotel on the outskirts of Houston, deciding to see the widow in the morning when children would be at school.

The doorbell was busted, and the woman who answered my knock peered suspiciously through a battered screen. *"Sí?"*

In Spanish I said, "Mrs. Guzmán?"

"Maybe—who asks?"

"A friend of Fernando's."

"He's not here."

"I know." I held up his driver's license.

Her hand came snatching around the screen, fast as a striking snake, but I drew away. "Give it to me!" she yelled.

"After we've talked."

Her eyes smoldered. "Where is he?"

I glanced around. "Want neighbors to hear?"

She kicked the door open and I went in.

The room was a shambles: sprung chairs with torn, stained upholstery; rug with a charred section near the fireplace; a gut-sprung sofa. Remains of an upright piano. Above it, a serene portrait of the Guadalupe Virgin surrounded by stiff sprays of long-dead flowers. Near the mantel, a hand-tinted photo of a thin-faced man wearing dark glasses and a fifty-mission cap. He had a pencil mustache and sideburns. Probably Fernando—and looking far better than my one glimpse of him. I gestured at the photo. "How long since you've seen him?"

"My husband? Six weeks—seven." She shrugged apathetically. "Is he coming home?"

"No," I said, "he's not coming home."

Swallowing, she stared at me. "Why not?"

I handed her the license. "Where do you think I got it?"

She let it drop from her hands and began wailing. While she was beating her chest and plucking at her hair, I went into the pigsty kitchen and found a half-inch of tequila. I wiped out a glass and transferred the tequila. She was slumped in a chair, shrieking and pounding the chair arms, but she stopped to toss off the liquor and glared at me. "Who killed Fernando?"

"I don't think anyone killed him. Plane crash."

That set her off again. I glanced through the screen and saw housewives gathering on the road. To cover myself, I stepped out long enough to say everything was okay. They responded with sullen glances, and I ducked back in.

"Mi esposo," she moaned. *"Mi pobre esposo. Muerto. Ay!"*

But the liquor was calming her down. I said, "Before I can help I need to know who he was flying for."

"Rafael," she whimpered, wiping her nose on a hairy forearm. "Always Rafael."

"Rafael who?"

"Rafael son-of-a-whore, that's who." Wet eyes fixed on me. "He never said. *Ayyyyy,* my poor husband, my Fernando . . . never to hold in my arms . . . make love . . ." Emotion overcame her, and I waited until the spasm passed before saying, "If Rafael hired him, Rafael has responsibility."

Her eyes widened. "Insurance?"

"Have you got Rafael's phone number?"

She heaved herself out of the chair, waddled into another room. From her size, she outweighed her late husband an easy two to one. She came back with a towel, wiping face and neck and arms, showed me a notepad with names and numbers. I copied down the entry for Rafael and said, "I'll follow this up, *señora.*" I got out a hundred-dollar bill and smoothed it between my fingers. She stared at it as though fearful I'd palm it as magicians do.

"Fernando was involved with some very bad people—you must know that."

"I? I know nothing of his business, *señor.*"

"He flew narcotics." The revelation didn't bother her. "So if anyone comes asking about him, don't say I came here first." I gestured at the license. "Put that away—you might need it."

"For what?"

"Insurance." I gave her the hundred. It would buy tortillas, rice, and beans for a month.

From one of the clustered houses came the thin, sawing sounds of *mariachi* violins, the tinny wail of a cornet. I wasn't in Old Mexico but I might as well have been. In someone's back yard a dog and chickens were at it. A woman yelled, I heard water splashing and the dog yelped. The chickens quieted down. She blotted her face with the towel. "You're very kind, *señor.* Fernando was a good man, a patriot."

I nodded.

"In Africa he flew against the Communists—before we married." That made him Cuban. But she wasn't, not by her accent. Nor Mexican. Farther down the line. I said, "Was it Rafael's plane he flew?"

"In Africa?"

"No, his last flight."

"Quién sabe?"

I'd drained her of limited knowledge; now was the time to leave her to grief and the comfort of neighbors. *"Vaya con Dios,"* I said and heard her repeat the parting as I went through the doorway.

Kids were hitting fungo balls near the car. Too near. Women moved aside, and I opened the car door. "She needs you," I told them. "Give her all the help you can."

Gathering their skirts, they fled into the house, and I started the engine. From a filling station I dialed Rafael's number. "Calexico Air Service," a man's voice said in accented English.

In Spanish I said, "Rafael there?"

"Not now. Who calls him?"

"When will he be there?"

"Maybe today, maybe not. He comes and goes."

"I get the picture. Well, I'll call later."

"Message?"

"I want to surprise him. *Adiós.*"

"Adiós, señor."

It was about as I expected. A shadow operation, planes not too well maintained. A hungry pilot willing to fly anywhere for a few bucks. The question was, who paid Rafael and Fernando? Diehl was the most likely candidate, but I had to make sure.

BAY TOWN WAS a hot hour and a half away. I found a café that looked as though it might cater to the action-oriented, ordered a T-bone steak, fries, and salad. The middle-aged waitress looked like a career employee, so I showed her a cutout photo of Astrid and asked if the girl looked familiar. "Like a cheerleader, that's what she looks like. Even the T-shirt," she said.

I laid five near her hand. "I'd appreciate your help."

She put on glasses and examined the photo more closely. "Maybe she's been here, maybe not—but she *looks* Texas, I'll say that. Lot of good-looking girls go to Bolivar High. Friend of yours?"

"Friend of a friend. Bolivar High?"

"Down the Peninsula. Best ball club in the Southeast. Triple-A champs for years. The Texas Terrors—everyone these parts knows the name. Bolivar High—some go to college. Anything else?"

"Not that you'd know from personal experience, ma'am, but if a girl wanted to strip dance around Galveston Bay, where could she find work?"

She smiled. "Lord, no shortage of joints. There's Marty's Place, the Cockatoo, the Lone Wolf, Paradise Now . . . yeah, and Fancy Feathers—just drive around, you'll see 'em."

"Much obliged."

The steak wasn't overdone and the fries were crisp. I downed two chilled mugs of Miller Lite, a cup of coffee, and was on my way.

Getting gas, I asked directions to Bolivar, and found it was at the far side of the Bay, across the cut from Galveston. Another hour, and I pulled into the high school parking lot. There were administrative people in the office, so I flashed Joe Milton's Treasury credential and Astrid's photo. "I need a name to go with this," I told the assistant principal. "We understand she was a student here maybe ten years back."

"I've been here three." He gestured at a shelf of class yearbooks. "Help yourself."

"Well, I haven't an excess of time. Perhaps someone here would have been around at that period."

He shrugged. A smallish man in a white-on-white shirt and a loose crimson tie. Crimson, I gathered was the school's color. Like Harvard. "Teachers come and go, you know. Administrators, too, and that's a good while back."

118

"I understand. So I need to speak with someone knowledgeable."

He squinted at me. "Tax case?"

"Can't say."

"Well, Louise Loudon's the most senior teacher we've got. I'll just see if she's in." He punched a call box and after a while a voice answered. Presently a large white-haired female came in and listened while my mission was explained. Miss Loudon said, "I'll be glad to help, of course," and studied the photograph.

Her first reaction was, "Natural blonde?"

"Definitely, why?"

"So many of them bleach their hair. Of course this styling wasn't fashionable a decade ago, so I can't be sure what she looked like then. Is she in trouble?"

I shrugged.

She tapped the photo. "Those looks . . . she could have been a trouble-maker . . . boys, y'know."

"Could she have been a cheerleader?"

From the shelf, she took several yearbooks and began skimming group photos. After the third scan she said, "I believe I've found her. Yes, I'm sure. Amy King. What do you think?"

It was Astrid. Hair longer, figure less developed, but the same nose and cheekbones. Kneeling on the turf, pleated skirt modestly across her knees, arms around the shoulders of adjacent girls, boys standing behind in antic postures. Tightly I said, "You've been very helpful, Miss Loudon."

She leafed to the individual class photos. Amy Astrid King. Extra-curricular activities: Glee Club 3,4. Cheerleader 3,4. Girls' Swimming JV 4. I said, "You have a pool here?"

"Team uses the Y."

Under her bio data, the class wish: *Our Vivacious, Curvaceous Amy Is Sure to Go All the Way. Lotsa Luck, Blondie.*

I wondered if the double entendre was intentional. "Could you copy the two pages?"

While Miss Loudon used the machine in an adjoining office the assistant principal said, "Is there anything else, Mr. Milton?"

"Unless you have her files and scholastic records."

"They'd be in Austin, probably impossible to find."

"Well, what you've provided is very informative."

"I'm glad we could help." He took the photocopy sheets from Miss Loudon and handed them to me. I thanked her again and went down the hall. Above the Auditorium entrance a long banner: *Bolivar High—Home of the Texas Terrors,* and to one side a large sign with crimson letters: *Beat Galveston!!!*

As I got into the car I reflected that if Astrid/Amy had been there for only her last two years, she'd transferred from another school. I wondered what name she'd used—and why—but it didn't seem worth pursuing. Not in the day's humid heat.

I TOOK THE channel ferry across to Galveston and followed Interstate 45 into Houston and over to my hotel.

A notice on my door read: *Please turn off air conditioning before leaving room.* I hadn't complied, so the room was comfortable when I entered. I poured Añejo over ice and sat on the bed drinking and evaluating what I'd accomplished. After a while I dialed Information and learned Calexico Air Service was located a few miles east of Bay Town. The operator didn't know if the field was private, and Yellow Pages didn't list Calexico. I phoned again but Rafael wasn't around; might have dropped by but the spokesman couldn't say. I said I'd try later.

The liquor relaxed me as I studied the two yearbook pages. Amy's photos hadn't reproduced well, but I didn't need the images now that I knew who she'd been. *Sure to Go All the Way.* Well, she had—all the way to the bottom of the Caribbean. The prediction couldn't have been more accurate.

Unanswered question: Who sent her there?

I lay back, closed my eyes, and slept until evening. Then I set out for the strip joints that bordered the bay.

EIGHTEEN

THE AIRFIELD WASN'T much out of the way, so I stopped off and found Calexico Air Service in a hangar on the far side. It seemed to consist of a cubicle, a desk with telephone, chairs, and a pay phone on the wall. A couple of light planes were in maintenance. One's engine had been pulled. The other was a Piper, same model I'd found off Cozumel. Spare wing-tanks for extended flying were stacked on a pallet.

While I was looking around a voice said, "Want something?"

"Rafael."

I turned and saw a man in slacks and *guayabera*. He had bushy hair, an Aztec profile, a long ebony cigarette holder between his teeth. "Friend of Rafael?" he asked.

"Never met him We have a mutual friend."

"Who?"

"Name of Guzmán. Fernando."

He eyed me. "You called before?"

I nodded. He wore heavy gold bracelets; a necklace of thick gold links glinted as he moved under the light. One of his eyes was frozen. "Got a job for Rafael?"

"I'll discuss it with him."

"I'm Rafael." He gave me his hand but not his family name. "How long ago you see Fernando?"

"Couple of weeks. You?"

He took out the ebony holder and picked his foreteeth with a thumbnail. "Damn near two months."

I looked at his waist and chest to see if he was carrying. "I didn't say where I saw him."

Rafael stopped picking his teeth. "Let's go in." He unlocked the cubicle door, turned on the overhead bulb, and we went in. He sat behind the desk and studied my face. "What was Fernando's condition?"

"Very poor. And very wet."

He sighed, shook his head.

"Charlie Bravo four-one-five Nan was the wing number."

He grimaced. "What's your interest?"

"You hired him. Who hired you?"

His lips made a sucking sound. "Federal?"

"Nowhere near."

"In the business?"

I pulled out greenbacks and riffled them. "Fernando's finished, plane's down, end of story. But you can still make yourself some bucks."

"Yeah?"

"You're short of planes, Fernando failed to make delivery, I deliver."

The greenbacks interested him. "The guy who paid the charter said it was one time only."

"How right he was. So I'd like a word with him." I detached a century and eased it within his reach. The money would buy a couple lines of coke; more, if cut. He dabbed a soiled handkerchief at his nose. Our thoughts paralleled. I said, "Or I can go elsewhere."

"Go ahead." The good eye seemed fixed on the greenback. He attended to his nose again.

"That would leave you outside looking in."

He coughed and made up his mind. "You know how it works, right? I get a message with a phone number, call at such and such a time—pay phone, right?"

"I'm with you."

"A flight to Mérida and back. Money up front."

"How much?"

"Five large. Okay, why not? Half for Fernando, half for me and the plane. In Mérida there'd be cargo, not heavy." He spread his hands, sniffed.

"Fernando made the Mérida pickup. He could have flown back direct. Why Cozumel?"

"Papers."

"You mean, he was coming back with—let's say—official documentation? That takes cooperation."

"There's an airport man helps out—for a price."

"The Captain," I said.

"You done business with him?"

"How else would I know? Okay, you haven't told me anything worth a peso. The guy who called you—tell me about him."

"Anglo—like you. Never saw him, just heard his voice."

"He gave you a contact number."

"Pay phone."

"Still got it?"

"Maybe."

I removed my hand from the bill. Rafael opened the desk drawer, pulled out a scrap of paper, and shoved it toward me. Using his phone I dialed the number. No answer. I dialed the operator and said, "I just lost coins in a nonfunctioning phone," and repeated the number. "Could you check it out?"

Before the operator could reply, Rafael snatched back the scrap. "Okay, wise guy, that's my girlfriend's." He got out his wallet and showed another number. "That's it, on my mother."

This one checked out, and the operator verified location. Replacing the receiver I said, "I have no sense of humor, pal. If you're jerking me around, I'll come back with a bat and break your fucking knees."

From the open drawer he snatched an automatic and pointed it at me. *"Carajo,"* I said disgustedly and overturned the desk on him. The pistol went off, barely missing the light bulb, and, while Rafael was yelling and trying to get out from under the desk, I twisted the automatic away, removed the magazine, and tossed it into a corner. I jacked the ready shell from the chamber and dropped the piece on the dusty floor. As he picked himself up I said, "That should cost you the hundred—but you're too dumb to know better. Get the desk up, chair, too."

Wincing with pain, he got them back in position and stared at me. I said, "Sit down, coker, we're not finished."

He tried brushing dirt from the *guayabera* sleeves, but it was there until next wash. I said, "You must have been curious about the caller because only a sucker would pay in advance. Maybe you figured you could stick him for more. Know what I'd do? Next time he was due to call I'd post a friend by the pay phone—then I'd have a description, maybe a license tag. Were you savvy enough to do that, Rafael? Did your girlfriend linger nearby taking everything down."

His good eye glared at me.

Reaching across the desk, I pulled his right hand toward me, picked up a switchblade from where it had fallen out of his drawer, and drew it across his palm. "There's a limit to generosity."

"Tall man," he spat. "Anglo. Light hair. Foreign car."

"German? Italian? Jap?"

"She couldn't tell. But she got the plate."

"And you'll give it to me." I put the blade point on the center of his palm, held it there.

"In my wallet," he grated, and got it out with his left hand. I dumped its contents on the desktop. Some of the ID showed his name as García, some as Julio Barros. I released his hand and let him extract the tag number, then took it from him. "Guy speak with an accent?"

"My English ain't that good. He spoke Anglo—what can I say?"

"Was he driving alone?"

"Woman with him."

"Blonde—brunette?"

"Too dark to tell—tinted windows."

"And you never traced the tag number?"

"When Fernando didn't get back, I didn't want to know who the guy was. I lost a plane, he lost a load. I figured he'd come looking for me." He shrugged. "I was plenty glad you weren't him."

I retracted the switchblade, dropped it in my pocket. "Keep the hundred, but if it gets back to me you've been talking about our conversation—I've got your home address. A couple of sticks through your window would give folks a big noise to talk about at your funeral."

I got up and started to go. As an afterthought I held Astrid's photo under the light.

"Ever see her?"

His eye studied the image. "No—but I'd like to."

"She's with Fernando," I told him.

He watched me walk away.

I LAID MONEY around the go-go bars: bartenders, dancers, night managers. The Cockatoo, Paradise Now, The Lone Wolf—all tapped out. I passed by several that looked like blood buckets and went into Marty's Place.

Like the others, it had a dance platform surrounded by an oval bar. Heavy rock music and good-figured dancers who looked like they were trying to shake apart at the pelvis. One girl danced with a drugged python that couldn't keep its snout from her crotch. A heat-seeking reptile. She got a good hand and a lot of horny whistles. The women in the audience looked embarrassed or too drunk to be. Navy days I'd seen plenty of nude dancing, but Marty's was something else. I wondered why the cops didn't close it down, then realized they were paid not to. Jaramillos everywhere.

I laid ten on the manager, who looked like he'd trained for bouncer, and showed the photo. "She used a lot of names when she worked the area."

"They all do. What's your interest?"

"My money's done my talking."

"I could barely hear."

I gave him another ten and his heavy eyebrows drew together. "Yeah, she was here—I think."

"Using what name?"

"Maybelle. Had little silver bells on her tits, see? She'd get 'em goin' like chimes. A real turn-on for the customers."

"I can imagine. How long ago?"

He took a choke, so I eased out another bill. "Four-five years. We got better girls right here." He waved his hand expansively. "But if you're collectin', forget it. Find your own talent."

I tapped the photo. "This Maybelle—was she a producer?"

"Every way. The boss hated her leavin', but"—he shrugged—"opportunity came knockin'."

"In what form?"

"Fancy Feathers was openin'—an' with the owner connected, my boss couldn't say no when they reached for her."

"We know how that goes, right?"

"Sure. Do the right thing."

"Same management at Feathers?"

He nodded.

"Did she coke?"

"Not on the premises—that's one thing the boss don't never allow. Grass? Hey, why not? Maybe a tab or two, but no hard stuff. Protection only goes so far." A waiter touched his arm. He said, "Pleasure—enjoy yourself," shoved my money in his pocket, and went away.

For a while I fooled with my beer and watched a cinnamon girl excite the watchers with simulated masturbation. Melody might have gotten a kick from the performance, but I wasn't in the mood for public sex, feigned or not.

I followed highway sign directions and left the car in the Fancy Feathers lot. The night was warm, dampness like tropic rain. Except for Manaus, Houston had to have the worst climate in the hemisphere. I paid a five buck cover charge and went in.

You didn't have to be told to know the place was a connected establishment. Thick carpets, discreet lighting at the tables, waitresses in saucily revealing costumes, and some very heavy-looking muscle posted around. A DJ booth and Dolby sound. The performers danced on a black glass panel, showcased by spot and strobe lights. A waitress handed me a small card with a food menu on one side, drink list on the other. "I'm Jennifer," she said engagingly, "and I'm here to serve you."

The high prices would keep out the crut crowd—that was obvious—and I had a momentary sense of being in a geisha palace. No beer on the list—natch—so I asked for a Cuba Libre and a steak sandwich medium-well.

"Fries or skins?"

"You decide." I gave her five with the menu. She thanked me politely and said the drink would be right along.

By the time it arrived there was music and a girl with long blonde tresses swirling over the black floor. It looked as if she were moving over total emptiness. She wore a glistening white Isolde robe gathered at her hips by a gold cord, and after a while she was beseeching a stern-visaged papier-mâché idol, body moving sensuously.

"She's very popular with the customers." Jennifer delivering my drink.

"Deservedly so," I replied, though not impressed by the act. "There was a blonde exotic who came here from Marty's Place some years ago. I wonder if anyone would remember her work name. At Marty's she called herself Maybelle." I passed her another five. "Would you ask around?"

"I'll be glad to, sir." She hesitated. "I don't suppose you'd want to say why?"

I shook my head very slowly.

While she was gone another dancer came out, cracking a lion-trainer's whip and costumed for the leather trade. Jennifer brought my sandwich. "Freshen your drink?"

"Duplicate it. Any reaction?"

"I'll know in a bit."

She walked away showing pretty buns. Maybelle—take away *belle* left May, a rearrangement of Amy. *You'll go all the way, Blondie.* A/k/a Amy King, with other aliases. A girl with something to hide—probably much more.

Rafael had turned into a downy bird and I'd plucked him. General description of car and driver, tag—and Jaramillo's support role. That made the fat captain suspect for shooting Joe Milton, booby-trapping my plane. Loose ends to tidy up in Cozumel.

Still, Diehl's behavior was hard to fathom. By profession and character he was not a risk-taker, and he could have monitored the operation from

Miami in air-conditioned comfort. Going to Cozumel was a departure from pattern, so his motive had to have been compelling.

Was Astrid—*Amy*—along as accomplice, or watchdog?

Someone slid into the seat beside me. "You want to know about Maybelle? Perhaps I can help you." The voice was soft, alto, seductive. Without the long blonde tresses I didn't recognize her at first. Her real hair was coppery and cropped, features harder than they'd looked while she was performing. Her arms were veined and muscular, and her body language suggested she wasn't totally feminine. Well, I wasn't going to lay her, just ask about a mutual friend. "Good," I said. "She was at Bolivar High with my sister, so—"

Her hand pressed my arm firmly. "If you want to talk we'll have to go outside—house policy, no mingling with customers." She looked around as though apprehensive of being seen.

"Won't take a moment." I laid a hundred dollar bill on the table. "Why did she leave here?"

"I'll tell you all that, where she is—outside." She rose and walked back to the entrance, moving solidly in Western boots. She hadn't taken my inducement, and I had a firm feeling she wasn't fond of men. Hell, being a nude dancer for a few years would sour almost any female.

I was finishing my ten-buck sandwich when Jennifer appeared with my drink. "Joey come?"

"Joey?"

"Josephine—everyone calls her Joey."

"Crazy," I said. "Keep the drink and I'll pay."

"Twenty-two dollars—including the drink. It's on my tab, see?"

I patted her hand and pressed thirty into it.

"Hurry back, hear?"

Leaving the table I turned my back on the current cat-costumed performer, went out, and looked around.

Joey was sitting on the parking lot fence, smoking something between cupped hands. With boots hooked over a rail and short-cropped hair she looked like a young male hooker. Catching sight of me she nodded.

From somewhere in the shadows behind I heard movement and started to turn, but my reactions were fractionally slow. A whistling rush of air and something exploded against the back of my head. My knees dissolved and I fell into empty blackness.

NINETEEN

"JOSEPH MILTON?"

The voice came from the top of a mile-deep mineshaft where I was lying crumpled at the bottom. *Milton?* Who he?

The question repeated and I became aware of light through closed eyelids. Was I on *Corsair?* Shot, sapped? What . . . ?

A hand shook me—not roughly. "There's been a mistake, Mr. Milton, a bad one. Try some water." Arms lifted me, fingers opened my mouth, and I tried to swallow, but my head was pulsing with pain. "Liquor," I croaked.

"Get something," the same authoritative voice commanded. Presently I felt glass against my lips. Vodka? The liquor was tasteless, warm and agreeable. I opened my eyes, surprised to find myself stretched out on a sofa in a paneled room.

I couldn't see the man who said, "You're free to go, Mr. Milton. If you want a hospital to examine your head, I'll have you taken there—no charge, needless to say."

"Where's Joey?"

"Don't hold it against her—she did as instructed."

Reaching back, I felt stickiness behind my head.

"What's your interest in Maybelle?"

I swallowed. "Friend of my sister's."

"That's bullshit. Treasury means a lot of things—trouble to me. What's the rap on Maybelle?"

"Counter—" I began. "Passing bogus bills." The man's face came into focus. He was young and well dressed. He sat behind an antique desk, and there were two other men, not as well dressed.

Their boss leaned forward. "I earnestly suggest you terminate your

129

search for the lady. Some time ago she left Feathers of her own volition, dropped from sight."

"Also of her own volition," I remarked in a cracked voice. "So why am I here?"

"Our policy has always been to protect female employees, present or past, from unwelcome attentions. It happened you inquired about one of our all-time attractions. Wrong place, wrong time." He paused. "As soon as I learned you were Treasury, I knew employee reaction had been premature, violence unnecessary."

"And damn near terminal."

He got up from his desk, came around, and bent over me. I scented expensive cologne on his smooth, olive-skinned face. Fitting an envelope into my hands, he said. "The money you spent is all there. I've added five hundred by way of partial compensation for pain and . . . inconvenience."

"Very courteous," I said. "Keep it in exchange for a sensible answer to one question." Slowly I propped myself on one elbow. He shrugged. "I want to be cooperative, Mr. Milton, even conciliatory."

"You people went to some trouble to get Maybelle here. You could have kept her—why let her go?"

"She expressed a strong desire for another way of life." He strolled back to his desk.

"Incomplete answer. I suggest she found favor in the eyes of a man able to provide her with an opulent lifestyle. A man influential enough to take her from Fancy Feathers without reprisal."

"Your theory."

"Tell me I'm wrong." I managed to sit up and get my legs over the sofa, shoes on the thickly carpeted floor. The way blood drained from my injured head felt like a rupturing dam. I said, "I know all about *omertà* and oath-taking, but let's bypass tradition in the interest of conciliation. Who was the man?"

His lashes were long and delicate—like a jaguar's. "Knowing that much, you'll understand our aversion to names."

Rising, I steadied myself on the sofa arm, let the envelope slide to the floor. "Makes no difference," I told him. "She's dead."

With that I made my way very slowly to the door. No one tried to stop me—or moved. A passage led to another door, then outside by the parking lot. Joey Dyke was no longer puffing pot on the fence rail. She hadn't suckered me entirely; I had to know where her invitation would lead.

Stooping over to get into the car, I nearly fainted, gritted my teeth, and got in. At a roadside stand I bought aspirin and swallowed several with

Sprite. That and the car's chill air conditioning made me feel a little better, but the drive back to the hotel seemed endless.

Bed was never more inviting. I took two more aspirin and turned in. Some of what Astrid had told me was checking out, though I never doubted it would. Tomorrow I'd trace a license tag to the man who paid for the Piper's final flight . . . and as I lay in darkness I wondered if Melody had reached Palo Alto safely—how she was getting along.

THE DOWNTOWN BRANCH of the state motor vehicle bureau declined help until I displayed my borrowed Treasury ID; then things moved along, and I was shown a computer printout. The tag had been issued to a black BMW sedan. Purchaser and owner were identical: Intierra Associates, a corporation registered in Texas, Louisiana, California—and Florida. States with heavy narcotics action. I photocopied the printout, thanked the clerk, and telephoned the capital to find out more about Intierra. Corporation officers of record were Paul Diehl, Lawrence Parmenter, and Delores Diehl.

Because none was a Texas resident, I asked for a local place of business and was given an address that turned out to be an old building on a side street near the courthouse. Signs laddered each side of the entrance, and most of them funneled into a second-floor office whose main business was answering telephones, forwarding mail, and renting desk space by day, week or month. I showed my T-card to the supervisor. "Routine check of corporate activity."

"Our books are in perfect order." He turned, but I said, "Intierra Associates. How long has the firm been using your services?"

"Oh, three, possibly four years," he said. "I can give you the exact period." He looked like a bright, ambitious young man who studied night-school law.

"How do they pay you?"

"By mail."

"Most people pay via mail. What *form* of negotiable instrument?"

He consulted a bound entry book, ran a finger down the page. "Sometimes cashier's check, usually money order." He scanned the entries again. "Punctual, too."

"Where is the monthly envelope mailed?"

"Here in Houston."

"Have you ever seen anyone purporting to represent Intierra Associates?"

"Actually I handled it—by phone. The caller wanted a local pro forma address and phone number."

"Mail forwarding?"

"I don't think there's ever been any mail."

"What's the forwarding address?"

He disappeared and came back with the information. A suite number on Miami's Brickell Avenue. I said, "So Intierra pays regularly but never receives telephone calls or mail."

"Right."

"Isn't that . . . unusual?"

He shrugged. "We don't question client's motives. Some like to receive specialized literature from Sweden and Denmark—if you understand me. Others correspond with persons they'd prefer their families not know about." He spread his hands. "We fill a need."

"Admirably too, no doubt. One last thing—because this is a confidential inquiry, you're not to mention it to your client. If you do, they'll thank you—and cancel the account."

"Discretion is our motto," he smiled. "Especially when it affects cash flow."

"Thank you," I said, "and good luck with the Bars."

Even descending the stairs made my head throb, so I walked back to a *clínica* that didn't look like a Feelgood shop and went in. The physicians' names were Hispanic, the dark-eyed young receptionist bilingual. She asked the usual questions—Age? Chronic illness? Medicaid?—took twenty dollars and said I'd be attended to shortly.

The young chicano doctor was neat and efficient. He had me strip to the waist and started examining my old shoulder wound. I said, "That's history, doc. Today it's the back of my head. Last night I took a nasty fall."

He fingered the shoulder scab. "Bullet?"

"Shower glass."

He cut a patch of hair from the back of my head. "Faintness, double vision?"

"After it happened. Today it just throbs."

"Shouldn't wonder. Nothing to stitch, so I'll clean it out and disinfect."

His hands worked with delicacy. He applied a small bandage and wrote a prescription for a painkiller. "If you take these, don't drink. Especially don't drink and drive."

A nearby pharmacy filled the prescription for six capsules. While waiting, I used the phone book to look up the office address of Vernon Saunders.

To hide the bandage, I stopped at a specialty store and bought a gray cowboy-style hat with a nicely rolled brim. Now I blended with the crowd on Preston Street.

The building was a new one with a spacious, air-conditioned lobby whose centerpiece was a semirustic ten-foot waterfall. The directory showed Saunders's office on the eighteenth floor, and when I got off the elevator I went to the drinking fountain to swallow one of my prescription caps.

I was standing with my head back when another elevator arrived and three people got out. They walked past, talking among themselves, and paid no attention to me. I watched them the length of the hall to Saunders's double-door entrance.

I didn't recognize the short, black-haired man wearing sunglasses, but the couple walking arm-in-arm, I'd seen before: Larry Parmenter and Melody's mother, Delores Diehl.

IV

TWENTY

ROM THE LOBBY I phoned Saunders's office. "Al Josselson, Tri-state Securities."

"I'm sorry, Mr., ah Jocelyn, but Mr. Saunders is conferring with clients."

"Umm. How long'd you say?"

"Why not call again in half an hour—unless he can return your call."

"I'm headed for lunch, Miss. I'll try from the restaurant."

Half an hour, and the trio would be leaving. I shoved back my hat to wipe my forehead. The pill was working so well that even my fingertips were numb—but my brain was processing data.

A picture was taking shape, though not one I'd expected. To make sense from it, I needed to know whether Saunders worked for his visitors—or if they and Paul Diehl worked for him. In short, the pecking order. Except for expensive clothing, the man in sunglasses looked like a run-of-the-mill Latino. He was nearly as tall as Delores, though he could have been wearing built-up heels. And he could be a legitimate investment client—but the company he kept suggested otherwise.

I bought a paper and scanned it from a bench by the waterfall where I could see the elevators. At the bottom of the clear pool lay a scattering of pennies and silver coins. A small sign promised contributions would go to the Heart Fund, but I suspected the maintenance man considered it bonus take-home pay.

The sports section carried a three-inch story from Palo Alto. Among contestants surviving the first day's diving competition was Ms. Melody West of Miami. No photo. It would be nice to be with her, I mused, but impractical. Despite her prediction, I felt we were already taking divergent ways.

Time passed. I wanted a cigar but didn't think my system was ready for the challenge of nicotine. So I bought a can of cold juice at the newsstand and was downing it when Larry and Delores left the elevator. They passed where I'd been sitting and went out to the street. Parmenter hailed a cab, and I moved up behind them. The cab stopped, and the driver barked, "Where to?"

"Hobby airport."

"Gotcha. Airline?"

"Eastern–Miami flight."

The door opened and Delores got in, Larry next. Without question, Melody's great figure derived from her mother's. Delores had to be a few years older than I was, but her form was that of a college girl's.

The taxi whipped away, and I went back to my bench. I knew where the widow and the lawyer were headed, but not the Latino, and he intrigued me. He was a little too flashily dressed to be a totally honest citizen. Who was he, and how did he figure in their plots and plans?

I was settling into a feature article on a Texas fat-farm when suspect Latino emerged from the elevator with a taller, conservatively dressed Anglo. He was in his early forties and smiled at several people as he walked through the lobby. A man of substantial success by his demeanor. He opened the street door for the Latino, and as I left the bench a battleship gray limousine eased up to the curb. The two got in, and the big Mercedes pulled away. The tag read: VOS-3. Translatable as Vernon O. Saunders, car number three.

Beside me a cab was unloading. I handed the driver ten, telling him to follow the gray Mercedes. "Easy, man, no way I can lose it. Plus fare, right?"

We moved off, and from the way he kept two cars between us and switched lanes, he'd done tail work before. I was pretty sure the limo wasn't headed for the airport, which was southeast, off the Gulf Freeway, because the Mercedes was going due east on Clinton. The driver called, "Must be going to the port."

Another mile and I could see the port of Houston on the right, pretty as you please. We followed the Mercedes in, and the driver said, "How close?"

"Don't be noticed."

So he pulled over, and I saw the Mercedes stop near a clear patch where a small helicopter waited. The Latino got out and jogged to the chopper whose rotors were already turning. The Mercedes turned around and drove past us. I watched the chopper spiral and climb and felt my stomach tighten.

I'd seen it before, at sea. Dropping on *Corsair* from the sun, auto rifle blazing.

THE NEAREST AIRPORT was just north of Bay Town. I paid the cabbie and said he could wait or not. A charter helicopter service agreed to cruise me around the bay for a hundred dollars, and by the time I spotted the big yacht four miles out, its chopper was being snugged down, and wake showed it underway. I had the pilot drop down close enough to verify the name—*Solimar*—and told him we could go back.

The cabbie was still there, so I got in, saying, "Meter rates this time."

He drove me to where I'd parked my rental earlier in the day, gave me a snappy two-finger salute, and melted into traffic. I found a clean-looking diner, ate the burrito special, and swallowed another pain capsule with iced tea. Then I went to the hotel and slept until dark.

RIVER OAKS IS a rather special community. Nuke it, and a quarter of America's wealth vanishes. Much like nineteenth-century Newport, River Oaks is a colony of great fortunes, whose residents are comfortable in each other's exclusive company. Unlike Newport, their wealth doesn't come from sea or Wall Street, but from oil, cattle, gas, and aviation. The mansions are set well-back from curving streets, fronted by handsome lawns and tasteful fencing. No property under two acres, and some estates seemed to go on forever. Obviously, privacy and security were prized, though not necessarily in that order. Tall oaks arched over the older streets, giving them the appearance of private arcades.

Vernon Saunders's spread was middle-size, and from a distance the manse could have been a tasteful version of Graceland. French-style lightoliers illuminated the frontal property, a motif extended along the crescent driveway, antique-looking bullseye lamps glowed yellowly on either side of massive entrance doors.

I didn't want to drive past often enough to attract interest from private patrol cars, so I toured the community before returning. Flowers were everywhere, in carefully tended banks. A half-moon rose behind massive homes, its pale light diffused through the warmly humid air.

Earlier I'd phoned and asked for Mrs. Saunders, representing myself as a member of the Symphony staff. A Mexican maid claimed she wasn't home and refused to say more.

I hadn't been able to come up with a plausible ruse to enter the house so I settled on reconnoitering the estate. Each time I'd driven past I'd scanned for dogs, but that didn't mean they weren't in house or kennel, just that they weren't visible to the unaided eye. The supersonic whistle I used for César and Sheba was in my pocket like a lucky charm; it might make hostile canines pause before attacking. Then again, it might not.

I considered these things as I walked back from where I'd left the car, and decided that if I missed Saunders tonight, I'd try his office tomorrow. He could hardly refrain from seeing a potential client who professed to be bulging with money and a frantic desire to invest.

The driveway gate was open, so I entered the easy way and began walking up the gentle slope. There were only a few interior lights visible through the windows, and at the end of the drive a four-car garage that could have sheltered a dozen wetback families. The rear of the mansion had a broad loggia facing an acre or two of lawn. Moonlight outlined the tall fencing of an *en tout cas* tennis court, glinted from the motionless water of a fifty-foot pool between court and house.

Standing in shadows, I surveyed my surroundings, wondering how many after-tax dollars it took to maintain—not buy—so opulent a place. From the extrinsic evidence of conspicuous consumption alone, Saunders was more than comfortably fixed. I wondered if Intierra Associates figured in his tax returns. Or an Antilles banking front.

Abruptly, noiselessly, the pool's underwater lights went on, their soft radiance giving an iridescent, mother-of-pearl cast to the still surface.

A loggia door opened, and I saw a figure come through lessening darkness toward the end of the pool. The walker wore a bathrobe, and at first I thought Saunders was coming down for an evening dip, decided from the body's undulations that it was either Mrs. Saunders or a servant girl.

From fifty feet away I saw her slip out of the robe and drop it. Naked, she moved to the pool edge and stood poised, hands reaching out and above her head. In the brief moment before she dived I saw her utterly feminine body, the light blonde patch between her loins that matched the gold of her pageboy hair, the snub nose and features that made her unique in all the world.

Astrid.

She left the pool edge in a graceful arc, entered the water smoothly, and disappeared below the ripples.

TWENTY-ONE

DISTORTED BY THE water's refraction, her body coasted the width of the pool before emerging at the far side. The sight hit me like a belly punch. I'd mourned her as dead; now she was alive—and in a hostile camp.

She tossed back her head, drawing wet hair from her forehead with one hand in a gesture I remembered achingly. Again she submerged, swimming unaware and without inhibition, gamboling in the water like a playful otter. If I'd wanted to call out I couldn't have, my throat was too constricted.

Turning over, she backstroked the length of the pool, returned underwater, and I remembered again her swimming beside me at the sunken plane. The pool lighted her body from below, the background was completely dark, and it seemed as though she were levitating like a magician's accomplice. But there were no silver hoops, no rolling drums—just an audience of one.

I considered going poolside for explanations, forcing them if necessary. Seeing me, she'd be too shocked to lie . . .

Seated on the edge, she palmed water from her hair and breasts and fluttered the water with her toes. I wanted to believe she was a prisoner; that every act, every lie was under duress, but I knew it wasn't so. And as truth came to me, I realized she'd saved my life that day—dropped me on deck and told the others I was dead like Diehl and Carlos. Because of her I'd survived the slaughter. I owed her my life.

Besides, I told myself, *she* wasn't my target; *she* hadn't killed Carlos, others had. But even as the thought formed I knew the reasoning was false.

She'd known what was coming and begged off the dive with me—then gone to the safety of the cabin just before the onslaught came.

But if she hadn't, I reminded myself, she wouldn't have lived to protect me.

If ever she thought of me, she knew that somewhere I was alive. And if she understood me at all, she would have realized I wouldn't rest without an explanation—the right one, the true.

If I approached her, would she melt into my arms—or scream and run? She was great on improvisation—why not put her to the test?

As I prepared to leave the shadows, I heard the loggia door opening. Astrid glanced over, lifted her hand, and slid into the pool.

The man walking toward her wore a blue terry wraparound, red and yellow blazes stabbing his thighs. He carried himself confidently, and as the pool light found his features, I saw a smile on Vernon Saunders's face. He pulled off the wrap and dived naked into the water.

They rose to the surface in close embrace, arms around each other's bodies, and I saw her legs break water as they circled his hips. He kissed her nipples, and her spine arched with a sudden spasm as they began to couple.

I turned away as though fleeing a macabre dream. Half-sick, I stumbled to the drive and made my way to the street in shadows.

The knowledge I'd gained I hadn't wanted. It exposed her complicity in fraud, murder, and narcotics. Worse—if possible—it told me what a credulous fool I'd been. My illusions were gone—along with what remained of self-esteem. She was Saunders's whore—had always been; the wife's complaint, fiction. The tale she'd told me in the El Portal—why remember all those lies? It dragged a saw-edge over open flesh.

A car was parked ahead of mine, lights out. Not just any car, but a marked prowlie with a light-bar on the roof. I didn't want to identify myself, explain why I was there. Only one man in the front seat, behind the wheel. I could see the glow of his cigarette. He was waiting for me.

I decided to end his wait.

Quietly and low I came up on his port quarter—as the pirates had on mine—and when he saw me, he jumped so hard his cap fell off. "Get the hell out of here," I hissed, and flashed my T-card. "Government business."

He gulped. Moonlight showed a white, uncertain face. "Federal?"

"Better believe it. I don't need to be showcased right now. Git!"

"Yessir!"

"No lights, pull away easy," I warned, and walked back to my rental.

The prowl car moved off almost noiselessly, and a block away the headlights went on. I'd resolved a minor inconvenience, but the problem of Astrid—and her protector—remained. As I got behind the wheel, I wondered if I could flip her—as in Cozumel I'd thought I had. But this time against Saunders and his associates.

I studied the rearview mirror, seeing only the distant gateway. Where was Saunders's wife? Obviously not home tonight or Saunders wouldn't have his girlfriend in the pool.

I thought of killing him while Astrid watched.

Jesus, when was I going to get her out of my blood? I couldn't go on seeing her as victim; she was part of an ongoing conspiracy— in the language of indictments. And of course I knew now who'd plucked her out of Fancy Feathers, had suspected before, seen confirmation in the lighted pool. Saunders was involved with the yacht *Solimar,* responsible directly or indirectly for three murders, one of which could have been mine. Had Astrid/Amy tried to dissuade him? Or having saved me once, had she found it impossible a second time.

What was Saunders's connection with Parmenter and Diehl's widow? Why had it been necessary to murder the *licenciado*? Was Diehl trying to end-run around their organization? Someone knew the answers—the onetime Amy King. *Sure to go all the way.*

Not *quite* the distance. She wasn't home yet.

But on the basis of what I knew and believed, no grand jury would indict Saunders. There had to be a witness, corroborating testimony.

The one I could reach for was Amy.

I drove quietly from the curb as far as a small station house on the fringe of River Oaks.

Briefly I showed the desk officer my Treasury credential and said, "I need a little cooperation."

"Sure, Mr. Milton—we don't like these tax-evaders no better'n you. Who's the alleged suspect?"

"Without in any way conceding he's an investigative target, Vernon O. Saunders."

He whistled. "Heavy. Whatcha need?"

"A house that size will have telephones with different numbers. I assume you people work conscientiously to protect River Oaks property owners, so you should have their unlisted phone numbers."

"That we do." He got a card file from a desk drawer, searched it, and produced the Saunders card. Extensions all over the place, separate call numbers for servants' quarters, study, bedroom, and—pool. Those were in addition to the listed house number I'd already used.

Joytime past, the sated couple would be sharing drinks poolside or on the loggia. I swallowed hard and copied down the numbers.

He returned the file to his drawer. "Arrest pending?"

143

"Afraid not—fraud gets pretty involved, takes mucho time to fit pieces together. Is Mrs. Saunders usually at home?"

"These people—they lead pretty private lives."

"Ever see her?"

"Oh, sure—a looker, too."

"The things money can buy," I remarked and went back to my car. Before starting the engine I breathed deeply, trying to shake off the zombie sensation. I was glad Amy was alive—even grateful—but not in the circumstances I'd found her; they were too damning. A vision of their lovemaking sickened me . . . well that was how things were—and had been, long before she showed in Cozumel. But I wanted her out of it now, finished with the past. Bolivar High, Bay Town, Marty's Place, the mob guys at Fancy Feathers . . . and sleek, successful Vernon Saunders. I wanted his *cojones* on a platter, and to get them I needed her.

I drove back to my room, took two more capsules, drank some rum, and hit the sack like a stone.

IN THE MORNING, I reached River Oaks early enough to see Saunders in the rear of his limousine as it drove off in the direction of downtown. Amy wasn't with him, nor had I expected her to be.

From a filling station I dialed the bedroom phone. It rang a dozen times before someone answered. Not the chicana maid, but a sleepy Anglo voice.

"Hello, Blondie," I said tightly. "At Bolivar they said you'd go all the way—and you almost made it."

"Who is this?"

"From Cozumel—fellow you used to dive with. Remember the exotic things we used to find?"

She gasped. "How . . . how did you find me?"

"Secrets, Amy. Incidentally,"—I took a breath—"at Feathers they remember Maybelle with nostalgia and affection. The place hasn't—"

"Cut it out—you *have* been snooping, haven't you?"

"You didn't leave a forwarding address when you skipped off *Corsair.* Under the circumstances I felt an obligation to thank Penny—I mean Astrid—no, *Amy* for saving my life."

"All right, you've thanked me. Leave it at that."

"Can't."

"Can't? Of course you can. Novak, listen to me, you have no idea what you're involved in. I saved you once, but I'd never have a chance again."

"Who's the Latin creep from the yacht, Amy? The one with the elevator shoes and the pimp suit? Or doesn't Vernon bring clients to the house?"

144

Another quick intake of her breath. I said, "I warned you about Diehl before I even realized what he was into or where it led. Believe me, Blondie, it's come together very nicely—and the outside of the package is striped. Iron bars for many folks you know."

Her voice softened, "I don't want you to be hurt. Stay out of it. That's all I have to say."

"Hurt?" I laughed shortly. "My plane was booby-trapped, and a marksman blew the head off a man he thought was me. Outside Feathers a hood cracked my skull after I asked questions about the Texas Terror who rang bells with her tits. So I don't need cautioning. What you haven't grasped is that you're heading for a long slide—and I'm the only hope you've got."

"They'll kill you!"

"They've tried. Would it surprise you to learn I know a little about killing? Anyone coming after me better update his will and wear a titanium jock. In Cozumel I offered you a deal—parts of it still stand, but the picture's enlarged. Now, we can meet away from Saunders's house at a rendezvous of your choice, or I can pound on the door and embarrass you with the servants, and ultimately Saunders, in two languages. But meet we will. You're involved with felony murder, Amy, and if you don't appear in half an hour, the next knock you hear will be cops with a warrant."

In the silence all I could hear was low, rapid breathing. Let her sweat, I told myself; if she thought this decision was tough, wait for the big ones down the line.

Finally she said, "Where are you?"

"Unimportant. Where do we meet?"

She named an intersection on the north edge of River Oaks.

"What's the color of your car?"

"Plum."

"Plum?"

"It's the rage this year," she said thickly.

"I'm sure. Be alone." I rang off, got into my car, and headed for the rendezvous to check for surveillants before she arrived.

If she came.

Plum, for God's sake. Maybelle and her musical nipples. Nothing conventional about her.

No prowl cars cruised the quiet residential area. A couple of produce trucks and a fishmonger made deliveries. No private prowlies I could detect.

Would *she* come?

If she didn't, what then? Was she brave enough to call my bluff? Or was she on the horn with Vernon, getting sage advice?

Five minutes to go. C'mon, Blondie, *all the way.*

A black compact idled past, with antenna and white lettering, Security. The driver glanced at me and kept going. I was watching him when I saw a low-slung sports car pull to the curb behind me. It was a Lamborghini painted in a lavender-crimson hue. The license plate was VOS-2; number two in the Saunders stable and probably assigned to Saunders's wife. I wondered if she'd like her husband's tart making free with her car.

The driver got out, rather elegantly dressed in linen culottes and a matching tennis top, expensive sandals on her feet. Clutching a purse, she came toward me and I saw the unmistakable cut of her blonde hair, the features I'd once thought had been devoured by crabs and eels. "Door's open," I told her, "get in."

Her expression was sulky. I started the engine and pulled into traffic. Glancing back she said, "Where are we going?"

"Open your purse."

Her fingers worked the catch and I felt the contents. No handgun. In a thin voice she said, "You don't trust me."

"After all the lies? C'mon, Amy, be realistic."

She laid the closed purse on her lap, looked out the window. "That's what I want *you* to be—realistic. You don't seem to understand the danger you're in. So drop the macho, go back to Cozumel and forget what happened."

I took a photo from my pocket and placed it on her lap. The scene showed her posed by the gunwale, *Solimar* in the distance. "With memories like that how could I forget?"

"You bastard!"

"The photos turned out nicely," I told her. "All of them. . . They link you to *Solimar,* the plane, and the coke you salvaged. Federal courts hand down twenty-five years for a lot less." I surveyed her coldly. "Say you only do fifteen—you'll be a lot less marketable than today. Not many wealthy men will want to make it with you in a swimming pool . . . like last night."

Her hand slashed at my face, but I caught her wrist and twisted it down. She was panting, chest swelling and subsiding. Suddenly I wanted her, and she saw it in my eyes. A slow smile moved her lips. I said, "Vern takes chances. Where do you get off driving his wife's car?"

Her nostrils flared. "Why shouldn't I? He's my husband."

TWENTY-TWO

O F COURSE, IT *had* to be that way. Nothing else made sense. But coming so suddenly it hit me hard. "How long?" I said huskily. "Two years—if it's any of your business."

"Everything about the two of you is my business. I'm not going to pretend remorse over Paul Diehl, but directly or indirectly you helped kill Carlos. Larry and Delores were part of that action, along with your loving husband. You're the only one who can be saved. Have you thought it over?"

She shrugged. "I can't testify against my husband."

"That why he married you? He got bad legal advice if he thinks that eliminates you as a witness. You can't be *forced* to testify, but anything you volunteer is admissible evidence." I turned into Memorial Park, followed the drive around past golf greens to the caddy shack, and pulled into a slot. Engine off, I said, "You'd be surprised how much is known about Intierra Associates and Paul's function—spreading money around the world. Your personal knowledge of that and other things is a negotiable asset, and I think you're smart enough to recognize it. Your career shows remarkable adaptability, Amy, but you've never faced anything like this."

Those marvelous lavender eyes were wide as she turned to me. "What are my choices?"

A mixed foursome was teeing off twenty yards away. "You can come over now, and in return for complete cooperation I'll try to get you the best possible deal from the U.S. Attorney. The alternative—a good deal riskier—is stay in place as an informant. I'm not sure you could do that and survive for the length of time the government would demand. So I recommend you disappear as far as Saunders and the others are concerned. No goodbyes, no explanations."

"Would I go to prison?"

"I'm ninety percent sure I could get you a suspended sentence."

"Can't you guarantee it?"

"I can't guarantee this car will start. But if you can hand over the others and provide solid leads to the money, dope sources, and so forth, any judge is going to be impressed." I looked at her. "Plus, you saved the life of a government agent—mine."

"Yes . . . I'd almost forgotten that," she said musingly. "Has to be worth something—even though it turns out my mistake."

"Why'd you do it? Because we'd made love a couple of times?"

"Probably. Female compassion, I guess." Her lips were a thin line.

"That didn't extend to Paul and Carlos."

Her hand gripped mine. "You've got to believe I didn't know they were going to be killed. Yes, I knew the cases were to be taken from your boat, but I didn't know there was to be killing. Then everything happened so fast . . ."

"You zapped me and let them think I'd caught a bullet?"

"Something like that."

"How come a desk man like Diehl was handling the drug recovery?"

"You haven't figured it out?"

"Maybe I have—and I'm asking you to establish good faith."

She sighed. "Paul invested money from laundry operations but used some to take a flier on the gold market in Europe. Gold prices fell, and he couldn't replace what he'd stolen. He was given time to make good, worked out his own deal to buy coke in Mexico and get it here. But the plane went down." She shrugged. "I was sent with Paul to make sure he didn't run with what he recovered."

"Why would he have tried that?"

"He knew he wasn't trusted any longer."

"How much were those cases worth?"

"Between two and three million dollars, enough to cover what Paul owed and give him a new life in some other country."

"Like Brazil," I said thoughtfully. "Delores lived in Brazil, she could have helped there—if she'd wanted to."

Amy said nothing. I said, "Fugitives think Brazil's a risk-free nirvana—and you can pass this along to Vern if you care to—but the record shows Brazilian cops bleed a fugitive until he's tapped out, then boot him back to the States."

"What will happen to my husband?"

"Depending on factors such as how badly Delores may want revenge for Paul's murder, he'll get minimum twenty-five." I shrugged. "Maybe life. It'll be longer than you'll want to wait."

Her mouth was bitter. "Then I'm to be yours, all yours—that part of the deal?"

"Why darling," I said tightly, "what a tender thought. We might make it for a few weeks or months, but sooner or later you'd reason that but for me, you and Vern would still have the big house and the good life, and you'd become very, very bitter. Alienated isn't a bad word—and before I knew it you'd be considering a choice of weapons—poison . . . knife . . . whatever's in vogue at the time."

"You think I'm utter trash."

"I worry about your soul, baby. You move quickly when you decide to, and always in a way best calculated to improve your lot. Unfortunately, I don't have much to interest a girl of your character, and my prospects aren't worth mentioning. So, I'll do my best for you, Amy, then we'll go separate ways."

Her gaze fixed on her folded hands. "I wish . . . we could have met under different circumstances."

"Me, too, but we play the hand we're dealt, right? As you always have. I'm holding top cards now and calling yours. Made up your mind?"

"I . . . I need time to think."

"You don't get any. Flip now or forget it. Only why go down the drain with Vern and the others? Think you could do twenty-five years stitching mattresses at Alderson? All that potential wasted . . ." I shook my head. "What's it to be?"

"You wouldn't be so vengeful if you hadn't seen me making love to another man—my husband."

"Maybe not, but it was a useful experience because it peeled off the last thin layer of illusion, and I realized how thoroughly I'd been used ever since you wandered into the café. By the way, does Vern know you slept with me?"

Her cheeks reddened. "That was *us*—you and me—nothing to do with my husband."

"But it got me on your side, didn't it? Kept me from suspecting you. So it had utility."

"Besides saving your life."

"Well, few things are black or white. And I'm waiting for an answer."

"I'll be . . . an informer."

"All right. I'll contact DEA and the U.S. Attorney." I gave her the name of my hotel and room number. "Call me and I'll tell you what's been agreed."

She swallowed. "Should I have a lawyer?"

"You couldn't have a better advocate than me." I started the engine and remembered something. "When you were on *Solimar* did you ever smell acetone?"

"What's that?"

"Like nail polish remover."

She shook her head.

"What about ether?"

She hesitated. "Yes—they told me a crewman's leg was being set."

"You believed it?"

"I would have—but I smelled it every day. Why?"

"Was smoking allowed?"

"On the ship? No." She swallowed. "What's that got to do with anything?"

"I'll ask the questions. Why no smoking?"

"They said it was because of gasoline—for the helicopter."

"Very neat," I remarked. "An answer for anything. And that confirms a lot of suspicions. If you didn't know it, ether and acetone are used in processing cocaine. Got it now?"

"If you say so . . . Jack." Her fingers touched the side of my face. "Do you want to take me to a motel?"

"Damn right I do—but I don't think it would be successful." I backed out and turned down the drive.

"Why not?" Her left hand stroked my thigh.

"I'd feel like an intruder—after seeing you and Vern making it in the pool."

"That's cruel."

"Lots of cruelty in the world, Amy—which isn't news to you. I'll be in my room no later than six. If you don't phone by nine they'll be coming for you—and Vernon. And just as a precaution, there'll be surveillance on your house, phones, and his office. So don't think you can run. Do what's required in good spirit. Think of it as working your way out of a hole you dug yourself into."

"You have no pity," she said scornfully, "no compassion. Not even my mother did. She let her boyfriends fondle me when I was still a kid. In strip joints, either I came across or lost the job. And everywhere I turned, everywhere I looked, there were men with their hands out, trying to finger me, play with my boobs. . . It made me vomit, until I got used to it. You don't know what that life was like, so who the hell are you to judge what I've done to get away from it, find security for myself? Look at you—you screwed me because it was going to help get Paul Diehl. You bastard, I should have let them gun you down with the others."

"Poor little Nell the matchstick girl." I said, but regretted it because so much of what she'd said was true. Then I saw the plum-colored Lamborghini and eased to the curb behind it. "Any time after six," I reminded her, "and before nine."

A slammed door was her response. I watched the sports car screech away, and then I drove downtown to the Federal Court House.

THE HOUSTON FIELD office wasn't glad to see me. All hands had read the bulletin Corliss issued after our Miami chat, and getting through to the supervisor chewed up most of my remaining patience. But when I began talking Intierra Associates, Netherlands Antilles fronts, Vernon Saunders, and the *Solimar* connection, my audience grew increasingly respectful. After an hour or so the supervisor said, "As I see it everything depends on the girl—Amy King, Saunders's wife. Without her we got zip."

"She's aware of her leverage, and she's using it to get a good deal—or *nada*."

"How good a deal?"

"She walks."

The supervisor—his name was Montijo—whistled. "I can't take that to Sensinich, Jack."

Tony Sensinich was U.S. Attorney for the district. I said, "I'll take it with you—and both of you ought to be glad I brought it here instead of the Miami office."

"Little revenge, eh?" snickered one of Montijo's lackeys.

Turning to him, I said, "I remember—you're the gofer they call the Perfect Circle." Turning back to his boss, I said, "Mainly proximity. The big action's here—Parmenter and Madame Diehl are bit players, but maybe they can be squeezed."

"Oh?"

"I slapped Larry around some, and the widow gulped it like an S-M scene."

Montijo thought it over. "You don't want to let Sensinich cast you as a vigilante. He's big on civil liberties."

"Me too—mine in particular."

"Is the girl trustworthy?"

151

"No—but too scared not to cooperate."

"Why were Diehl and Carlos killed?"

"Carlos, because he was there. Diehl? He'd screwed them, and they didn't want to spend time arguing over the split. So they took it all. How long you figure Sensinich will want Amy in place?"

"I don't know—how long you think she'll be needed?"

"A month, maybe two. I want her to locate any documents Saunders may have that outline the conspiracy."

"*You*, Jack? You have no official capacity in this."

"Don't want any. I know the setup, you don't. So like any good citizen, I'm free to make an occasional suggestion, right?"

Montijo nodded. "For a long time we've been hearing rumors about a floating laboratory, a factory ship where raw stuff is refined for middlemen. We've been thinking in terms of some old, rusty Liberty ship, but a *Solimar* would be far better. Who's going to figure a luxury yacht as the home of a lab operation? Think the girl knows about it?"

"She's been on board," I said. "They choppered her there after the shooting--though that doesn't mean she saw what went on below decks."

He shook his head. "And you pulled this together on your own, Jack, strictly private. You're a fuckin' wizard."

"Until there's a payoff, I'm an amateur fumbling with a two-buck magic set."

He punched an intercom and asked for an appointment with the U.S. Attorney. Then he turned to me and smiled. "Coffee and danish?"

SENSINICH WAS HOSTILE and hard-assed as I expected him to be. He was one of those U.S. Attorneys who won't prosecute without a guaranteed win. He didn't like me because I wasn't on the payroll, and he resented what I'd done since quitting. I let him erode my store of patience until finally I snapped, "Let's sweep away the bullshit, Tony. I can take the case elsewhere, since you're reluctant to strike a deal. Your counterpart in Miami lusts for a Federal judgeship. He could run this from Florida and come out a big winner." I let the annoying thought sink in.

He said, "She has to do time."

"She says no deal. Besides, if you come down hard on her, where's the incentive for the next informant? We've walked real scumbags and you know it. Compared to them she drifts by like jasmine in the night."

He gnawed at a thumbnail, bit too hard, and stared at the thumb as though it had attacked him. "When the defense gets down to attacking her credibility, they'll surface every sordid thing she's ever done." He shook his head. "Erotic dancer, druggie, part-time hooker, participant in high seas murder. . . Damn!"

"So who's perfect? I never said Amy was a candidate for den mother. If she were, she wouldn't have the kind of knowledge you need."

"One thing, Novak, *you* don't handle her, understand?"

"Hey, I'm out of it. I'll tell her the deal's firm and pass along reporting arrangements. Doubtless, she'll want a lawyer to stop by and pick up a signed copy of the agreement."

He looked at Montijo. "Work out details." They shook hands with each other—not with me. As an afterthought, Sensinich said, "Tomorrow you pull out, Novak, no further contact with her."

I stood up, and the U.S. Attorney eyed me, "One thing that got glossed over—what do you want out of this?"

"Just the satisfaction of aiding my betters."

Montijo walked me back to his office and when the door closed he began to laugh. "Jesus, that was worth money—the way you served it to Tony, he'll be brushing his teeth for a year."

"You let him intimidate you. What's he got you haven't? A law degree from a cow-chip college—and an uncle who passes the loot bag for Senator you-know-who. That doesn't add up to character."

Montijo shrugged. "You got what you wanted, right? Okay, here's how Amy's contacts will go—and do me a favor, brief her on telephone discipline. Now that we got our witness, I want her alive to testify."

He laid it out; I made notes and left.

At the newsstand I bought a paper and turned to sports. The story was a little larger today, but still no photo. Melody West, the young Miami competitor, had survived the quarter-finals but would face vastly more experienced competition in the semis. One unnamed coach, however, thought that if Melody had a couple of exceptional days, she might well go all the way.

I didn't like the prediction: too close to what once had been printed about Amy—and look what she'd been and was about to become. Tossing away the paper, I went down to my car and found it ticketed. I decided to mail the ticket to Sensinich; either he'd square it or I'd be a fugitive—I didn't care which.

There was a sandwich bar not far from the courthouse. The chef cut me a thick slice of prime and laid it on a large warm poppyseed. I found a table, and a waiter with the solid, ugly features of Pancho Villa brought me an icy Carta Blanca. The sandwich was so big I needed a second bottle to wash it down.

Then I drove east, paralleling the Houston ship channel, and got out near the San Jacinto battleground. I'd never seen the old USS *Texas,* but there she lay with her basketweave masts, just as she'd looked in Academy photos. I was tempted to go aboard and tread her decks, but I thought old Navy memories might surge, and I'd do something foolish like signing up again. So I sat on the grassy knoll, watched children playing on her holystoned decks, and reflected on how many better men than I had shed blood aboard her. Last of the dreadnoughts, now a state shrine. Deservedly.

A hum like a distant wasp attracted my attention, I looked up to see a small chopper beating inland at two thousand feet. It was too far away to make identification, but I wondered if it was *Solimar's.* More likely it was on a routine run from one of the offshore rigs.

I lay back, pushed the cowboy hat over my face, and promptly fell asleep.

Something moved my foot. I jerked aside the hat and saw a young boy and girl peering down at me. They held hands like brother and sister. "You okay, mister?" he chirped.

"Just fine," I yawned, "and thanks for asking." I put my hat back on. "Enjoying yourselves this fine afternoon?"

"Sure am," they said in unison.

"Tell you what . . ." I got out a dollar and handed it to the boy. "That's one of the great all-time battleships. I'd like you two to go aboard her. Would you do that for me?"

"Sure would," the boy said, and the girl curtsied. "Thanks, mister." Turning, they scampered down the knoll. My muscles were stiff, and as I worked soreness from my shoulders, I noticed the chopper flying back. It didn't head out to sea as I'd expected, but beat to the east in the general direction of the strip I'd visited the day before. So I got in the car and followed it past the Goose Creek Country Club and the Bay Town refinery until I saw the chopper begin a spiraling descent.

By the time I reached the airfield, it was on a hardstand beside one of the old hangars, not far from where I'd conversed with Rafael. I drove close enough to identify it as the two-man gunship that assaulted *Corsair,* left the car in the shade of a hangar, and strolled back. Sure enough, Rafael had visitors. Through grimy windows I saw two men, one holding a pistol on him, and he looked terrified.

I slipped into the empty maintenance hangar and grabbed a bunch of rags from a workbench, found a spray can of starter juice, and drenched the rags. Then I circled back and approached the chopper from the off side, climbed up to the engine housing, and packed rags very tightly around the rotor shaft, jamming the can of high octane into the gear train. If all went well the jammed rotor shaft would heat from friction and ignite the rags. Gears would crunch the spray can and—well, let's see what happens. Climbing down, I spotted an M-16 assault rifle with extension mags between the seats.

Then, walking back to my car, I heard the soft pneumatic report of a silenced handgun. *Adiós,* Rafael, I murmured and slid behind the wheel.

Two men came out of the Calexico office and, without looking right or left, made unhurriedly for the chopper. They got in and rotors began to turn, accelerating to liftoff. When the helicopter was about a hundred feet up it banked and headed toward the Bay, still gaining altitude. I followed it around Bay Town and was beginning to think I'd failed when I caught sight of the chopper again. Flames were flaring up from the engine housing, and the craft was losing stability. Either that, or the pilot was sideslipping to keep flames from the tank. Suddenly the upper part of the chopper vanished in a huge orange ball, and the fuselage plunged nose downward. It vanished below the skyline as the sound of the tank's detonation reached my ears.

At a filling station I bought a can of cold juice and sipped as I dialed the Bay Town police.

"A chopper just went down," I told the officer.

"Yeah, yeah, we got the report, thanks for calling."

"The report you *haven't* got comes from the airfield. In the Calexico office there's a dead guy—Rafael somebody. Don't spend a lot of time on the case because the guys in the chopper just wasted him."

"Yeah? Say, who *are* you, mister. Lissen, you better come in an'—" I replaced the receiver and finished my juice.

The dash clock showed close enough to six that I ought to be in my room for Amy's call. Would she? I'd taken her up on the mountain and shown her the precipice. Three to one she'd call.

I got my key at the desk and rode the small self-service elevator to the third floor. As I opened the room door I noticed the shades were down. I didn't remember lowering them, but a maid could have. There was enough light in the room that I could see something on the bed. A naked woman. Blonde hair.

Amy.

Her eyes were open and I wondered why she didn't speak.

It was my last thought because something slammed the back of my neck, and the scene dissolved.

TWENTY-THREE

I WAS IN cold, dark depths without an air tank. If I rose too fast, I'd burst lungs and brain; if I ascended slowly, I'd exhaust what air remained in my lungs—and drown.

Far above me, lighted as through etched glass, swam two naked figures. One dangled an air tank I desperately needed, but she seemed unaware of me. Both figures were caressing each other while my life flowed away.

I didn't know how long I'd been holding my breath; long enough for pain in my lungs, much greater pain in my skull.

I decided to risk shooting up, snatching the tank from her grasp, and descending quickly—but when I glanced up again, they were gone.

No, Astrid was coming down—naked, blonde hair streaking back from her forehead. No facemask, and I could see the lavender eyes. She'd almost reached my outstretched hand when she drew away the tank. I tried to follow but the tank was always just beyond reach. Her body lost substance, became transparent—vanished. The tank dropped into a black void, and I drifted upward.

Dying.

My lungs expelled the last of my air, and I let them fill, resolved to drown quickly.

Instead, air entered. I opened my eyes.

My head and neck throbbed. I was sprawled on carpet. Below my mouth it was wet from saliva. I must have been there a long time.

Rolling on my back I stared upward, trying to find the swimming figures but there was only blackness.

I began remembering.

My hand touched her foot on the bed, flesh cooler then mine. On my

157

knees I groped for her carotid but there was no pulse. A sob echoed through the room. Mine.

Using the edge of the bed, I pried myself off the floor and covered the bedlamp with a towel. Window shades were still down but I didn't want to chance a watcher's spotting light.

I turned it on.

The blonde bangs were partly off her forehead and her eyes and mouth were open. Near her right hand lay a hypodermic syringe. I gazed at her eyes a final time, and the color had gone. Gently I closed her eyelids, went to the toilet, and vomited.

Then I packed my bag.

When that was done, I turned off the lamp and moved the window blind enough so I could look down on the parking lot. Perspiration trickled from my forehead. My neck felt as though it was broken.

For a long time I stared at the cars below, saw no watchers, bent over, and kissed her fingertips. "Goodbye, beautiful," I whispered and went out, wiping the doorknob clean.

I found the service stairway and walked down slowly and carefully. My bag was unbelievably heavy. Carrying it flashed pain through my spine, and as I opened the exit door I heard the siren of a police car. Walking through the lot I realized it was nearing. Another siren wailed, both were converging on the hotel. I managed to start the engine and drive out the back way as the first patrol car hauled up in front, light bar flashing.

My vision was uncertain, images kept doubling and crossing until I felt like throwing up again. I thought of Astrid alone in the dark room and tears welled in my eyes. No point trying to figure things out; hell, I could barely keep the car on the road.

At the bus station, I left the car in the parking lot, keys under the floormat, and bought a ticket on the next interstate bus.

New Orleans.

Except for pit stops, I slept all the way. Rest was only physical because my brain formed endless nightmares, and when I got off at dawn my mind was still too tired to function.

I caught a bus to the Vieux Carré, found a cheap hotel on Decatur Street, and signed a false name, paying in advance. Once in the room I made an ice pack and took my last two pain capsules. When I woke it was evening, and the pillow was soaked from melted ice. But I felt well enough to shave.

The mirror showed a gaunt, alien face. I grimaced and it scowled back. Dehydrated, I drank a quart of cool water and realized I needed to eat. So I found a one-star restaurant on Iberville and got down a piece of sautéed liver with mashed potatoes and limp asparagus, two cups of coffee, and yesterday's pecan pie. The meal replenished energy, and as I strolled through the Old Quarter, I saw how badly it had deteriorated since I'd visited in uniform. Hookers and panhandlers everywhere. Rock music and lewd dancing—I thought of Astrid and forced her out of my mind. I wondered if I was on a police bulletin, having made the mistake of using my true name at the Houston hotel. Well, Joe Milton's ID would continue to serve.

From the hotel, I took a limo to Moisant Airport and bought an Eastern ticket to Ft. Lauderdale where I had a better chance of getting through unnoticed than at Miami.

THE REDEYE FLIGHT landed after midnight and I rented a not-so-new Plymouth from one of those cheapie agencies that wasn't fussy about credit cards. The place was half a mile south of the airport, so I had a start toward Miami even before driving.

As I headed south on I-95 I realized my mind was beginning to function again—though on a primal level—and I wasn't sure why I was in Florida again. From Houston I could have flown to Cozumel and been free of Texas jurisdiction. But some cortical circuit had brought Miami to the fore and I was almost there. Wherever I went I couldn't stay long—had to keep moving until I was off the Houston wanted list.

If I hadn't seen *Solimar*'s chopper destruct, I would have thought its occupants the most likely suspects for killing Amy. Still, I mused, it was possible they'd snatched Amy someplace, injected her, and left her body on my bod—before stopping at Bay Town to terminate Rafael en route the yacht.

Publicly, Saunders would blame me for his wife's untimely death—even if he knew otherwise. Had she tried to get him to abandon the business and turn himself in? If she truly loved him she might have, rather than stay under his roof as a Justice spy. Perhaps she had principles I was unaware of. But the bottom line was she'd been murdered—and the frame fitted me.

No point trying to explain to Sensinich and others what occurred. They might give me fair words, but only to lure me in for prosecution. The government could be cold hearted about refuge to fugitives, so if I were ever to be cleared of murdering Amy, I'd have to do it alone.

My residual leads were Larry Parmenter and Delores Diehl. Two days ago they'd been in Houston with Saunders and the creep Latino.

I wondered if they'd care to tell me why.

TWENTY-FOUR

FROM A BEACH motel near the Morningstar, where Melody and I had gotten acquainted, I phoned the Diehl home. A dozen unanswered rings and I decided the widow was out for the evening; an abbreviated mourning period—not even a month.

For Delores was resilient, I reflected, a survivor by instinct and talent. Melody was a beneficiary of that trait, but I found no other resemblance between mother and daughter.

How did Larry and Delores perceive each other now that Paul was gone? Were they together for the long run, or temporary confederates on the road to riches? Little as I knew about their relationship I could identify areas of common interest that might bind them closely for a time.

The room was comfortable enough; the a/c tossed the curtains around like paper, and I didn't mind the worn furniture. I hadn't requested a double bed, but in that neighborhood, single males weren't expected to lie alone.

That made me think of Melody and wonder if she was abiding by training rules, or out on some moonlit beach with a preppy blond hunk. I hoped she'd honor team discipline and abstain.

Two o'clock. I was only a mile or so from the Diehl house, so I decided to cruise by and see who was up and around. The clerk gave me a knowing smile when I tossed him my key; he figured I was going out trolling. What he didn't know was that my damaged neck ruled out pleasures of the flesh.

Moonlight gilded the water as I drove to Bay Harbor Island; the Miami skyline glowed red in the distance. A hot and sultry night, not unlike Houston, I mused as I turned into the wide entrance. When I found the

161

house, I parked in the shelter of sabal palms and entered the Diehl estate.

The house showed an upper hall light, one or two on the main floor. The garage doors were down, but I saw a steel-gray Corvette glistening in the moonlight. Melody's cantilever diving tower loomed over the dark pool like gallows, and I remembered the last time I'd come across a pool in the dark. The episode hadn't been pleasant.

The Corvette meant Parmenter was around. But if the two of them were in bed, why the lights? Conversely, if they were having a private party in the beige-carpeted playroom, why not stereo music or TV? The night was soundless.

I stood in shadows and considered what to do.

I was tired from the cross-Gulf flight and the tension of evading the law. Tomorrow would be better for looking into their affairs. I'd be in less pain, and my mind sharper.

I began retracing my steps when I heard the rising snarl of a powerful engine on the waterway. Halting, I glanced at the family dock, saw Melody's Saber missing, and decided to wait.

From a quarter of a mile away I could see the boat's rooster-tail white in the moonlight. The Saber? Too distant to tell. The big speedboat bore on.

At first I thought it was going to overshoot the dock, but it heeled over in a tight turn, leveled off, and throttled down. A bow searchlight caught the dock, and the wet hull glided home. When the boat was secured, they got out and walked arm in arm past the tennis court. Nearing the pool, they paused in shadows for a long embrace and I heard Delores laugh.

From nearby and to my right, a muffled sob.

I froze. There wasn't supposed to be anyone around. Crouching, I moved quietly and heard the sound again. Vision fixed on the source.

A figure so close to the trunk of a palm I hadn't seen it before—but then I hadn't been looking for another surveillant. Dark slacks and sweater, a brief gleam of jewelry. As Larry and Delores strolled on, the figure left the shadows, and I saw the unmistakable glint of gunmetal. The figure moved jerkily, uncertainly, gun thrust out ahead, and I decided to act.

So I made a soundless flanking move, came up behind fast—as I'd been taught—and did three things simultaneously: left palm over mouth, right hand securing the revolver's hammer, knees buckling the other's from behind.

We fell back together on the thick grass. I twisted the revolver free and got out from under.

Eyes blazed at me, and even in the dimness I could see high color in her cheeks. I kept my hand over her mouth, and when she tried clawing my face, I slapped hers. "Bad idea," I grated, "all of it. I'm not fond of them either, but I can't have you spoiling my plans."

She lay staring up at me, fire dwindling from her eyes. I wondered if she was coked out of her skull or whether we could talk peaceably. Her features were sharp but not unattractive. Turning, I saw Larry and Delores passing by, ten yards away. She saw them, too, and began struggling. So I pressed that special nerve at the angle of her jaw, and her body went limp. Even so, I kept my hand over her mouth until Larry opened a rear door and followed Delores inside.

Expelling breath, I sat up, reached for the revolver and extracted the shells, gazed at the gunwoman. I'd disarranged her frosted, expensively coiffured hair. She sat up, rubbing her lips, and spat, "Who the hell are you? His bodyguard?"

"Who're you, lady?"

"Cheryl Parmenter—the bastard's wife."

I helped her to her feet, noticed her hips and thighs were trim though her tummy needed work. "That tableau we just watched suggested both were free as birds. No domestic entanglements."

"He wants to drop me for that . . . bitch." Her lips curled. "After all I've done for him."

"He's going to marry Delores?"

"He *thinks.* Just because you stopped me this time doesn't mean I won't kill him next chance I get."

"Easy," I said. "I followed them from Texas. Before you do anything, I've got business with them—especially Larry."

"What kind of business?" Sulkily, she rubbed the wrist I'd twisted.

"Federal."

"Huh?"

"Treasury," I said. "Diehl's death left a lot of unanswered questions. Whenever a large estate changes hands the government wants to know where the money came from—was it all reported, that sort of thing." She seemed to be swallowing it, so I continued, "Some of Paul Diehl's clients had very heavy money. Paul moved it around—as you probably know from Larry. The government is interested in those clients, and one way to get information is through the estate."

She said a surprising thing. "Would there be any money in it?"

"Money?"

"Reward—you know. If someone tells about tax fraud."

"In case of evasion and fraud, absolutely." I brushed grass from the back of her sweater. "Perhaps we should talk about it."

"Why not? I need a drink anyway—a big one." She gestured. "Got a car?"

"Where's yours?"

"Taxied here—I was planning to drive back in his Corvette."

HER CONDO WASN'T far away—the Belle Vista. Fountains on landscaped grounds, guards at barrier gates. Seeing her, they waved us in. It was a massive, modern building with a row of townhouses at one side. Hers was a triplex with an empty parking slot—the Corvette's I presumed. Beside it was a white Mercedes roadster with a shiny black top. "Yours?" I asked, and she nodded. Her plastic card got us into the elevator for the one-floor ride, and we were in a cobbled hallway half-choked with lush tropical plants. She got a key out of the mailbox, turned off the alarm system, and we went in.

The place looked like an architect's dream. The main room rose forty feet to a translucent skylight; at the far end a formal dining room over-looked Biscayne Bay. Her sandaled feet moved easily over the thick piling, but for me it was slow going—like undergrowth in 'Nam. She was already at the lacquered Japanese-style bar, uncapping a bottle. Her hands trembled as she splashed premium scotch into a silver goblet, lifted it with both hands, and drank. She didn't drain quite all of it, but paused to breathe before continuing. Liquor was an old friend to this baby.

"Ice?" she finally said.

"With rum flavoring."

"Rum's too sugary for me, and I never use ice. I take my liquor room temp, and I like the taste."

I moved behind the bar and shoveled cracked ice with a monogrammed silver scoop. The Añejo was easy to find, bottle nearly full. I dribbled some over ice and touched my goblet to hers. She poured more Chivas. "What'll we drink to?"

"How about compatible interests?"

"Not bad. But before we exchange confidences, how about some ID?"

I flashed Milton's T-card and returned it to my hip pocket.

There was a free-form stand of shrubs and flowers thrusting up from the carpeting, about where a fireplace would be, anyplace but Florida. I almost tripped over it, following her to a low sofa that looked twenty feet long and four feet deep. When we were settled in it, I said, "For reasons of your own you want Larry dead. I don't know your provocation and it isn't relevant—just the timing."

She said, "You mean—you don't mind if I kill my husband?"

I got out her cartridges and laid them beside her thigh. Then I sipped rum, realizing it had been a long time since anything tasted as good. "We need his cooperation, Cheryl—after that he's yours." I got out her revolver and tossed it to the far end of the sofa. "Of course, Larry may not want to disclose Diehl's activities—in which case I'm reasonably sure he'll go to prison." My words fascinated her. She drew up her legs catlike, and I could almost see her lapping heavy cream. "Prison?" she murmured.

"Five to ten years. And a convicted felon can be divorced without recourse, on a simple court motion. That might interest you."

She thought it over. "It might indeed. And I'd get"—her hand swept the setting—"all this."

"Perhaps much more."

She drank what was for her a small ration, loosened the scarf around her throat, and let it drift away. The hard features were softening; for my hostess a bottle was the fountain of youth. Almost purring, she said, "What do I have to do?"

MORNING

Cheryl was wearing a saucy French-maid wraparound that barely covered her buns. We were in the kitchen, and she was whipping up a cheese omelet. She poured the mix into a double pan and said, "I hate to ask this, but I have to."

"Shoot. Uh . . . I mean, go ahead."

She smiled. "Last night . . . did we . . . do anything?"

"Not that I remember."

She sighed. "That's a relief. You see—I'm . . . unprotected. With Larry away I haven't needed anything. I mean protection, y'know."

"Put your mind at rest."

"You're positive."

"Too tired, too much liquor. Take an oath."

She leaned across the counter and kissed the tip of my nose. One breast nearly dunked my coffee. "I like you, Joe Milton, and I think we're going to be great friends."

"Fantastic," I said. "Most of my contacts are hostile."

"You're sure about the uncontestable divorce?"

"Ask your lawyer."

She spread unsalted butter on muffins and served the omelet in a way that suggested she lacked intimate knowledge of cooking and kitchen. But when I'd put her to bed, I'd noticed her body was well cared for; lacquered toenails and a full-length tan. What I'd seen as a hard set to her features

165

turned out to be the results of cosmetic tightening. Her breasts had either been augmented or reduced—the hairline scars weren't telling—and she'd had a tushy-tuck. A forty year old bimbo with enough money to try for thirty.

Before eating she added an ounce of Chivas to her coffee and offered me Añejo. "I had enough last night," I told her. "With all you've told me, I've got a challenging day ahead."

She sipped her scotch-coffee and covered my hand with hers. "This is going to be fun, Joe. God, I can't *wait* to stick it to him!"

"Patience," I said, "and all will be well."

"I haven't felt this up in *ages*. If you hadn't stopped me last night I'd be in jail today—wondering how the hell to get out. Just a damn miracle you were there."

She was working slowly through the omelet. Even the Crabtree & Evelyn preserves didn't tempt her. In daylight I could see the eye puffiness, the flabby underarms of the alcoholic. For her, a drink was like a slice of bread. I hoped she'd be around for the payoff.

"Joe, why not stay here—make this your headquarters? There's no one but me—the maid only comes half-days to pick up."

"Well, thanks," I said, "but I have to stay loose—go here and there all hours. Besides, if Larry chanced by, it wouldn't look good finding us in, ah, intimate circumstances."

Maybe it was reflection from the Bay, but I thought she actually blushed. "Do him good," she said coldly. "Half the condo husbands would like to bust his balls. And to think I put up with it." She shook her head. "Thank God we didn't have kids."

"Sounds like an authentic ingrate," I remarked, "after you and your family put him through law school, bought into Diehl's practice, paid for the condo." I glanced around. "How much does a place like this go for?"

She shrugged. "A million five—unfurnished. In all, about two."

And nearby were a couple dozen like it, I reflected with a sense of awe. Well, Diehl's bayside spread was worth about the same. I ate the last of my muffin. "Larry told you Saunders didn't really marry the dancer, Amy—that her name?"

"*She* thought they were married, but Saunders tore up the papers, and they never got registered. A real prick. His wife lives in some Colorado clinic—Vail, I think. *If* she's still alive. Bad heart."

I finished coffee, dabbed my mouth with an Italian napkin. "I'll take those office keys you mentioned, be on my way."

"By now Larry's probably changed the safe combination—to keep me out. He wanted me to store my jewelry there, but it's here where I can get at it." She looked away. "I'm going to have to start selling to keep this place up—might as well, never go anyplace I can wear it." She looked back at me. "How about dinner?"

I got off the chair-stool. "I'll phone."

Cheryl seemed to have forgotten the keys, so I reminded her. She went to the bedroom we'd shared, and came back with a gold key ring and several keys. I thanked her, chastely kissed her forehead, and left.

Driving down Biscayne toward my motel, I reviewed what she'd told me, and while all of it was interesting, very little was usable with a grand jury. Cheryl knew something about offshore corporations established to launder and invest money belonging to clients of Diehl and her husband. Apparently Diehl did most of the foreign travel and money transfers. All of it—as far as I could judge—in violation of federal statutes. If Cheryl knew of narcotics operations involving the firm, she didn't tell me—and most of her inhibitions were down. Just before she went glassy-eyed, Cheryl said she'd heard Larry mention a big client yacht—but she didn't know who really owned it or what went on aboard. Aside from cruising tropic seas.

I wanted Saunders and the man aboard that yacht. If they were vulnerable, it would be through records of their transactions. Cheryl told me Diehl kept them in his office.

And I had the keys.

TWENTY-FIVE

ELORES DIEHL SAID, "Why, Mr. Novak—I doubted we'd meet again . . . but do come in." She stepped back, and the houseman closed the door.

"Thank you—things ended on an over-emotional note the other time. I thought it might be worthwhile to clear the air—particularly since I've come into some new information." I followed her toward the reception room. "New to me, at least."

"Whatever could that mean? Coffee? Bloody Mary?"

"Coffee will be fine."

She gestured at the houseman, and we entered that big beautiful romper room. I wondered if Melody was often allowed in. Her mother led the way to the sofa at the far end, but I veered off to the party-size cellarette. She said, "Changed your mind?"

"That was just for appearance's sake—you know how servants talk."

"How right you are," she sighed, "and as long as you're there, you might build me a Bloody Mary."

"Easy on the vodka?"

She smiled tolerantly. "Whatever made you think a thing like that?"

I made our drinks and carried them to the low cocktail table. *"Pesetas,"* I said.

"Tiempo," she responded, and we drank.

"Now, then, what is this information you mentioned—or was that also for Thomas's benefit?" One finger stroked the side of her glass.

"It's true. But first, are you really going to sue me—as Mr. Parmenter suggested?"

169

"Oh, that was just Larry. And under the circumstances, I feel I should regard you as a family friend." Her gaze caressed me.

"Splendid. Then we can consider Larry's outburst null and void."

"Bravado." She sipped delicately. "Just in from Cozumel?"

"No—why?"

"Because it seems my daughter, Melody, went there shortly after your visit. It occurred to me you might have seen her."

"I flew in from Houston."

"Houston?"

"I was following a lead Paul's companion, the girl calling herself Penny Saunders, gave me—unwittingly, I guess. And to my surprise, it paid off."

"Oh? In what way?"

"Crazy," I said. "She wasn't killed on my boat. In fact, she's very much alive. Imagine that?"

She sat down her glass firmly. "Are you *serious,* Mr. Novak? I mean, you told everyone—including me—she'd been slaughtered, too."

I shrugged. "Because of appearances, all circumstantial. It was quite a shock to find she'd survived." I drank again while she thought it over.

"And that's the new information? Just that, Mr. Novak?"

"Call me Jack—since I'm considered a friend of the family."

"Delores—please."

I cleared my throat. "She had other things to tell me I thought you ought to know—and I'd prefer you not tell Larry."

"Not if I mustn't."

"You'll understand why. Larry doesn't come out too well—according to what the young lady had to say. Her name, by the way is Amy King, used to do nude dancing in scummy Bay clubs. The man she pretended was her father—Vernon Saunders—turned out to be her husband."

"Really?"

"At least she *thought* they were married. But when she found out he'd deceived her, as they say, it upset her considerably. Which is why she was willing to confide in me."

Delores swallowed. The trend of the conversation was worrying her. Not wanting to ask the wrong question, she let me continue. I said, "Apparently Saunders used the girl, exploited her shamelessly in connection with certain criminal activities involving narcotics and money-laundering."

"Oh?" Her tongue flicked into the glass and withdrew. "I don't believe I know the term."

"It means sanitizing the profits of illegal transactions, such as narcotics. According to Amy, your late husband was one of the chief conspirators— aided and abetted by Larry P. Doubtless, you had no idea of Paul's criminal activity, but it happens to be a fact. And as family friend I'm passing the information to you—however unpleasant it may be."

Her cheeks whitened. "Paul...? Larry...?" She seemed unable to grasp my message. Finally she said, "Couldn't the girl have been mistaken— vindictive?"

"Why would she want to slander Paul and Larry? What's the advantage to her? We have to look at it objectively."

"This is . . . terrible news. I   I hardly know what to say."

"Before I left Houston, Amy was preparing to denounce Saunders. She also revealed that Paul was killed in a plot to rip off a couple of million dollars in cocaine he'd been trying to smuggle here. I know—sounds impossible, doesn't it? But she convinced me. And the sunken plane—Paul hired it, and when it crashed with his cocaine, he had to try recovering it."

"This is all . . . just incredible." She pressed a cocktail napkin to her lips and closed her eyes. Her bosom rose and fell.

"My reaction, too," I said sympathetically. "We have to deal with facts, though—don't we?"

Throatily she said, "I knew Paul was going through . . . certain difficulties, but I had absolutely *no* idea his desperation led him to crime. You see, Jack, he never confided in me. I was Paul's chatelaine, the centerpiece of this home, his social life. I knew nothing of his activities, his clients, or associates."

"Except Saunders." I drained my glass and set it down.

This was a bad morning for my prospective mother-in-law—if anyone took Melody's fantasy seriously—but Delores was trying to cope. "Why do you say that?"

I leaned forward. "You're not saying you and Larry weren't in Houston with Saunders the other day?"

"As a matter of fact, we were. Larry had a business conference and invited me—we both agreed I needed a change of scene."

"Who was the little Latino with the built-up heels?"

"Mr. Chavez? He was in Vernon's office—I gathered, some sort of flunky." It was killing her not to ask how the hell I knew so much. But she stayed with her role, and I with mine.

"Chavez, eh?"

"Nestor Chavez, I believe."

"Well he's more than Saunders's flunky. He travels on the yacht *Solimar.* That's where the helicopter came from that killed your husband and my captain." I paused. "And almost killed me."

Lifting her glass, she downed the last of her drink. "I think I'll have another." She thrust the glass at me.

I obliged, and when we were facing each other again, she said, "Mr. Novak—Jack—this is dreadful news you've brought. Really, I could almost wish you hadn't come." Her gaze traveled over my face appraisingly. "But here you are—and I don't really know what to do. Could you advise me?"

Not wanting Melody homeless, I said, "First off, there's the estate. Get yourself a legitimate, non-Larry-type attorney and have him establish that this property wasn't bought with the proceeds of illegal transactions."

Her eyebrows drew together. "Why . . . ? I don't understand."

"Everything can be confiscated—cars, boat, bank accounts . . ." She could complete the list herself.

"My God, I had no idea!"

I said, "This is going to place you in an adversary position with Mr. Parmenter—of necessity. He'd like to control Paul's wealth through marrying you, but I have it on good authority, his wife won't let him. That's moot, anyway, because if things are only half as bad as I've described, Larry will be spending the next two decades making license tags in Atlanta. So, break clean, Delores—that's the best advice I can give you. And I think your new attorney will agree."

"Why are you telling me all this? Being so helpful? You couldn't have liked Paul alive—and now he's dead you have far less reason to want to help his . . . survivors."

"From what your daughter told me, she was a neglected child. She's at an impressionable age right now. If you were dragged down with Mr. P., unjustly, it would destroy her."

"Why should you care about her future?"

"She has Olympic aspirations. Our young athletes deserve every consideration." I glanced through the window at the pool. "Where is she, anyway?"

"Stanford, actually, competing for a place on the Olympic team."

"That's great," I said enthusiastically. "I hope she makes out like a bandit."

Her eyebrows arched. "Melody's so talented I'm sure she'll get whatever she wants. But we were talking of very serious things. I should get an attorney—and stop seeing Larry. It does sound like excellent advice." Her hands spread. "It won't be easy—Larry's been so comforting in this trying period, we've become . . . close." She swallowed. "*Much* closer than I intended . . . I was vulnerable, you understand?"

"Completely."

"So now—everything you've told me, I'm overwhelmed. But I must protect myself, mustn't I—and Melody. Shouldn't we just go back to Brazil until things straighten out?"

"I'm afraid departure would have the color of guilty flight. No, I'm confident a capable attorney can safeguard your interests." I got up. "Of course you're under no obligation to accept my advice."

"But I *sought* it." She gazed upward. "You seem to have such comprehensive knowledge of . . . the situation."

"Thanks to Amy. That's in confidence, of course."

"Certainly. Do you expect to see her again?"

"No."

"Larry . . ." she said musingly. "Not brave, I'm afraid. I wonder what he'll do?"

"You know him better than I, Delores. Sometimes it's hard for a man to see just where his interests lie."

She nodded. "Where are you off to? Cozumel?"

"Probably."

"I understand it's a pleasant little place. Perhaps we'll meet again."

"Let's hold the thought," I said, and left as Thomas brought in the coffee tray.

I got into my car feeling that Delores had been convincing. A man as close-mouthed and involved as Diehl would have no reason to burden Delores with guilty secrets—and in her self-described role, no reason to inquire. She was ready to dump on Larry.

So was I.

I drove south toward his Brickell office—to case it before dark.

TWENTY-SIX

AFTER THE WATCHMAN made his ten o'clock rounds I went in.
There were still a few workers on the eleventh floor, and that
was good. The char force had come through at eight, and I'd been
noticed in a lavatory stall where I'd perched with a paperback titled
Airborne. I'd bought it at the lobby newsstand thinking the book covered
parachute training, but it was about sailing the Atlantic.

The keys on Cheryl's gold ring worked smoothly. First I deactivated the
alarm, then opened the entrance door. I closed it from inside, flicked on my
penlite, and located a video scanner in the upper corner of the reception
room. I hung a Dixie cup over the lens and turned on the light.

Tiled floor, sumptuous leather furniture, strong regional paintings on the
walls. The inner door was controlled by an electric lock I bypassed with a
plastic card. There were work cubicles for stenos, paralegal assistants, and
billing clerks. A few open offices for law associates, then three mahogany-
framed doorways with gold-leaf lettering: Law Library, Mr. Parmenter,
Mr. Diehl.

Another key unlocked Larry's place of business. The marble-topped
desk was semicircular, furnishings conventionally modern. An unlocked
connecting door led into Diehl's office. I pulled down the blinds and turned
on the desk lamp.

What had been Paul's desk was larger than Larry's; the walls were hung
with diplomas, testimonals, and racing prints. By now Parmenter would
have removed anything worth examining, so I went into the other office,
shoved Parmenter's chair aside, and rolled back the carpet.

The safe was sunk flush with the concrete floor, the 3-way combination
dial recessed. I drew on racquetball gloves and tried the combination
Cheryl had given me. No dice. He'd changed the numbers.

I'd brought a few things with me, including a small Walkman-type player. To it I rigged a phone-type suction mike and jacked in earphones. Positioning the mike next to the dial I began turning until I heard tumblers fall at 14. Reverse direction. Forty-three. Right again: 27. Zero, and *open.* I lifted the heavy steel lid, shined my penlite, and looked in.

Ledger books and bundled documents, bankbooks, an unsealed manila envelope bulging with hundred-dollar bills. (His getaway stash?) Plus two safe deposit keys. And a 9mm Beretta pistol.

I took a black Minox camera from my pocket and tilted the desk light to photograph the documents on high-speed Ilford film.

The first book seemed to be the regular office expense ledger. A second contained client billings, and I photographed pages with entries for Vernon O. Saunders. The third ledger was labeled *Intierra Ass.* and I photographed every page.

Changing film cassettes, I photographed corporation documents from around the world: Curaçao, Lichtenstein, Zürich, Panama, Geneva, Madrid, and—Florida. More than a dozen fronts, and enough information to allow Justice to pierce the corporate veils.

What I'd thought to be only a vinyl-bound notebook had a name scribbled on the inside page: *Parra.* Luis, I thought, and scanned the pages. Entries looked like a weighmaster's report with figures in kilos, and dollar amounts. Probably gross sales. *Tierra* was Spanish slang for cocaine, *caballo* meant horse and heroin, *pasto* was grass. Dollar total over eighty million. I turned to the last page and saw radio frequency notations and call signs. For *Solimar?* Parra's Colombian redoubt?

I was preparing to photograph the pages when I heard a key turn in the reception door lock.

I turned off the lamp, picked up the Beretta, and tiptoed beside the door where I tied a handkerchief over my face, bandit-style. The reception door opened.

Security guard? Hell, he'd toured the floor half an hour before. Any law associate would have a key—but why return so late at night? Had I tripped some hidden alarm?

The inner door opened and a man came in. As he reached for the wall switch I whacked the back of his head with my pistol butt, caught him as he collapsed.

Light from the work area showed the face of Larry Parmenter.

I pushed the door shut, and the spring lock clicked. For a time I gazed at Mr. P., deciding how to exploit his unexpected visit.

His pulse was strong. I patted him down, but he was clean. In the mailroom I found rolls of heavy twine and plastic wrapping tape. I tied his wrists behind his back and bound his ankles, leaving enough slack so he could hobble if not actually walk to the phone.

I taped his mouth and blindfolded him with his handkerchief. Then I dragged him behind a corner chair, and photographed the Parra ledger.

That completed, I decided to arrange a scene that would suggest burglary to the police—if Parmenter brought them in.

I replaced the office ledger. The manila envelope contained something over a hundred thousand. I extracted twenty thousand to cover past and future expenses and put the envelope aside. From my pocket I took one of the film wrappers and dropped it into the safe. When Parmenter found it, he'd realize why his office had been invaded.

In Diehl's office I shoved back carpet and found a duplicate safe. This one was unlocked—and empty. I set a combination involving the letters of my name and deposited the special ledgers, money envelope, documents and keys. Lastly, I set the Beretta among the ledgers, closed the lid, and spun the dial. After replacing carpet and chair, I went back to Parmenter's office. By now he was groaning, and I heard a shoe hit the chairleg. It would take him awhile to orient himself.

I took two more photographs: one of the desk and open safe, the other of Parmenter, trussed and gagged. In my pockets I put the player, mike, headset, the Minox, and exposed cassettes. Then I went out, locking each door behind me, and took the fire stairs down to the ninth floor. From there I rode the service elevator to the garage—bypassing the lobby guard—and strolled to the parking lot where I'd left my car. As I got behind the wheel I checked the time—only eleven-ten, but I was tired. My work product— the film cassettes in my pocket—were bargaining chips. Properly applied, they were leverage on Larry Parmenter to flip him against Saunders and Luis Parra. And in return, the government would erase any charges against me for Amy's murder.

I was starting north on Brickell when, without warning, a car heading south turned abruptly in front of me and into the drive of the building I'd just left. A white Mercedes roadster with black top. The driver wore sunglasses, but light from the front of the building gave me a glimpse of her face.

Cheryl Parmenter.

She must know her husband was at the office, I reflected. Well, let her find him bound and gagged, victim of a burglary.

As I drove away I wondered what she'd do.

TWENTY-SEVEN

T HE ANSWER CAME in the morning. I was shaving and listening to radio news. A prominent attorney, Lawrence Parmenter, had shot to death in his office during what police described as a burglary. Parmenter's wife arrived shortly after the killing, called a building guard and went into shock. "*Son of a bitch!*" I blurted at my mirror image, and listened to the rest.

The guard had let Mrs. Pamenter into her husband's office and gone back to his post. Minutes later a frantic call from Mrs. Parmenter summoned him to the scene. Police spokesmen declined to speculate on motive for the lawyer's murder, although it was known that the firm represented numerous narcotics clients. In a recent incident the firm's senior partner, Paul Diehl, had been killed in Mexico when his chartered boat was attacked by pirates.

There was the usual cliché about clues leading to arrest of the perpetrator, then a fast-food commerical. I turned off the radio.

Naughty girl, I thought as I finished shaving. Cheryl, you used me to set the scene, shot Larry when the guard was far away, and got yourself a divorce without the aggravation of waiting. Plus double indemnity insurance.

The murder left me in a dilemma. The photos I'd taken—particularly the final frame of Larry lying bound on the office floor—were incriminating to the Nth degree. When I'd left him he was alive and uninjured, but Cheryl hadn't told it that way. Still, self-preservation required her to stand by the burglary-murder story without involving me.

Only the two of us knew the truth, and so long as neither went public, the fiction would endure. I had no reason to clarify matters, and I had the exposed cassettes and knowledge of where the ledgers and documents were stashed. It seemed unlikely the police would rummage under the carpet of Diehl's adjoining office.

So I could regard the cache as secure—unless Parra's henchmen came looking. The materials had no positive value for Parra—he couldn't *do* anything with them—but he'd know they could be used against him in a very dangerous way.

That Cheryl, I thought, as I patted after-shave on my face, what a vicious opportunist she turned out to be. I was pulling down the curtain on our brief relationship. Forever.

Delores? What would she make of Larry's murder? She knew I was interested in him, but was she likely to inform the police? I could perceive nothing gained, and I was betting she saw it the same way. Nevertheless, an exploratory call might be in order—after I'd taken care of other things.

Using the bathroom, I developed my nine cassettes in the special Minox unit, hung the 8mm strips on a towel rack. While they were drying, I walked a couple of blocks to a shaded pay phone, waited while an elderly Cuban lady screamed all the way to Cienfuegos. After she hobbled away, I got a handful of change from my pocket and dialed Montijo in Houston.

It was a while before I heard his voice. "Jack—where are you? You better come in, *amigo*."

"I'm in Tulsa, and as far as coming in—you mean you bought that frame?"

"Circumstantially, you killed the girl."

"I'll tell you what really happened, and I hope you're taping this—but whoever had her killed learned she was going over. Maybe she tried to persuade Saunders or warn him, and it wasn't well received. They weren't legally married, by the way."

"So it develops. Listen, Sensinich is up the wall. The U.S. Attorney wants you charged with witness tampering—and of course the state has you down for murder one."

"About what I expected." I told him what happened in the hotel room and said I'd run, rather than attempt to work out of an obvious frame. I described my film strips and said I was willing to send them to him for action.

"Where are the original documents and ledgers? Parmenter's safe?"

"Not exactly—and under the best-evidence rule, you'll need them. I have them."

"What do you want?"

"Dismissal of all charges against me."

"Can't promise anything."

"Well, that's the deal. As a show of good faith I'll send you negatives."

"Sounds fair. But I still think you ought to come in, Jack—so does Tony."

"Not convenient—or practical. I've done considerable work for you fellows, and I'd like a show of appreciation—sooner than later."

"I'll see what I can do."

"Unfortunately, Parmenter won't be around to testify."

"Is he gone?"

"A long way. Last night his wife killed him." I sketched the background and said, "Everything played into her hands, and she'll get away with it. Conceivably she might be indicted, but never convicted."

I heard him sigh. "The target list is getting pretty short, Jack, you say your stuff will nail Saunders, for sure?"

"Definitely. And he's your gate to Parra."

"I'll get you as good a deal as I can."

"Not just good," I told him, "it has to be perfect," and hung up as the operator began asking for more quarters. Well, maybe the deal would fly, maybe not. My chief worry was whether Parra's people would find and destroy the evidence before I could retrieve it. I fingered the gold key ring in my pocket. It had gotten me in once; it could get me there again.

I HAD FOLDED the dried film strips in tissue paper, and at the branch post office I bought a pre-canceled envelope and mailed it to Montijo. Two days and he'd have something substantial to consider. He and Tony Sensinich. I'd give them a day or so to mull it over and then I'd call in.

At a corner cafe I ate a *media luna* and swallowed two cups of Cuban espresso before going back to my room. I removed my twenty-thousand from the base of the air conditioner and fingered the bills. One felt a little too crisp, and when I examined it under a lamp I saw it was counterfeit. I set it aside and vetted the other hundred and ninety-nine, not wanting to be arrested for passing bogus bucks. In all, I extracted fourteen counterfeits— low percentage for drug deals—and burned them in the john. Leaving me eighteen thousand six. Compared to the sums Parra and Saunders could command, it was trivial—but it might be enough to outlast them.

If there was enough left over, I'd get the Seabee's engine overhauled, install radar on *Corsair*, and maybe cruise down to Bonaire for a month's diving. But right now I didn't want to make long-range plans. I was living hour to hour, and I had more calls to make.

I drove north on Collins, spotted a sheltered pay phone, and dialed Cheryl's number. When a man answered, I said, "Who's speaking?"

"Morry Farnham—Mrs. Parmenter's attorney."

"I'm Paul Diehl's cousin. Tell her Joe wants to extend condolences."

"I'll see if she's up to answering."

I held on and shooed two kids from my car before they could snatch my hubcaps. "Hello, Joe? That you? So thoughtful of you to call." Her voice was confident and strong.

"Yeah." I cleared my throat. "What a sly boots you are Cheryl. I just want to say this—I won't go around talking about you, if you'll do the same for me."

"But of course, Joe. After all, you were *enormously* helpful."

"Please don't thank me."

She giggled as though she'd mixed pills with her scotch. "You take care of yourself, hear?"

"I'm certainly going to try." I hung up, thinking that if she ever made me another omelet it would be laced with cyanide.

I telephoned the Diehl estate.

After some sparring with Thomas, the houseman, I heard Delores come on an extension. She said, "I suppose you've heard the news."

"Tragic. Poor Larry."

"Yes. But, maybe it was for the best."

"In view of what faced him. But dead, he can't be as helpful as he could have been alive. Testifying."

"I understand. You see, Jack, I was afraid you had some part in last night's tragic affair. So I'm very glad you called."

"Seemed the thing to do."

"The police have been here and gone. I'm afraid I wasn't very helpful. Do you think they'll come back?"

"I doubt it. And of course I have nothing to volunteer."

"I thought you might have returned to Cozumel, but since you haven't, perhaps you'd stop by? We might have coffee together, a bite to eat. You're a very personable man, you know."

"That's kind of you to say." I sensed where she was leading, but I'd been preempted by her daughter. Delores was elastic, I reflected, bouncy as a tennis ball. "I'm glad you're not grieving too deeply. Larry's intentions weren't entirely disinterested."

"Alas. But now I'm more alone than ever. And I'm not at all a recluse type. I've always led a very active social existence."

"That's evident," I said. "By the way, how's you're daughter doing?"

"Melody? She phoned last night—she keeps on winning."

"Isn't that gratifying. Well, I wish her the best—both of you. Sorry I can't stop by."

"You'll . . . stay in touch?"

"Definitely—as a family friend I have that obligation."

On that note I hung up—the only way to end her overtures.

So far two widows were very big winners from all the bloodshed and deceit. I wasn't sure how long their unattached prosperity would last, but both had a world of options.

Meanwhile, I had no further business in Miami, and Captain Jaramillo was overdue for attention. I took the next flight to Cozumel.

TWENTY-EIGHT

CHELA WAS ASLEEP in the guest room. I was dead tired but I stayed up long enough to feed a bonus to my ever-hungry hounds who made it known they resented my absence and were happy I'd returned.

Around dawn I felt a warm female body beside me, and almost before I realized it we were making love. Afterward I slept again, and when I awoke I was alone. There was a bowl of sliced fruit in the refrigerator and a tumbler of orange juice. Fresh coffee warmed.

The day was bright, sea glassy. From the pier I noticed strands of kelp on the Seabee's hull and decided to scrape them off underwater. But first I inspected the plane for booby traps and weakened control cables. Everything shipshape as far as I could tell.

Off the end of the pier was the usual crowd of gaily colored parrotfish nibbling at barnacles; almost impossible to catch by hook, and insufficiently tasty to justify the effort. But as I gazed downward, I saw a striped grouper that had strayed in from deeper water.

With a short rod from the plane I angled a fiddler crab. At first the grouper wasn't interested, but when the wiggling crab brushed his nose, he struck. In a few seconds I had a four-pounder on the pier. Sitting there, I gutted and scraped him, rinsed fillets, and took them to the refrigerator. Chela had a special way with baked fish, and I hadn't had fresh seafood in too long a time. A chilled bottle of Riscal white would go well with her Yucatecan recipe, and I'd pick up one in town. Shading my eyes, I gazed at the horizon and realized I was unconsciously searching for the *Solimar*. All I could see were a few fishing craft, and one of the cruising love boats making for port. I didn't expect the yacht in Cozumel waters, but if it came, there could be dangerous times ahead. By now they'd have replaced chopper and pilot, I felt sure.

Jaramillo. Was the captain at the airport shaking down tourists or lending a helping hand to drug-laden plans transiting Cozumel? I got my .45 from its cache and strapped on a shoulder holster, then a lightweight jacket to conceal the harness. *El Capitán* had tried to waste me twice, and I supposed the contract was still open.

At the café I asked Chela if she'd seen anyone nosing around. She shrugged. "Twice at night the dogs barked, and one evening Jaramillo wanted to come in."

"But you didn't let him."

"Another man in your home, *padrón*? Certainly not!"

"He won't be around again," I told her. "By the way, was there any mail for me? *Cartas*?"

Her eyes lowered. Reluctantly she reached into her skirt pocket and brought out a letter. "I thought if it was from the *niña* you might not want it, Juan."

"As it happens, I do. Thanks for guarding it."

"*Para servirle.*"

Walking over to the little waterfront park, I opened the envelope. Palo Alto postmark, and addressed in the stylized script fancied by private school misses across the country. Small circles in place of dots—that sort of convention.

> Lover—Because you are my destined soulmate and husband I have a continuing concern for your well-being and I order you to do nothing that could conceivably impair it. Avoid all hazards and danger. And while leading this good and tranquil life know that I am following all team rules and regs, and doing everything possible to make you proud of me. Mother seems to be surviving without me so I plan to join you after the competition ends.
>
> I'm still not used to nine o'clock bedtime, so I lie awake and think of you and get very horny. Please keep up your strength so we can make love endlessly.
>
> Your adoring
> Melody

The thought of seeing her again cheered me, and I wondered how long the diving trials would last. Winning might encourage her to finish her education, so I had a particular reason for wanting her to win. I tucked the letter away and strolled down the fishing pier, thinking of Captain Jaramillo.

The glass-bottom tour boat was coming in, so it had to be close to noon. The pudgy captain would be lunching.

I drove to the airport, saw him walking around inside the Arrival enclosure, and went into the lunchroom where I ordered a Tecate.

He came in after a while, sweat stains under the arms of his khaki uniform shirt, pot belly protruding over a braided leather belt from which hung an ornate leather holster. In it was an ivory-handled Colt .45. Catching sight of me, he halted, his face a mix of changing emotions. Finally, he tilted back his cap and sauntered over. "*Señor* Juan," he said expansively, "so you returned. There were those who thought you would not."

"Sit down," I said. "Keeping well?"

"Especially as my wife is visiting in Guanajuato." He straddled a chair as the waiter came over. Jaramillo ordered beer—and a full meal.

"I've been in Texas."

"Oh?" He looked at me uneasily.

"I saw some of your business associates."

"I . . . business . . . ?"

"Rafael, the chicano who rents planes, told me you could certify cargo for me—for a price."

His mouth opened and closed.

"Unfortunately, Rafael won't be doing business any more. Unfortunately for you." I drank from my sweating glass.

"He was . . . arrested . . . ?"

"Terminated. Not by me, Captain, by people who thought that he knew who supplies the coke and gives the orders. He didn't." I sipped briefly and stared at him. "I do."

He swallowed. "Dangerous knowledge."

"The point's been made. Someone tried to sabotage my plane, and when that failed a *gringo* was shot by someone thinking he was me."

He licked his lips. "You did not report these things to the authorities."

"That's true," I said, "because I've lost confidence in the law as a means of justice. Accordingly, I do what I find appropriate. As the occasion arises."

The waiter brought his beer, but Jaramillo ignored it.

"The point," I said, "is that I'm probably going to overreact to even the most innocent happenings. Anyone watching my house, hanging around my boat, or coming after dark could be in danger. Yours is a violent

187

country, *Capitán*, and I've become accustomed to violence." I let my jacket hang open so he could see the holstered .45. "I'm comfortable with it—as you are."

"Are you threatening me? Me—an officer of our army?"

"Does that offend you? All I want is to continue living comfortably and peaceably—but if I feel threatened I'm going to terminate the threat."

As I rose he looked up. "Why tell me?"

"I'm putting out the word. Naturally I wanted you to know."

The waiter arrived and unloaded several dishes in front of him. Jaramillo glanced at his lunch with distaste.

"No night visits," I told him before I walked away, "don't even drive past by day."

JARAMILLO'S HOUSE WAS luxurious for an army captain. Single-story ranch of stuccoed masonry, red-tiled roof. Atop it soared a TV antenna that ought to pull in signals from Cancún, if not Mérida. His domain comprised several lots fenced by iron grill set into a yard-high masonry wall. Beyond it was a good-sized free-form swimming pool, water pale green under the midday sun. A shiny blue BMW sat in the shadows of a portico, and out in the garden a *lavandera* hung out wash to dry in the warm breeze. Captain Jaramillo enjoyed a life of ease and comparative affluence, and I reflected that if he was smart, he would ignore the open contract on my life.

But having baited him, I didn't think he would.

TWENTY-NINE

CHELA BAKED THE grouper fillets with red and green peppers, plantains, and spices, and we ate it with icy Riscal white.

While she was clearing up, I turned on the short-wave receiver and scanned two of the frequencies I'd found in the Parra account book. One was working, and transmission was in open voice code: a *bulto* of *tierra* was ready for delivery to *llmón*, another to *naranja*, and so on. Trouble was, I couldn't tell where the transmission originated or who was receiving it. But when DEA had the full schedule of frequencies, transmitter locations could be determined. Tomorrow or the day after I'd call Montijo and hear what he had to say about amnesty for a murder I didn't commit.

If I hadn't had on earphones, I might have heard something to warn me. Instead, suddenly a window shattered as something smashed into the room. In a frozen moment I saw a fragmentation grenade hit a chair leg and bounce back. Diving behind a sofa, I saw Chela framed in the kitchen doorway. I yelled, saw horror grip her features, and the thing exploded.

Something hot hit my calf. Stunned, deafened, I saw through smoke that all but one light had been knocked out; where Chela had been the doorway was empty. I staggered toward it, found her body crumpled where the blast had hurled it. Blood streamed from a score of wounds, and her face had been blown away.

Outside, my dogs were barking maniacally as a car sped away. Chela's body jerked and lay still. I reached for her wrist. No pulse. My shoulders began to shake uncontrollably, breath came in gasps. Tears flowed down my cheeks, but I wiped them away, bent over, and kissed a lock of Chela's

189

hair. I wanted to scream at the enormity of her death, beat my chest in agony, but there were other priorities. Her murder had to be avenged.

Breathing spasmodically, I got up, took a step, and my foot squished in its shoe. Hobbling through smoking debris, I got to the bathroom, taped a pad on the skin flap, and slowed the bleeding. My impulse was to call the police, but with Chela dead that could wait. I got my M-16 assault rifle from its hiding place, turned out the remaining lights, and limped out to my jeep.

The bomber had a head start, but that wasn't going to count because he had no reason to believe I'd survived. As I raced toward the outskirts of San Miguel, grief gripped me again, and I thought of how Chela had changed my solitary life, freely giving me her love and affection, caring for me, and sharing my days and nights. Through her my refuge had become a home—and now it was destroyed, along with the girl who had created it. That I'd survived the blast was a miracle. That she'd been the innocent victim was a tragedy I wasn't yet able to absorb.

Lights festooned cruise ships at the long pier. Over the engine I could hear strains of music from the saloons. The contrast was macabre.

I parked a block from Jaramillo's house, shouldered the rifle by its sling, and kept to the shadows as I made for the rear of his property. No outside lights, a dim glow within. Moonlight showed the BMW in the portico. His army jeep was missing.

The back gate was locked, so I pushed the rifle through the bars and pulled myself over the fencing. The effort made my leg throb, but the hell with it. I circled the house, peering into windows, saw no signs of life; he'd said his wife was in Guanajuato.

I was picking a spot to wait when an engine roared close by and headlights splashed the house. From where I stood, I could see him come around in front of the headlights to unlock the entrance gate. A rifle hung over his shoulder, grenade-launching attachment still in place. He got back into the jeep and drove up behind the BMW, went back, and locked the gate.

Whistling, he walked toward the front door, and I fell in behind him for two short strides before poking my rifle barrel into his spine. "*Alto!* Drop the rifle."

He seemed to stagger from shock; the rifle slipped from his hand, clattered to the ground. I jerked the ivory-handled Colt from its holster and dropped it beside the rifle. "We're going around back," I told him, and when we reached the rear entrance I made him unlock the door.

From there, I prodded him to the edge of the swimming pool and told him to strip. By then he was blubbering, but I remembered Joe Milton's corpse, the bloody body of Chela. "You know why you're here," I told him. "I warned you, *chingado*."

Shoved him into the pool.

He came up gasping and floundering—a poor swimmer, as I suspected. Every time he tried to reach shallow depth I jabbed him with the rifle. Soon his lungs had more water than air and the corpulent body began to sink. I watched the surface become calm, waited a few minutes to make sure he wasn't going to bob up, and then I gathered his boots and clothing and went to the house. Before going in, I collected his rifle and pistol and carried everything into the master bedroom. After folding his clothes neatly I laid the bundle on the bed, replaced the pistol in its holster, and hung it over a chair.

I carried his rifle downstairs and set it in an open gun cabinet. Beside it a large metal chest was unlocked. In it I found a dozen blocks of C-4 plastic, fuses, and a box of detonators, all identical to what I'd found on the Seabee's engine. There was an 8-power scope, five grenades, and several hundred rounds of rifle and pistol ammo. I took four blocks of explosive, some detonators, and a coil of fuse and put them in a kitchen bag.

From the rear door lock I extracted Jaramillo's keys and laid them on the kitchen table. Then I left, leaving the door ajar.

As I crawled over the fence I had a last look at the free-form pool. Its surface was flat as polished glass.

All the way home I tried to keep from thinking of what still faced me. Blood loss and emotion drained my strength, but Jaramillo wasn't a factor. I'd finished him as casually as stepping on a roach. But the death of Chela overwhelmed me.

I stowed the explosives in an ice chest outside my kitchen door, returned my rifle to its cache, and dialed the police for help.

I fed the dogs and locked them in a bedroom, went back to the sofa. The raucous klaxon of a police ambulance speared the night.

THIRTY

A T THE *CLÍNICA* they stitched my leg wound, stuck me with antibiotics, and gave me an overnight bed. In the morning I told *comandante* Elpidio I knew no more about the attack than he did and declined to speculate on the bomber's identity. "Maybe someone who doesn't like *gringos*."

"Like *Capitán* Jaramillo?"

I shrugged.

"He drowned in his pool last night."

"Drunk?"

"Possibly. You didn't like each other."

"That's no secret."

"I'm sorry about Chela."

"So am I." God knows I was sorry. Guilt gnawed me with sharp ferret's teeth. I hadn't warned her of danger—perhaps because I was so accustomed to her presence—and by not keeping her from the house I'd let Chela come into harm's way. Jaramillo was her killer, but I could have prevented her death if I'd only given her the thought her love and loyalty deserved. Guilt would be with me forever, a constant rebuking companion.

Almost blindly I went to the funeral home and paid for her services and interment. Her widowed mother embraced and blessed me, and we wept together for a long time. That purged me enough to wander out into sunlight and locate a contractor willing to start home repairs that afternoon. Until the place was habitable I'd have to live aboard *Corsair*, so I cruised my boat from the marina to my pier and tied up across from the plane. I brought bedclothes from the house, food and drink, and moved aboard, letting the dogs join me.

The grenade blast had shredded the life-saving sofa and destroyed the radio, so I told the workmen to junk them along with other ruined furniture. I carried the ice chest aboard, unsure why I'd taken the C-4 from Jaramillo's place, but certain he wouldn't need it again. I might—if only to stun fish at sea.

I stowed the ice chest forward by the head where temperatures were normally stable; I didn't want nitro leaking from the C-4 blocks. Two drops could topple a tree.

From the shaded deck I watched workmen bring supplies and haul out debris, sipped Añejo, and reflected on the carnage that had become my companion ever since Amy sought me out in the café. I remembered her floppy violet boots, the thrust of her beautiful breasts under the T-shirt. Texas Terror. Bolivar High . . . How long ago it all seemed, so many bodies since then.

Vernon Saunders was still mobile though, and Luis Parra, wherever *he* was. They were the principals I needed to think about. Separately or together, they were responsible for Amy's murder—and by their agent, Jaramillo, the slaughter of Joe Milton and Chela.

Well, the chopper crew was finished, Jaramillo, too. But three for four weren't enough, and it would take Justice years to unravel and penetrate all the corporate shields Paul Diehl had established around the world. With an overnight flight, Saunders could take refuge in Paraguay or Bolivia, and I doubted the government's ability to nail Parra after trying for seven years. He had a private army guarding his *estáncia,* a fleet of mother ships, aircraft, and informants everywhere. But part of the time he lived and worked aboard *Solimar*, so that was the place to look for him.

If anyone knew the yacht's location it would be Vernon Saunders—safe in his River Oaks retreat, now that Amy had been disposed of. Except that no one is always completely safe. Not even a President.

I badly needed a change of scene, so I flew the Seabee over to Cancún and tied up to a buoy in front of one of the newer beach hotels. The cocktail hour was underway—in resort hotels it never formally begins or ends— and there was plaintive mariachi music, a table of hot canapés, and a planeload of American office girls wearing big Charro hats and colorful *serapes*, looking around for males while pretending they weren't.

There were half a dozen slim-hipped young Mexicans wearing flounced bolero shirts V-cut to the navel, adorned with Taxco silver rings, neck chains, and bracelets. Their tango trousers were tailored to display their sex, and most of them wore long curving sideburns and Valentino mustaches. One had a furry, long-tailed kinkajou draped over his shoulders and fed it morsels from the buffet. The entire contingent was available to either sex by night or week, and none was in danger of starving.

I was sipping Añejo at the long bar and watching my tethered plane swing slowly with the tide when a combo began a pulsing Afro beat and couples flowed to the small dance floor. A man in an embroidered *guayabera* bowed to one of the seated American girls, and they began to dance. His footwork was amazing, considering his elevator heels. The girl was taller, so she kicked off her shoes and danced barefoot. As they turned I glimpsed his face for the first time: Nestor Chavez, the Latino I'd seen in Houston. I felt my fingers clench the glass, then relaxed. He'd never seen me, didn't know who I was.

The number ended, and I saw him walk over to a patio table where he joined another man.

I'd seen him before, too: the grammatical young hood who ran Fancy Feathers, whose money I'd declined. He was well turned-out in a pastel leisure suit, sky blue Ascot at his throat. Chavez seemed to be encouraging him to pick out a girl and dance, but the hood shook his head. Chavez shrugged and left the table. I watched him select another partner and begin dancing. The hood sipped Coco Loco and surveyed the scene.

I gave the bartender twenty bucks to send an adulterated drink to the hoodlum, another twenty to say nothing about it.

The mickey hit in about five minutes. I saw his face whiten; he began gasping and doubled over clutching his belly. Chavez came off the dance floor, wasted time asking questions, and finally got a waiter to help him half-walk, half-carry the victim toward the men's room.

They were there so long, I decided to follow. The hood was on his knees in a stall, barking and retching. Chavez was washing his hands at a basin. He used a damp towel to get bits of foreign matter from his trousers.

Presently Chavez got his friend from the stall, and with one arm across his shoulders moved him to the elevators. Neither was paying attention to strangers, so I rode the elevator and got out with them on the sixth floor. Chavez walked the hood to the corner suite, and I returned to the bar. After a while Chavez appeared and resumed dancing. I took the elevator to the sixth floor and used a plastic card to open the suite.

Chavez had gotten him to the bedroom; the hood lay on his back snoring. I went through his pockets, found the billfold, and shook it out. Five thousand in cash, Texas driver's license in the name of Frank James Pirelli, and some Feathers business cards. There was an engraved card: Vernon O. Saunders and a smudged hand-written phone number beneath the name.

Half a dozen credit cards, four in Pirelli's name, two billable to Fancy Feathers. I decided Frank James Pirelli was living too comfortably, so I pocketed his billfold. He could replace the cash but replacing credit cards would be an annoyance.

Near his bed was an expensive steerhide valise with gold locks and trim, initialed FJP in gold. I thought Chavez might be sharing the suite, but I found no other luggage, and Pirelli's monogrammed shaving kit was the only one in the bathroom.

My bladder was full. I was preparing to use the toilet when a better idea occurred. Standing at Pirelli's bedside, I watered him down, and he was too deep in sleep to notice.

Going through his valise, I found a nice-looking Walther 9mm automatic. The bluing was intact, magazine full. I shoved it in my hip pocket and was getting ready to leave when I heard the hall door open.

Spinning around, I saw a maid enter, arms loaded with towels. She took them to the bathroom, and through the hinge crack I saw her come to the bedroom. She'd been planning to turn down the bed covers, but when she saw Pirelli's condition, her face screwed up. She spat on him, cursed, and strode out. Another ugly *Americano*.

I waited until the hall was quiet, left the suite. When I got back to the patio bar, Chavez had paired off with a short blonde at a candlelit table where they were ordering dinner.

I took another table and ordered broiled *langosta*, a green salad, and a bottle of Paternina white.

Chavez and the giggly girl were holding hands and blowing covert kisses. I pointed him out to my waiter, said, "Find out what room number he signs," and tipped him ten.

When he returned with the winestand, he said the patron was paying cash. "Is there a problem, *señor*?"

"He looks like a *ratero* who stole tourists purses in Guadalajara. He was forced to leave the city."

"Thank you, *señor*. I'll remember should there by any difficulty."

I was cutting into my *langosta* when I noticed Chavez rise. He lingered a few moments exchanging sly repartee with the blonde, then began strolling toward the men's room. I was there ahead of him, and as he pushed the second door inward I smashed it against him, hearing the crunch of bone. He yelped and sprawled on the tile floor. I dragged him further in and stuck Pirelli's credit cards in his shirt pocket, placed the empty billfold in his left hand. Taking Pirelli's Walther from my hip pocket, I transferred it to his.

The shattered shades were strewn near a spreading pool of blood. The kick I gave his thigh wouldn't improve his *salsa*.

I went back to my table and continued my meal. The blonde was getting unhappy and starting to feel she'd been stood up. I saw her beckon to the waiter and point at the men's room. With a nod the waiter set off. He didn't come back directly but spoke agitatedly to the maitre d'. Presently I noticed a gathering of hotel people and guests outside the men's room. Two pool lifeguards appeared with a stretcher and by the time they carried Chavez out, police had arrived to organize the scene. Finally, everyone moved toward the exit, and I started on the salad.

My waiter came over, bent low and whispered, "A very strange occurrence. Apparently the man—his name is Chavez—slipped on the floor and damaged himself." He glanced around. "He was found with the possessions of another person."

"Some people never learn," I remarked. "Amazing."

The blonde looked upset and very angry. I sipped wine and strolled over. "Pardon me, are you American?"

"I am, and I don't—"

"Please—I'm not trying to pick you up. But I noticed your companion was evacuated and you seemed distressed."

"Well . . . I am. If I'd known I was going to have to pay, I'd have ordered tortillas and a coke. Instead, there's this huge steak for two-bordelaise . . ." She seemed ready to cry.

"Don't worry about the check, Miss, I'll take care of it—as a fellow American—no strings."

"That's very nice of you."

"I heard someone saying the fellow was a purse snatcher who preys on tourists."

She looked bewildered. "Nestor—that's his name—bragged he lived on a big yacht and spent his time cruising the Caribbean."

"Those confidence men will say anything. Did he mention the yacht's whereabouts?"

"No—but he said it was coming soon to pick him up. The creep even offered to take me on board for dinner."

"Well, no sense waiting for that. Enjoy your meal."

I worked things out with the waiter and saw one of the local dancing boys slide into the chair vacated by Chavez. The blonde didn't object.

Unless Chavez was simply running his mouth to impress her, *Solimar* was back in the Caribbean, and I began to grasp his role. Chavez was the jobber who scouted around and visited wholesalers, took narcotics orders, and had them filled. More and more, the yacht seemed like a factory ship. Operating on the high seas, it was immune to search or seizure; the helicopter picked up raw materials and delivered refined coke.

I wondered what kind of play there'd be between Pirelli and Chavez when Frank learned the Mexican had been found with his billfold and credit cards—but not the five-thousand cash. It would annoy me, I reflected, but five Gs to Pirelli were like five bucks to anyone else.

It was too late to fly back to Cozumel, so I took a hotel room for the night, and in the morning as I was checking out I saw Chavez arrive by taxi. His face was heavily bandaged, and he limped badly as he climbed the hotel's entrance steps. I didn't think he'd seen me when I slammed the door against his face, but I kept my face turned from him as I paid my bill.

On the sand, I negotiated with a beach boy to row me out to my plane, looked back, and saw the blonde sitting alone at a patio breakfast table. Her face wore a mournful expression, and I suspected she'd gone through shock when the young Mexican asked prior payment for companionship.

I was getting into the rowboat when two men came down on the beach. Chavez was one, grotesque in his bandages, the other, Pirelli, looking pale and weak. He glanced at me, spoke sharply to Chavez, and looked back at me again. He shaded his eyes, and his mouth opened as though he couldn't believe what he saw. Ignoring him, I told the rower to approach the leeward side of the plane.

I started the engine, and as the plane swung seaward I saw Pirelli still staring at me while Chavez limped back to the hotel.

I took off into a gentle breeze, flew low over the hotel, and banked for home. Time to call Montijo and find out whether I was still a fugitive charged with the murder of Amy King.

THIRTY-ONE

ONTIJO WAS SAYING , "Jack, it would be more than slightly helpful if you had some idea who actually killed the girl."

"I don't know names but I have to assume they worked for Frank Pirelli, and the order came from Saunders."

"Best you can do?"

"It's better than anything you guys developed. So I'm off the hook?"

"You're clear, but Sensinich is yelling about the entry job you pulled to photograph the stuff. He's worried the evidence is tainted."

"You haven't got the evidence yet. What I sent you proves evidence exists."

"So—where's the evidence?"

"Stashed in the safe under Paul Diehl's desk in Miami. Parmenter's murder is bound to worry Parra and Saunders. They know Diehl and Parmenter kept books and accounts, and they'll want to recover them. Maybe you can get there first—have the Miami office use a search warrant." When he said nothing, I said, "Or is that asking too much?"

"Unless you believe in miracles."

"Not since I was ten. Well, that's your problem, right? Pirelli's not in Houston. I came across him in Cancún with a *chicano* creep named Nestor Chavez who was cozy with Saunders in Houston. According to Chavez, the *Solimar* will be in these waters fairly soon. If you could get our Coast Guard or the Mexicans to board her, you might find a good-sized drug lab. Maybe Luis Parra."

He whistled. "How the hell do you get that kind of info?"

"By not sitting on my ass behind a desk. By moving around and asking questions. That's how it's done."

"Parra, eh? I'll check it out." His voice softened. "Sorry about your housekeeper. Your own luck seems to be holding."

"Yeah. I was expecting another try—but not the way it came."

"I'll level with you—I doubt I'll be able to have the yacht boarded unless it comes into U.S. waters. If not, the regional supervisor would have to be persuaded, then he bucks it up to the interdepartmental committee in Washington. The Coast Guard would have to agree, and if we ask the Mexicans then State has to consult the Mexican ambassador, and it all goes back to Mexico City, then Vera Cruz, and pretty soon everyone in the Caribbean knows what's going down."

"So nothing's changed."

"You don't *know* the boat's cookin' coke."

"Under your procedures the only way anyone will ever know is when the boat rusts down to the waterline. I love you dedicated office workers."

After paying for the call I left the *Centro Telefónico* and sat in my jeep, staring out at the water. I was going to miss Chela, miss her more than I wanted to admit. She hadn't played games with me as Amy had, although I'd thought that in time Amy would have leveled with me . . . but there was no point in speculating. I was sorry about Amy's life, sorrier about the way she'd died. So needless . . . so senseless . . . I'd never see those incredible lavender eyes again.

My hand tightened on the steering wheel.

Saunders had given her some good times, but he'd exploited her and ended her life. I'd always remember him going to her in the pool and . . . I started the engine and drove away.

THE HOUSE REPAIRS were progressing. Another day and walls, ceiling, and woodwork would be restored. Two coats of paint and the place would be habitable—except that the paint would stink from its fish-oil base. But I was in no hurry to move back in. Without Chela it was going to be very lonely. Haunted.

Unless Melody returned. And I didn't want her back until danger ended. Within a few days I'd lost two women I cared for, and I had to be sure Melody wouldn't be the third.

But with Saunders playing out his schemes in Houston and Parra cruising his yacht in the Caribbean I was still a target.

According to Chavez, *Solimar* was to stop at Cancún long enough to pick him up. Pirelli, too. A sea voyage would speed their healing. So all I had to do was wait for the yacht to make Cancún.

What then?

I'd wiped out their helicopter . . . why not the yacht as well?

I went to my boat and got C-4 plastic from the cooler, stripped off the blocks' protective wrapper, and molded two nine-inch cone-shaped charges from the puttylike explosive. After setting electric detonators in the nose of each shaped charge, I wired them into acid-copper timers and strapped nine-volt batteries to each. As I'd learned in the SEALS, the cone shape focused explosion so that most of the force came from the base of the hollow charge. The penetrating blast was greater than an artillery shell.

I placed the charges back in the ice chest and climbed on deck. Plenty of daylight remaining. I untied the Seabee's bow line and got aboard, took off, and flew toward Cancún, gaining altitude until I leveled off at eight thousand feet.

With binoculars I began scanning, searching the northeast quadrant along a fifty-mile course, well off the Yucatan peninsula.

At cruising speed I flew north for twenty minutes, retracing south for another twenty. Below on the light green sea were fishing boats, a few sailing craft, and a large cruise vessel setting out from Cancún for an overnight stop at Cozumel. But no sea-going yacht.

If and when *Solimar* reached Cancún, it would either anchor offshore or tie up at one of the deepwater buoys. If the stop was only to pick up Chavez and Pirelli, the yacht wouldn't stay long. Its chopper could bring the men in a few minutes, or they could cover the distance in a lighter. Once the yacht was underway, there was nothing I could do to it. I had to catch it dead in the water.

I thought of these and other factors, checked the gas gauge, and saw the level getting uncomfortably low. There was enough fuel for another ten minutes search before I had to head home—and I didn't like dead-stick landings.

After completing the northern leg, I turned south and flew farther to the east, making a crescent sweep that would bring me on course for Cozumel.

I passed through a bank of clouds, rested tired eyes, and when I looked down again I made out something in the far distance that looked like a cruise ship from the bow wave.

Banking toward it, I climbed and found cloud cover. Then, free of clouds, I focused my binoculars on the vessel, and as we closed I saw its gleaming white length and the distinctive helipad amidships. The flag was Liberian.

More clouds. When I broke clear I was beyond the yacht, and to make identification positive I dropped to two thousand feet and approached from astern until I could read the name.

Solimar.

Banking southwest, I set course for Cozumel. The yacht was heading toward Cancún, and at present speed would make harbor in four to five hours.

I had a busy night ahead.

THIRTY-TWO

T HE GAS GAUGE showed close to empty when I touched down a hundred yards off my pier. As I taxied toward it, I could see through the twilight a figure standing near the end.

Wipers cleared spray from the windshield, and I made out the face of Melody West. She was waving at me. I gunned the engine then cut it, coasting to where she could toss out line.

I climbed onto the pier and she came into my arms. Our lips joined and her body fitted against mine. After a while she murmured, "Surprised?"

"I guess I lost track of time." Touching her forehead I let my fingers trail through her hair. "Did you—lose?"

"I *won*." She smiled happily. "Aren't you proud?"

"Exuberant."

She gestured at the house. "Redecorating for me?"

I helped her aboard the boat, and as I told her what had happened her tanned cheeks paled. She pulled up my trouser leg and touched the bandage gently. "You could have been killed. Poor you."

"Poor Chela."

"Yes, poor Chela. I'm so very sorry. But now everything's going to be all right, yes?"

I looked at my wristwatch. "I'm taking the boat to Cancún, and I'm not sure you'd be safe while I'm gone. So take the jeep and find a hotel for the night."

"What's so important about Cancún."

I took her hand and explained about Saunders, the yacht, and Luis Parra. "They're responsible for Paul's death and Carlos's. And they've had a foolproof system for manufacturing and distributing narcotics. That sea-going lab is probably responsible for the deaths of hundreds, the ruin of thousands. It's invulnerable to the law, but something has to be done."

"But—why you?"

"Look, honey, I've got to get going." I drew her to her feet and pointed at the pier. "See you tomorrow."

She drew her hands from mine. "I'm going with you." Her mouth had a stubborn set. "We have to share things."

"Cast off the lines."

"LOVE ME?" SHE lay beside me on the narrow bunk and kissed the point of my chin.

"Yes." The wheel was tied on course. Running lights on we cruised the dark sea.

"You'll marry me?"

"In due course."

"When's that supposed to be?"

"When things settle down—when you're at least partly educated." I kissed her forehead. "Your mother won't like it."

"She doesn't like lots of things. I didn't like Larry, but that didn't stop her making a fool of herself. Sort of evens up—except that I'm not being foolish." She stretched, arching her body. "Besides, I had a birthday three days ago so now I'm an adult."

"Welcome to the club." I swung my legs off the bunk. "Someone's got to run the boat." I looked at my wristwatch.

"I'm afraid—for you."

"Just do what I told you." I climbed up on deck and adjusted course. The current was stronger than I'd thought, but I could see distant lights now, beachfront hotels. I pointed them out as she took the helm. "Hold steady."

I lugged diving gear to the stern and went below to pull on dark trunks and T-shirt. Then I carried up the ice chest with the shaped charges. Underneath the yacht, in darkness, I would need all my gear. I checked each item again.

Melody called, "Something big over there—and moving."

I put the glasses on it and saw *Solimar.* The big yacht was well out from the buoys, and it was anchoring. In deep water.

"Okay," I said, "point for the stern."

"Aye, aye, sir." Looking back she smiled at me. "You'll be careful?"

"I'm always careful."

"But sometimes not careful enough."

I fitted the charges into a bully bag and strapped an underwater compass on my wrist. Melody said, "How can you be sure those things won't explode before you're safe?"

"Nothing's certain—but I'm reasonably sure."

"Have you used acid fuses before?"

"Often. A very simple principle, honey. The sulfuric's in a glass tube. When the tube's crushed the acid starts eating copper wire. Dissolving the wire releases a spring. That closes the battery circuit to the detonator. It explodes and so does the plastic. *Boom!*"

She shivered.

I said, "I'm depending on you to hold position, because I'll be swimming by compass, and I want to find this boat where I left it." I studied the yacht again. "About a hundred yards off the port quarter." I handed her the binoculars. "Understand triangulation?"

"Not really," she said, so I explained the principle.

The yacht's screws had been shut down. *Solimar* swung on its hook, bow to the current. By the time we covered the last mile it would be dead in the water. Then I could get to work.

Melody said, "You're very brave, love, and very crazy. Just remember we have a long and fantastic future together—with loads of children. There's a dynasty to found, so you have to get back—understand?"

"Yeah."

"How deep will you go?"

"Oh, thirty feet for the round trip. I figure to blow her open about ten feet below waterline."

She gestured ahead. "They've turned on deck lights."

"Festive spirits. Decadent old Rome, eh? And me the Vandal at the gate."

"Don't joke about it—*I* can't."

"Just stay the hell on course."

Plumbers tape, knife—oh, oh, flashlight. I got the black rubber-covered light from the cabin and added it to the rest of my gear. I already had on diving watch and compass. Fins, weight belt, gloves, BC, tank . . . I fitted regulator to tank, and the gauge needle zoomed to 2800 psi. Perfect. I purged the regulator, spat on my face mask, and coated the inside to prevent fogging.

Melody said, "I think maybe you should take over now, captain."

We were about three hundred yards astern. *Solimar* was lighted more brightly than any Love Boat. Vertical lights shined all around, brightening the depths. If anybody looked down, they could probably spot me working on the hull.

But this was a pleasure port, no reason for the yacht to mount security alert.

"By the way," I said, "the shotgun's in the overhead rack. Know how to use it?"

"I hope I do—I've shot skeet and trap since I was nine."

"But not lately."

"Who can forget?"

I pointed at the yacht. "If you see any shooting and my yellow tank pops up, you get the hell out of here. Because if that tank becomes visible I'll be dead. Don't linger."

"Hell I won't—I couldn't abandon you."

"Those are my orders."

"Fuck you," she said in a steely voice.

I grinned at her. "I'd like that—and I'm counting on a lot of it. But I'm not marrying an undisciplined brat."

"Chauvinist."

I blew her a kiss. "I'll see you later. Now—half throttle and two degrees left rudder. That's right. About fifty yards more. Okay, as she goes, clutch neutral."

I stood behind her and put my right arm around her breasts. With my left I pointed at the shore beacon. "That's one triangulation point, the yacht's bow staff is the other." I checked my wrist compass with the binnacle card. A true bearing of six degrees, reciprocal one eighty-six for the homeward leg.

Turning, she stood on tiptoes to kiss me, and her cheeks and eyes were wet. "You crazy bastard," she said huskily. "If you don't come back I'll kill you."

We both laughed, breaking the tension, and I said, "That's a threat I can't ignore. The current's parallel to shore, so keep pointing into it."

"You get your ass back here, mister," she blurted, and hugged me tightly.

I lowered my gear onto the dive platform, sat down, and donned fins, backpack, B.C. weight belt, and knife. The tape was in the net bag with the explosives. I tightened the flashlight lanyard around my wrist. Because of the yacht's underwater lighting, I probably wouldn't need it—but I might. What I didn't tell Melody was how much of a hazard the lighting would be. I hadn't planned on it—hadn't even thought of the possibility. The side of the yacht was thinner than the heavily sheeted bottom and easier to penetrate. But from the side I could be seen. Under the bottom I'd be invisible, but my two charges weren't enough to kill the yacht. To make certain I'd have to run the risk.

She handed me my mask and I put it on, clamped my teeth on the regulator mouthpiece, and checked my wrist compass a final time. The radium dial and needle showed my course. I set time-elapse on my watch and slipped off the platform into black water.

At thirty feet I established neutral buoyancy and kicked around until I faced the compass heading. Arms trailing by my sides, I began swimming toward target.

THIRTY-THREE

A NIGHT DIVE is always eerie, especially when you're alone. Without gravity, up is the same as down, and lacking visual references the senses can become disoriented. The rise of air bubbles is the only reliable signal, and you consult them when in doubt.

But I had the dial of my wrist compass to point my way, the depth gauge kept me horizontal to the surface, and I concentrated on them, suppressing other concerns.

I'd gone about halfway when I saw a dim glow ahead—*Solimar's* girdle of light. Directionally I was okay, and the depth gauge showed a steady thirty feet. Pressure about 2600 psi. I was using too much air so I regularized breathing, taking slow, deep breaths. I'd have to limit air bubbles while I worked, lest their breaking surface attract attention.

Around me I could see nothing. There could have been sharks or 'cuda four feet away and I wouldn't have noticed. Elapsed time under three minutes. Ahead the glow increased, and it reminded me of an etched-glass dance floor I'd once seen in Rio.

Rio. Melody would know Rio. Perhaps we'd visit Copacabana together, Ipanema, Pan do Azucar—fly to Iguassu and view the falls by moonlight . . .

My mind was wandering when it shouldn't. This was a life-threatening situation, and I needed full concentration to complete my mission and survive.

The air bubbles seemed to be rising on a slant, meaning I was swimming at an angle. I leveled off and the next exhalation rose vertically. Good.

I didn't need to check my compass heading—the glow ahead was all too distinct—and soon I began noticing fish nearby. Small ones. No large ones wanted.

Vision cleared, and I saw the rudder, the motionless twin screws. White paint ended slightly below waterline, and from there down red anti-fouling paint, as expected.

I went under the rudder and rose until I could grasp the keel, moved forward about twenty feet. Riveted construction on the underside meant plates too thick for spot welding. The charges might penetrate, but they might not. So, leaving the keel, I moved slowly to port, and when I was at the hull bulge I looked up. The light was strong.

Just above the bottom seam I found a metal guy hole protruding about two inches. That meant internal reinforcement, so I went forward another yard and began placing charges, using plumbers tape to hold them to the skin. Luckily the hull blocked current from me as I fastened down the cone-shaped explosives a few feet apart. If only one fuse worked, its detonation would set off the other charge almost instantaneously making two torpedo-sized holes in the hull.

I was getting ready to crush the fuses when I saw chains of tiny bubbles descending around me. Bullets. They were firing at me from above.

A bullet hit my tank, gave off a slight *ping*, and I crushed the fuses. Another bullet glanced from my head, but it lacked energy to penetrate. One struck my compass, shattering the glass. I bled air from the BC and dropped under the hull. I was breathing fast—too fast. Mustn't panic. Glass had cut my hand, and little whorls of blood rose. I pulled on gloves, checked my watch, and kicked down to fifty feet. Even from there I could hear clanging noises above.

My ears hurt so I blew tubes, equalizing pressure, puffed a little air into the BC, and headed toward where I thought *Corsair* would be. A five-minute swim would cover the distance, and if I surfaced off course, I still had whistle and flashlight to attract Melody's attention.

Of course, there was a chance the chopper would attack, while a diver removed the charges.

I wondered if there was a bomb-disposal volunteer in the crew. He had twelve minutes to do the job, and I wished I'd set the fuse for only five. Glancing up, I saw light move across the dark roof of the sea. The yacht was searchlighting, looking for me, and they'd notice *Corsair* a hundred yards away.

I tried swimming faster but my left thigh was aching badly. I turned the flashlight and saw the tip of a bullet embedded. It came out easily but blood flowed, and I stopped long enough to cover the wound with water, then swam on.

At four minutes from the yacht I slanted up to ten feet, swam another half-minute, and slowly surfaced. The first thing I saw was the chopper's searchlight playing over the water. It showed *Corsair*, too, about thirty yards away.

Down again, I swam as fast as I could toward the far side of my boat. By then, the chopper was hovering fifty feet off the stern. No way I could reach the diving platform unobserved, so I made for the shadowed side, dropped the tank and pulled off my fins. The rotors were beating too loudly for Melody to hear my call, so I blew the whistle three short blasts and clung to the gunwale. Moments later a rope ladder dropped over the side and I saw her face, shotgun barrel beside it.

From the chopper a burst splintered the deck around her feet. I ducked back, but unhesitatingly Melody shouldered the shotgun and swung toward the light. She fired three times very quickly and the searchlight went out. Silhouetted against the lighted yacht, the chopper looked like a giant moth. It veered as though wounded and began sliding from the sky.

She watched it, hand over mouth until it hit the water.

"Good shooting," I called. "Now get us the hell out of here!"

In the dark water men were yelling. The rotor blades were all I could see of the chopper, then they were gone. *Corsair* lurched forward as Melody hit the throttle. I looked at my watch, picked up binoculars, and turned them on the yacht. Crewmen were on the forward deck, and I could see the hook rising from the sea. Maybe they were going to try to beach it.

But I saw no evidence of divers where I'd set the charges. And only a couple of minutes to go.

I limped to the chart drawers, got out a pint of Añejo and took a long, long pull. "Hey," she said through chattering teeth, "how about *me*?"

I handed her the bottle and took the wheel. She was shivering from nervous reaction, so I put my wet arm around her shoulders and drew her close. *Corsair* was pounding over low waves, spray dashing aft across the transom. At flank speed my boat was almost standing on its stern.

Time to glance at the compass and set course for Cozumel. Melody clung to me, sobbing. Kissing her I said, "You're wonderful—I admit it."

Her tear-stained face lifted. "You . . . really . . . think . . . so?"

"Absolutely—but you'll go into shock if you don't drink more booze. Keep pulling on it—I'll get us back." I kissed her again. "My God, that was marvelous shooting!"

"Instinct," she said a little more calmly.

I looked at my watch. "Just about now," I said, and pointed aft.

Solimar was underway and starting to turn when a fountain erupted below the port side, thrusting water high above the radar mast. The detonation was thunderous even at our distance, and I saw Melody's shocked face. As we watched, the yacht began canting to port. Deck lights went out, then running lights, but we could see its bulk silhouetted against the shore lights.

It was still knifing the water, turning as it settled lower and lower. I saw the next detonation before I heard the blast over the water. Half the upper deck lifted and peeled aft. A vicious blast shook the hull like paper—tanks of ether and acetone letting go. The shock wave whipped past, the sound nearly deafening. I opened my mouth and swallowed fast, too late to avoid pain.

We were a mile away when I saw the last of it: a series of huge foaming bubbles that ruptured and spread until there was nothing to break the dark horizon. Some of the topside crew might survive, but not the below-decks chemists, the drug-makers.

I drew a blanket around Melody's shoulders and slowed to cruising speed. "How do you feel?"

"Better. Maybe a little drunk."

"You're with friends."

"But I'm on curfew—eleven o'clock. What about mother?"

"She'll have to find her own friends. You're staying with me."

Her laugh was strained, but more normal than I had a right to expect. "You mean—all night long?"

"Uh-huh. As planned."

"And I never guessed." For the first time she noticed the tape across my thigh, the cuts on my hand. With a little cry she began kissing them. Finally she said, "All that shooting—I knew they'd hit you."

I fingered the top of my head, found a blood clot. It wasn't big enough to bandage. The sea air would dry it before we were home. "Anyway," I said, "results were worth it."

"I still can't believe I shot down a . . . a helicopter."

"Believe it," I told her. "Saving your life—and mine."

"I know . . . but . . ."

"Have another drink."

She did and passed the bottle to me. I had another pull and left some. Her skin was warm again, blood pulsing through her veins. My future wife was not going into shock. "Take the wheel," I said, "and hold course."

I tossed the rest of the demolitions gear over the side—in case anyone came looking—and returned the shotgun to its overhead rack. Tomorrow I'd dig bullets from the decking, fill in the holes.

Turning on the radio, I found the Mérida station—marimba music embellished by a deep-throated Vera Cruz harp. We listened for a while, and then Melody said, "I think that's the Cozumel beacon over there."

"So it is." I made course correction. "The next pier you see will be ours."

"I like that. Never more to roam."

"Ummm. When does the team start training?"

"Two weeks."

"You'll have a busy year."

"So long as we're together, it'll go fast."

I began pulling tape from my thigh. Hair came with it and I winced. The shallow wound was blue. I poured Añejo on it and covered the spot with a bandage.

She said, "Think what you did tonight—sank a big goddamned ship. Just like that. Blooey!"

"Couldn't have done it without you, precious. And I certainly wouldn't have come out alive if you hadn't blasted the chopper. Call it a combined operation."

While she steered I stood behind her, arms circling her body, feeling closer to her than ever before. What we'd survived gave hope of a future together. Just a few more things to do.

In the distance I could see the outline of my plane, the straight thrust of my pier.

Corsair glided smoothly over the calm dark sea.

WE SLEPT ON the boat, and in the morning heard radio accounts of the yacht's sinking. None of the few survivors identified themselves before leaving Cancún, nor was it known whether there were any victims. Port authorities speculated the explosion resulted from failure of a boiler valve, but noted that the cause of the sinking would probably never be known since the yacht sank in deep water half a mile from shore. The helicopter was not mentioned.

"How convenient," Melody said as I switched off the receiver. "No names, no interest, no nuthin'. I suppose the police were paid to ignore things."

"If the owners weren't interested in the incident, why should the cops work overtime?"

"Sounds very Brazilian. Now, how shall we spend the day?"

"We'll take the boat down the coast to a beach where we can swim and sun by ourselves. I'll spear something for lunch, and we'll have beer and light wine."

"Perfect. For two whole weeks."

213

I looked shoreward. "Well, not quite, honey. Two days and I'm putting you on the plane for Miami."

"Why, for God's sake? Haven't we earned time together?"

"We have," I admitted, "but . . ."

"Then,"—her dark eyebrows drew together—"you must be going somewhere without me."

"Houston."

THIRTY-FOUR

I WAS BECOMING familiar with Houston airport. From a pay phone I called Saunders's office, said I was Billy Bob Buxton, a potential client from Shreveport, and asked for an appointment with Mr. Saunders.

"I'm afraid I can't make one, sir. Not at this time."

"Humm. Vern travelin'?"

"I really can't say, sir."

"Well, is he to home ailin' or sumthin'?"

"I'm sorry, but I have no information on that. Perhaps Mr. Rose could discuss business with you."

"Doubtless. But it's Vern I'm needin'. Y'see Paul Diehl told me he was just the man for me. Confidential, y'know."

She thought it over. "You might call back in, oh, two or three days."

"He'll be in town then?"

"So I . . . ah . . . understand."

"Thanks, sugarpie. I'll call again. 'Bye now."

I hung up and dialed Saunders's unlisted telephones. A *chicana* maid answered the second, said he wasn't home. In Spanish, I asked if he was out of town.

"I think so."

"How long?"

"Since some days ago."

I loved the Hispanic concept of time; flexible as a rubber band. "Can we narrow it down?"

"Please—you ask his office."

Short of torture, I wasn't going to get more from her, so I gave up.

215

Change clinked in my hand. What the hell, why not call Montijo?

When he answered he said, "Been in town long?"

"Why?"

"That yacht we were talking about met an unfortunate accident off Cancún."

"Unfortunate?"

"Well, an accident . . . or was it? Occurred to me you might have had a hand there."

"Matter of fact I did—but that's confidential."

"You're a heavy hitter. God!"

"There were survivors but nobody got their names. Saunders doesn't seem to be around Houston, so it might be he was aboard. Any ideas?"

"His jet flew out of here two days ago."

"Was he on board?"

"We don't keep that kind of tab on him—the plane showed up missing one morning, that's all."

"Splendid. One final item—did the Miami office recover what I stashed in Diehl's safe?"

He coughed. "I understand they're working on it. Or will be."

"Beautiful. Don't be surprised if someone else gets there first."

"I'm all out of surprises, but here's one for you: Mrs. Parmenter has been fished up in Biscayne Bay."

"She did dangerous things, stretched too far."

"Yeah. She'd been knocked around and tortured." He paused. "How much did she know?"

"Not enought to help them—they must have figured she killed Larry and was holding out."

"Well, that's police business."

"Not entirely. Plenty of cocaine cowboys available to handle Cheryl. But someone gave the order."

"Saunders?"

"Or Parra."

"Listen, Jack, I've got a Washington call coming in—stop by, buy you a drink."

"Rain check," I said and hung up.

Not much satisfaction in Houston, and in Miami Cheryl Parmenter hadn't had long to enjoy her inheritance. So a measure of justice had been meted out to the murderess. But I didn't like her being tortured.

I took a deep breath and decided to check with General Aviation Operations.

Milton's T-card got cooperation. I asked for the last flight plan filed by

Saunders's pilot, and while the clerk was looking I decided there were three likely destinations: Colombia, Cancún, or Miami. The flight plan showed Miami.

As I left the counter I wondered whether Saunders had gone there to claim the ledgers and documents I'd put in Diehl's safe. If he found them, would that satisfy Parra, or would the drug king want custody? Whoever possessed them had leverage over the other.

I knew only one Miami contact of Saunders—Delores Diehl. But as far as I'd been able to establish, she'd had no guilty knowledge of Paul's transactions—or Saunders's. Still—I'd seen her at Saunders's office with Nestor Chavez, and Chavez was Parra's man . . .

Maybe Saunders was romancing Delores—she was attractive enough, and she had enticing ways. But Saunders had killed Amy . . .

Suddenly I wished I hadn't sent Melody back home.

THE PAN AM jet reached Miami in the early evening. I telephoned the Diehl residence, and when the houseman answered I asked for Melody, saying I was one of the diving team coaches.

"Miss Melody is out, sir."

"Back for dinner?"

"I can't say. Is there a number where she could call you?"

"Well, I'm at the airport en route New York. Please tell her Joe Milton called and I'll try later."

I stowed my bag in a locker and rented a car.

THE GROUNDS OF the Diehl estate were dark, but inside the house there were plenty of lights. Parked in the drive was an elongated Cadillac limousine. All I could see of the driver was the glow of his cigarette. Garage doors were closed, pool dark.

Keeping to the border shrubbery, I made a wide circuit around the house. In the dining room, dinner was underway. At the head of the table Delores was being served by the houseman, but from where I stood, foliage outside the window screened the rest of the table. And the guest who'd come by limousine. I wondered if Melody was with them.

Delores didn't seem her usual chatty self; her face had a strained expression, and her gaze focused on her plate. Doubtless she'd heard about Cheryl Parmenter's last swim; the news would depress anyone.

At the rear of the house an outside staircase led down from the second floor. Not a fire escape, but graceful railed access to pool, court, or garage, bypassing the first floor.

Keeping the house between me and the limousine, I crossed the lawn,

217

went up the staircase. As I began turning the door knob, I glanced to the right, and there in the corner of the room was Melody. She was sitting at a vanity buffing her nails, wearing nothing but pink panties. Rock music blaring.

I entered the corridor and went to her door.

In the mirror she saw me come in, shot to her feet, and turned. I put a finger to my lips and closed the door behind me.

She rushed to my arms and kissed me feverishly. "Lover, you've come for me? We're eloping?"

"Not tonight, sweet. God, you look adorable."

"Because I am. I got that screwed-up message from Thomas, so I've been expecting contact." She rubbed against me kittenlike. "What happened in Houston?"

"Dry well." I disengaged her arms. "Who's the dinner guest?"

"A Mr. Saunders—from Houston. Of course! You followed him here."

"Anyone with him?"

"I don't think so."

"Any idea *why* he's here? What they're talking about?"

She shook her head. "Want me to find out?"

"No. The guy is very bad news, honey, and I'm worried about your mother. She could end up like Cheryl Parmenter."

"How? I don't understand."

After explaining a few things, I said, "Cheryl didn't know where the ledgers are, and neither does your mother—but I do."

"So—?"

"Get some clothes on."

She kissed me again. "What an odd request. Then?"

"Go down and draw your mother out of the dining room."

"Then what?"

"I'll sort of sneak up on Saunders and cold-cock him."

"I suppose it's useless to ask you to be careful." She glanced at the ornate bed. "Time for a quickie?"

"Trade for an all night longie."

She slipped into sandals and pulled on a silk robe with Japanese designs. I scanned her shelves: floppy animals, dolls from around the world, souvenirs, and—a miniature baseball bat branded *Louisville Slugger*. I took it down and hefted it. Good solid hardwood—about right for the job. "Let's go."

We went down the main staircase in unison, and at the bottom, she walked toward one dining room entrance and I took the other. Looking around the doorjamb, I saw Melody whisper to her mother at the far end of the table. Saunders's back was to me.

Delores said, "Excuse me," and got up quickly. As she disappeared, I went up quietly behind the Houston visitor and whipped the bat hard against the back of his silver head. He pitched forward, chin flippig his plate onto the carpet.

Melody rushed in, followed by her mother. "Good job," Melody said.

"Get some rope, twine, or tape, honey."

Delores Diehl stared at Saunders, then me, and gasped, "What on earth's going on?"

THIRTY-FIVE

I SAID, "I'VE been chasing Saunders for a long time. Why did he come here?"

"By phone he said he just wanted to pay a social call—so I invited him to dinner. Then he began asking about some files of Paul's, saying he wanted them, had to have them."

"And didn't believe you had no knowledge."

She stared at me, eyes wide. "How did you know?"

"Cheryl was tortured and killed because they didn't believe her. You were next on the list."

"Oh, God!" She slumped into a chair.

Melody handed me a spool of nylon boat line and electrical tape. I pushed Saunders to the floor and bound wrists behind back, tied his ankles, and ran a snub line between them and his wrists while Melody taped his mouth. Delores gasped, "What are you going to do?"

"Haven't decided. The priority was protecting you."

"I don't know what to say."

"'Thank you' would be nice, Mother," Melody suggested.

Delores looked from me to her daughter then back again, and her eyes narrowed. "Is there something between you two?"

"Quite a lot," I said. "I'm afraid we've been deceiving you, Delores, but my intentions are basically honorable." I stood up. Saunders's wineglass hadn't spilled so I grasped it as Melody brought her mother's.

"*Melody!* How far has this gone?"

"All the way, Mom, and we're devoted to each other."

"Jack," she said furiously, "she's just a child, and if you've deflowered her that could be statutory rape."

"Mother," said Melody in a patient voice, "reconcile yourself," and handed her the glass. "This is one hell of a man, and I'm not letting him get away."

I touched my glass to Delores's and sipped. At my feet Saunders was beginning to stir.

Melody said, "Any ideas, champ?"

"His driver's outside. Try calling him in."

I stood to one side of the entrance while Melody opened the door and went partway down the steps. "Mr. Saunders wants you," she called, and came back in, leaving the door open.

I glimpsed a black suit, white shirt, and swung hard just above his belt. He snapped over clutching his belly. I laid the bat across the back of his neck, and he was out before he hit the tiles.

Stepping across him, Melody closed the door.

In his shoulder holster was a .38 Special. I pocketed it, trussed, and gagged him. The houseman came in and glanced at the unconscious chauffeur.

"Think nothing of it," I told him. "You saw nothing, heard nothing, know nothing. Right, Delores?"

My future mother-in-law swallowed. "Quite right. Thomas, these men were planning to harm me. Fortunately, Mr. Novak intervened."

"We're finally getting organized," I said. "Thomas, I'll need help getting these fellows outside."

"Certainly, sir."

I liked his reactions. Thomas seemed like a man who had seen a good deal of life and took things as they came. Not unlike myself.

Melody's fingers twined with mine. "Mother, the *least* you could do is thank my fiancé."

Her eyes studied me. "Thank you," she said. "Jack, you appear to be a man who knows how to accomplish things. Since it's come to this, I'll confess I'd rather have Melody with you than those young freaks and oddballs she used to bring around."

"I'll do my best to care for her, Delores. I haven't much to offer—strong back and willing hands—but we do get along."

"And her education . . . the Olympics?"

"As scheduled. We'll have lots of time for discussion but very little at the moment. Saunders there had a major role in your husband's murder, and he killed people I was fond of, so don't feel any pangs about him."

Thomas said, "I take it we're not calling the police, sir?"

"Not hardly."

Between us, Thomas and I carried the driver out to the limo and locked him in the trunk. As we walked back to the house Thomas said, "I suppose he won't suffocate in there."

"I don't think anyone cares."

Saunders was conscious and struggling when we picked him up. I said, "The hell with this," and untied his ankles. "Walk!" I jabbed the .38 in his spine.

We went out the back way, crossing the dark lawn past pool and tennis court to where Melody's Saber nosed the pier.

To Thomas I said, "That's all for now. Tell Miss Melody I'd like a word with her—and the keys."

He went back to the house, and by the time I'd maneuvered Saunders into the boat Melody was running up. As she handed me the keys, I said, "Get rid of the limo—leave it in some restaurant parking lot on the Causeway. Have Thomas take another car and bring you back."

"Whatever you say, love." She kissed me lengthily.

"Any private reaction from Mom?"

"Nothing verbal—but I think she's jealous."

"Do tell. Well, I'll be back after a while."

"Shall I keep dinner warm?"

"Just your bod." We kissed again, and I got down behind the wheel.

The huge engines started with an ear-numbing roar. Melody cast off lines, and I backed out from the pier, turning into Biscayne Bay. Not wanting to attract Marine Patrol attention, I held the Saber at twenty knots, cruising north between mainland and Miami Beach with its glittering hotels and condos. After ten minutes I slowed to turn through Haulover Cut, and we were in the Atlantic.

A mile offshore I stripped tape from Saunders's mouth and he spat, "Who the hell are you? What's going on?"

"I'm the turkey Paul Diehl hired to recover his lost coke. Along with Diehl, my captain was killed that day, and that's why you're here."

"That wasn't intentional—listen, I can square everything."

"Too late," I told him. "Through Amy, I offered you a chance to save yourself. Your response was killing her and framing me."

"So *that's* who you are! You couldn't stand that she was my woman." There was a sneer on his lips.

"I couldn't stand it that you killed her."

Waves higher now, smacking the hull. Spray drifted over the windshield, wetting us both.

Saunders blurted, "I can get you millions, Novak. I know where Diehl put all of Parra's money."

"Along with plenty of your own. But secrets are perishable. Kept too

223

long, they stink up the place." I glanced over the side. The waves were tipped with phosphorescence. A good night for catching dolphin, dipping shrimp.

"You and Parra figured the two widows had the ledgers and corporate papers, but they never did. You were going to work Delores over the way Cheryl got it, but Diehl's widow couldn't have told you anything. You see, I got there first."

"*You!*"

"Where's Luis Parra?"

His cheeks looked sunken. For the first time he realized he had nothing to trade.

"Parra," I repeated. "The last of the lot, probably the worst. Tell me where he is, and I'll let you live."

"I don't know—Colombia, probably." He wet his lips. "Unless he went down with the yacht."

"It went down pretty slow. There was time."

"You—*saw* it?"

"I didn't have enough explosive to blow a bigger hole, but I kept hoping you were aboard." Waves were breaking over the port bow. I turned the boat into the wind, feeling tired, dull. "I'm not a big important guy like you—never was, never really wanted to be. I worked for what I got, went to the Navy's trade school because tuition was free. I never had much money, so I'm unfamiliar with its lure. You talk millions, I want Parra."

He licked his lips. "In return for him, you'd let me go?"

"I didn't say that, Saunders. I said I'd let you live. You'll stand trial—what happens is up to the court."

He shook his head. "I couldn't do time. I never have—too late to try, anyway." He looked away. "Parra could be anywhere. I might be able to locate him if I liked your deal, but I don't. Find him yourself."

I knelt on the seat. "You shouldn't have killed Amy. You used her, cheated her—God knows all she did for you—and her life was never more than a mirage. Such beauty—"

"You're a fool," he said harshly. "She used you the way she used men all her life. I saw through her proposition—she was trading me to you for *her* freedom. Don't be a goddam romantic. She hired you, didn't she? Got you to find the plane, kept you and Diehl where the chopper could reach your boat." He struggled up on his elbows. "She arranged the episode."

"And spared me," I said leadenly. "I can't forget that. I don't care what her life had been, whether she loved you or not . . . We found something in

224

Cozumel . . . together." I looked away from him. Dark on the horizon was a tramp steamer, low in the Stream. No other lights around.

"For that you'll kill me?" His voice was tinged with fear.

Slowly I shook my head. "Not for Violet Eyes or Carlos—he was my captain, and a good man—or even the others. But because as the law goes, you're unassailable. You won't give me Parra and cop a plea because you'd have to confess other things. And without a confession, you'd walk."

The bow was turning. I spun the wheel and brought it back into the wind. Astern I could see the lights of Miami Beach, a string of golden dots against the darkness. An orange blur hung over the distant Miami skyline. The boat began to roll.

"You'd walk," I repeated, "and be available to men like Parra—his corruption's everywhere. But you'd go on, a respected citizen taking in clandestine millions and laughing at the rest of us chumps. There has to be a break in the chain, and it's going to be you. If I let you get away, I'd never sleep well again. I'll find Parra without your help."

"He'll find you, kill you," Saunders grated.

I shrugged. "I've done pretty well against the two of you. I sank the yacht, remember, and that interrupts production until he finds a new boat and rigs another processing lab."

"How did you know that?"

I bared my teeth. "Amy told me. Yes, Amy, ever-loyal to you. Laid it out for me, Saunders. How do you like it?"

He spat at me, but wind whipped away the spittle.

"So I can't let you get away, and that's why you're going to die."

"Be honest—you wanted Amy and I kept her from you. That's why you hate me."

"Maybe," I said, "and I'll have time to ponder who was right. On your feet."

"Why should I?"

"Because drowning is less painful than a bullet in the belly. Of course it's possible you're a strong swimmer. Every now and then they pick up a Cuban out here, or a handful of Haitians. You've got a chance."

Slowly he got up. I placed the .38 muzzle against his spine and untied his wrists. As I expected, he whirled around and tried to hit me, but I'd backed out of reach and he stood there, air whistling in his nostrils, wind whipping his silvery mane. His face was handsome and evil, and I realized how over-matched Amy had been.

"Over the side," I snapped.

"*Make me!*"

I fired. The bullet splintered the gunwale beside his hand. He yelled, jerking his hand away. I fired wide, and he bent over and rushed me. I stepped aside, the boat rolled and with a yell he pitched over the gunwale.

I didn't look for him. I shoved the throttles forward and turned in a wide circle, heading back to shore. The roar of the engines covered any sound there might have been from the dark water.

I DROVE THE Saber fast, not only for the feel of controlling a high-performance boat, but to keep my mind off Saunders and what he'd said. I came through Haulover Cut so fast I nearly swamped an outgoing fisherman, turned south, and cut speed as I neared the Diehl estate.

There was no one on the pier as the Saber glided alongside. I looped a line over the nearest bollard and snugged it, drawing the speedboat against the fenders. I secured a stern line and walked up the pier toward the lighted house.

A man stepped in front of me holding a MAC-10 submachine gun. The snout pointed at my belly.

THIRTY-SIX

A T FIRST I thought the gunman was Saunders's driver looking for his boss, but he was taller and less bulky than the man we'd locked in the trunk. "Freeze," he said. "What you doin' here?"

I held up my hands. "I was returning the boat."

"Yeah? Where you been?"

"At Mrs. Diehl's request I took a friend of hers to a hotel."

"What hotel?"

"Doral."

"What guest."

"I didn't ask and he didn't say. I just work here, man. Jobs don't come easy. You some new security guard? The lady didn't tell me."

He looked at me uncertainly. I said, "I'm off for the night, here's the boat keys." I jangled them in my upraised hand. "If I stole the boat would I be bringin' it back? Hey, be reasonable."

I was watching his eyes—and the gun. My fingers flicked the keys at him, and his gaze followed them. Instinctively he caught the keys, the MAC-10 wavered, and I kicked the wrist that held it.

He yelped, and the submachine gun disappeared in darkness. Before he could come at me I had the .38 in hand. "On your belly, sucker," I said, and as he got down I shoved the muzzle against the base of his skull. "One more hood tonight isn't going to ruffle me," I told him. "Looking for Saunders? He's swimming, but I don't think he'll make shore. Who brought you here and why?"

He swore.

"I'll waste ten seconds on you, no more." I drew the muzzle along his spine and dug it into the small of his back. "One shot makes you wheelchair for life. What's going on?"

For two seconds he thought it over. "Parra's in there," he gasped. "Jesus, man, don't cripple me—that's inhuman!"

"You're human?" I struck the back of his head with the barrel, and his body went limp. I searched for the MAC-10, spotted its cold glint, and picked it up. Full magazine, action cocked and ready. The cocaine cowboys' weapon of choice. I left its recent owner on the grass and bolted for the house.

Snaking along the foliage, I saw the dining room was empty. The gathering was in the living room. Seated near the far end were Thomas, the cook, Delores, and Melody. Facing them were two men I recognized, and both held guns on the family; one was Nestor Chavez, the other Frank Pirelli, the Galveston hood. A third man held no weapon. He lounged comfortably in a chair. He wore a thin moustache and a well-trimmed black goatee. Between them his teeth flashed as he spoke. Pockmarked cheeks and an old scar at the end of his jaw. For a Colombian he was lean and tall, and from the Freeport snatch I recognized Luis Parra.

He must be desperate to risk coming, I thought, and wondered if more than one bodyguard was posted outside. It wasn't like the drug king to travel with under a pair.

Slowly I eased around the corner of the house, and there in the drive was a long black Mercedes. Crouching, I thought it over.

There were three men terrorizing the family—and there was me. I was prepared to kill the invaders, but I didn't want them harming the captives in a sudden shoot-out. That risk was unacceptable, so I had to lower the odds.

I looked at the Mercedes. No one behind the wheel, but the windows were tinted and I could be wrong. So I approached low and from the rear, peered in, and saw the interior was empty. Cradling the MAC-10, I got out my handkerchief and rolled it cornerwise. Then I unscrewed the gas tank top and lowered the rolled fabric until I felt it slacken as it touched gasoline. I set the metal top on the handkerchief to hold it in place and got out a butane lighter.

Flame caught the lower end of the fabric, and I sprinted toward the house. I made it as far as the shrubbery before the gas tank blew.

Concussion shoved me against the shrubs, and as I knelt to aim, a wave of heat blew by. Flames erupted in the sky, their light nearly blinding as I sighted along the submachine gun's short barrel.

The front door burst open, and two men came running out. Chavez had the heavily bandaged nose, Pirelli was the other, and both had guns in their hands. I held low and squeezed the trigger. The MAC-10 chattered, vibrating in my grip. Pirelli went down, but Chavez staggered forward as though trying to reach the flaming car. I squeezed off another burst that blew his head apart.

I waited for Parra. Waited, but he didn't come.

Back to the window. He stood behind Melody, one arm around her neck, pistol against her temple.

Delores and the servants lay on the floor.

Parra was shouting, but I couldn't hear his words.

Melody's face was taut, eyes closed. She wasn't struggling.

Parra kicked Thomas, who got up and shuffled out of sight. I heard the back door open and close. Thomas was heading for the garage. Parra wanted a getaway car, and he was going to take Melody along.

A garage door went up, lights on. Thomas began backing a gray Audi from the stall. The burning limousine blocked the drive, so he drove toward my side of the house, saw me in the headlights. I put a finger to my lips and motioned him past.

Where the hell were the fire engines?

Thomas braked the Audi and got out, leaving the door open. I was counting on shooting Parra as he crossed the open space, or when he started getting into the car. Flames from the Mercedes lighted the scene more brightly than high noon. Half a chance, and I couldn't miss.

But animal cunning brought him out whirling Melody from side to side like a doll, screening his body. Behind them I could see Delores's ashen face. If I shot out the tires, that would stop him, but he was cornered and could easily kill Melody. Because of me she was in mortal danger.

As he forced her into the car I stepped into the open. "Parra," I shouted, "you want Diehl's ledgers. Leave the girl and I'll take you to them."

His head snapped around but he kept the pistol at her temple. "Drop your gun or I kill her."

"Kill her and I kill you—where's the profit?"

He was thinking about it, thinking fast because the throaty noise of fire engines was nearing.

"She goes with us—you drive," he shouted.

Lowering the submachine gun, I walked toward the car.

Melody's eyes were bright with fear. I said, "Stay cool. I'm giving the man what he wants."

Parra said, "She rides in back with me. I'll kill you both if you try to trick me."

"Straight trade," I said, and they got into the rear seat, the pistol never leaving Melody's head.

I got behind the wheel and fitted the MAC-10 between my knees, shifted, and drove past the sprawled corpses and the burning car. We were barely out of the gate when the fire engine bore down on us and I had to veer around it. Melody gasped. Parra snapped, "How far?"

"Diehl's office."

"You lie."

"Cheryl Parmenter didn't know, so she couldn't tell you."

I was watching him in the rearview mirror, thinking of a backward shot through the seat with my .38, but the bullet might deflect and he'd kill Melody reflexively. I turned onto the Causeway, heading into a long straight stretch, knowing that once I'd turned over the ledgers he'd kill us both. Through set teeth I said, "Take it easy, honey. If he hurts you I'll take off his balls."

Parra grunted. A moment later he said. "I know you—right? Yeah— you're the narc snatched me in Freeport." I could hear him chuckling. "This time I'm in charge, baby. You're smart, but I got the iron— remember that."

"That makes you plenty smarter," I told him. "Prove it by keeping the deal."

"I said I would, narc, and Luis Parra never lies."

"Good. Tomorrow you'll be back at the *hacienda*, all this forgotten."

I was talking to distract his attention from Melody because I saw one slim chance for our lives.

Ahead was a gap in the concrete railing marked by wooden barriers. Now or never.

I spun the wheel hard, and the Audi splintered wood as we sailed into space. I braced on the wheel and saw dark water rising.

The impact was stunning. I barely had time to fill my lungs before the car sank. Water rushed through open windows and I reached back to pull Melody forward, kicking open the door, hauling her out and up. I couldn't see Parra, didn't look for him. Thrusting Melody above me, I kicked for the surface, reaching it as a big air bubble broke beside us. The Audi was fully submerged. Supporting her head, I stroked for the shallows, saw cars stopping at the shattered barriers.

Her eyes were open, but she was unconscious, a bruise across her forehead. My feet struck mud, and I got her into my arms, staggered up the slanting bank. I laid her level and found she was breathing. Calling her name, I kissed her wet cheek, rubbed her palms, and wept as rescuers gathered around us. A policeman knelt. "How is she?"

"Alive. Get an ambulance."

"On the way." He took off his leather jacket and covered her torso. With a glance at the still-bubbling water he said, "Lucky to get out."

I was breathing hard and trying to get oriented when Melody retched and water spewed from her mouth. The policeman said, "That's good. How about yourself?"

"I'm okay."

Then the seesaw klaxon of an ambulance. I sat dazed while paramedics brought down stretchers. After they lifted Melody onto one, they forced me onto another. Just then she looked at me and smiled. "You're an awful driver—when you want to be."

In the ambulance we held hands while they gave her oxygen.

I heard the radio crackle and in a few moments a paramedic came back to me. "There was another man in the car."

"He tried to hijack it."

"If you'd told us, we might have saved him."

"Must have forgotten."

He eyed me curiously and moved back to where he'd been.

Lights glared at the emergency entrance. We were moved in quickly and efficiently. My arms felt as though they'd been pounded by jackhammers. Attendants cut off my soaked, muddy clothing, fitted on a white gown before wheeling me off to X-ray where Melody was.

When they brought her out I saw a bandage across her forehead. One of her eyes was blue-green, a cheek was bruised. I lifted her hand, kissed the fingertips. "I love you."

She smiled. "I love you, too—and next time I'll drive."

The attendant left us together while the X-ray machine was adjusted for the next patient—me. I said, "We're going to tell a story, all of us, and it goes like this—while you were dressing for a date with me, your mother was dining below. Armed men burst in, and from the way they were yelling in Spanish, they were coked to the ears. They were going to kidnap your mother and you for ransom. Then, for reasons none of us comprehend there was a four-man shootout on the front lawn. About then I arrived, all innocent and expectant, just as bullets hit their gas tank. The survivor grabbed you and forced me into the car. You fainted then, and I'll take it from there."

She squeezed my hand. "Fantastic. Will it be believed?"

I said, "If everyone's vague. Hell, all the cops need is something to satisfy reporters. Stay away from details, let them speculate. Two days from now there'll be something even gorier to write about—that's Miami. So have the cops bring your mother, and tell her the tale. As soon as possible, we all leave town."

They wheeled me in and X-rayed my skull and limbs, transferred me to a private room, and gave me a pill to make me sleep. Sometime before dawn I was wakened by Delores at my bedside. She said, "You're such a violent, unpredictable man. I certainly hope living with Melody will calm you down."

"I hope so, too. How is she?"

"Concussion, but she can leave in the morning. How are you feeling?"

"Stiff."

"I'm sure we owe you our lives—all of us, Jack, and I'm very grateful. I've told the police what you suggested, and the servants did, too."

"Thomas deserves a large bonus."

"Of course." She touched my hand. "I'm afraid to ask about Vernon."

"Don't. When the FBI starts going through those papers of Paul's, they'll find your signature on several. Your position is you signed whatever Paul asked you to—he was a lawyer, after all, as well as your husband. Beyond that you know nothing."

"I . . . well, really I don't. How can I ever repay you?"

"By being an affectionate mommy to your daughter, and a tolerant mother-in-law to me."

"I'll certainly try." She swallowed. "Melody said you wanted us to leave town. Where will we go?"

"Cozumel."

I INSTALLED DELORES in a suite at the Sol Caribe, and for a week the three of us dined together nearly every night. The rest of the time Melody and I kept to ourselves. Socializing at poolside, Delores discovered a male companion, and announced they were boarding the *Skyward* for the balance of its Caribbean cruise. Melody and I agreed it was a splendid idea and saw her off one morning.

My intended fiancée decided to redecorate the house, and did so with Pirelli's money. From my remaining sixteen thousand, I gave half to Carmelita's priest for parceling out as needed. For her and Carlos's fatherless children.

Montijo flew in from Houston and spent an afternoon with me while I told him the whole story. Melody made drinks and brought us tacos on the terrace, went back to the kitchen to prepare dinner. Looking seaward, Montijo said, "That's a hell of a story, Jack. Wish you'd let me write it up—do you a lot of good in DEA."

I shook my head. "Too many guys to pick it apart, say 't'warnt so."

"Then what do you get out of it."

"The girl."

I could hear her in the kitchen, humming as she whipped batter for conch fritters. "Yeah," he said enviously. "Get 'em young, train 'em right, keep 'em barefoot. The Mexican way."

"This being a Meskin household. And in light of my contributions to law enforcement, I'd like the plane and the boat."

"Keep them," he told me. "With family obligations you'll need to earn a living."

SO THAT'S THE way it's been. I hired a young boat captain named Ramón to do the charter work and bought into a small company that provisions cruise ships. Every other weekend Melody flies in from Miami, and sometimes I go there for a few days at her home. Thomas is always glad to see me, and Delores doesn't seem to mind. Her prenuptial agreement with Diehl brought Melody a lot of money, and some of it's paying for college tuition.

After we're married we'll head for the Olympic Games while Delores starts a six month 'round-the-world cruise calculated to bring new romance. Then Melody and I will be looking for an apartment in south Miami near the university.

What I don't do is drop by the El Portal café as I used to. The ghost of Chela swirls among the tables, and if I went there I'd be half-expecting a blonde from the sea with violet boots and lavender eyes to enter the doorway, come to my table, and ask my name.

For me she lives in dawns and sunsets.

Always will.